"I would n̲ ̲ ̲ ̲ ̲ ̲ ̲ ̲ ̲ ̲ ̲ ̲ ̲ ̲ t̲h̲ ̲
Can't you b̲ ̲ ̲

Sloan was st̲ ̲ ̲
murmur rais̲ ̲ ̲

"It's not a matter of my believing y̲ ̲ ̲ ̲ ̲, can't
believe in myself. My judgment has proved to be so
flawed that I'm afraid to trust it anymore. It tells
me you're not like other men, but I don't know if that's
true, or if it's wishful thinking, or if it's just lust."

"Well, at least you admitted you want me," he said
with a gently teasing grin. "But you're wrong, Crystal.
Never assume that because one man hurt you, the
next one will, too.

"And never—" he bent closer "—ever think you
can casually mention lusting for me and then just
walk away...."

MONTANA MAVERICKS: WED IN WHITEHORN

Brand-new stories beneath the Big Sky!

MONTANA MAVERICKS

MARILYN PAPPANO

brings impeccable credentials to her writing career—a lifelong habit of gazing out windows, not paying attention in class, daydreaming and spinning tales for her own entertainment. The sale of her first book brought great relief to her family, proving that she wasn't crazy but was, instead, creative. Since that first book, she's sold more than forty others to various publishers and even a film production company, and she's come to love almost everything about writing, except that she would like a more reasonable boss to work for, which is pretty sad since she works for herself.

She writes in an office nestled among the oaks that surround her country home. In winter she stays inside with her husband and their four dogs, and in summer she spends her free time mowing the yard that never stops growing and daydreams about grass that never gets taller than two inches.

You can write to her at P.O. Box 974, Tulsa, OK, 74101-0974.

MONTANA MAVERICKS

BIG SKY LAWMAN

MARILYN PAPPANO

Silhouette Books

Published by Silhouette Books
America's Publisher of Contemporary Romance

Special thanks and acknowledgment are given to Marilyn Pappano for her contribution to the MONTANA MAVERICKS: WED IN WHITEHORN series.

 SILHOUETTE BOOKS

ISBN 0-373-65050-7

BIG SKY LAWMAN

Visit Silhouette at www.eHarlequin.com

Printed in U.S.A.

MONTANA MAVERICKS

Wed in Whitehorn

*Welcome to Whitehorn, Montana—
a place of passion and adventure.
Seems this charming little town has some
Big Sky secrets. And everybody's talking about...*

Sloan Ravencrest: Sheriff's deputy Sloan made finding Christina Montgomery's murdered body his #1 priority. And he wasn't above seeking help from secretly psychic Crystal Cobbs, a woman long the object of his affection....

Crystal Cobbs: To put the *right* culprit behind bars, Crystal would use the gift she'd long considered a curse—and the surest way to remain single. Because not many men found a woman with "visions" marriage material. But Sloan was proving to be the exception in so many ways....

Rachel Montgomery: The news that her sister Christina may have given birth before her untimely demise sends Rachel on a mission to locate the lost baby.

Lexine Baxter: Though still safely behind bars, this wanton Whitehorn villainess is up to no good. And the apple doesn't fall far from the tree....

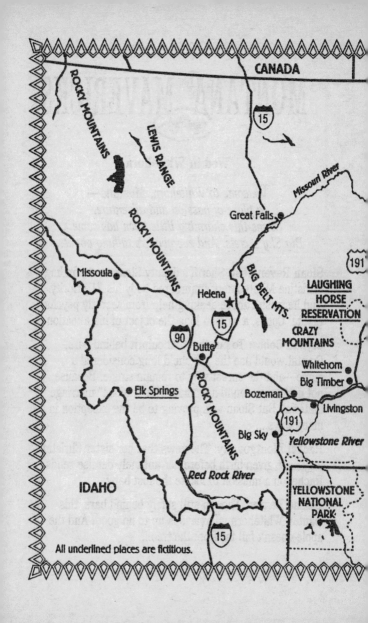

CANADA

ROCKY MOUNTAINS

LEWIS RANGE

15

Missouri River

ROCKY MOUNTAINS

Great Falls

191

BIG BELT MTS.

LAUGHING
HORSE
RESERVATION

Missoula

Helena

15

CRAZY
MOUNTAINS

90

Butte

Whitehorn

Big Timber

Elk Springs

Bozeman

Livingston

ROCKY MOUNTAINS

191

Big Sky

Yellowstone River

IDAHO

Red Rock River

YELLOWSTONE
NATIONAL
PARK

15

All underlined places are fictitious.

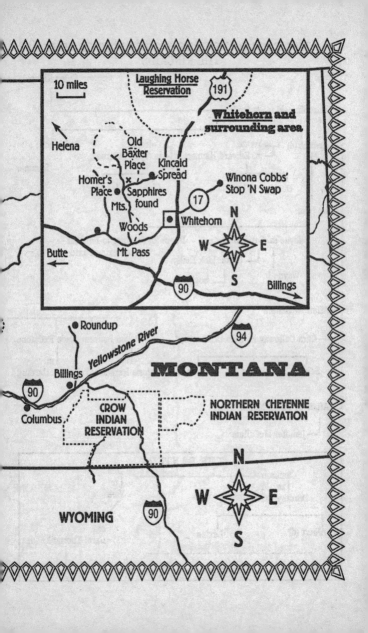

MONTANA MAVERICKS: WED IN WHITEHORN
THE KINCAIDS

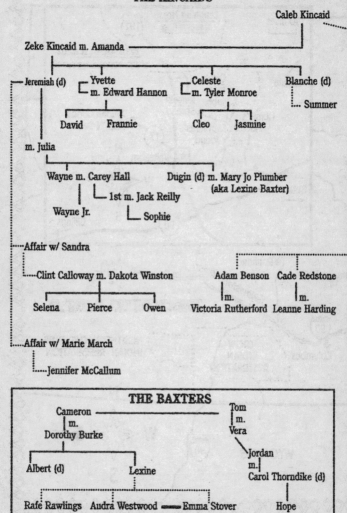

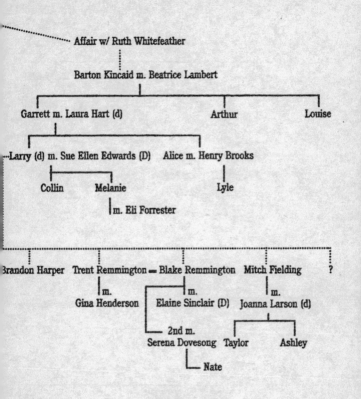

Affair w/ Ruth Whitefeather

Barton Kincaid m. Beatrice Lambert

Garrett m. Laura Hart (d)　　　　Arthur　　　　Louise

Larry (d) m. Sue Ellen Edwards (D)　　Alice m. Henry Brooks

Collin　　　Melanie　　　　　　　　　Lyle

m. Eli Forrester

Brandon Harper　Trent Remmington ━ Blake Remmington　Mitch Fielding　　?

　　　　　m.　　　　　m.　　　　　m.
Gina Henderson　Elaine Sinclair (D)　Joanna Larson (d)

　　　　　2nd m.
　　Serena Dovesong　Taylor　　Ashley

　　　　　Nate

Symbols
..... Child of an Affair
━━ Twins
d　Deceased
D　Divorced

Prologue

On a bright, sunny Tuesday afternoon, with the Montana sky a clear, perfect blue and a gentle breeze blowing the scents of fall from the north, Crystal Cobbs opened a book and saw a vision of terror.

With trembling hands, she set the ancient, leather-bound first edition down, staggered back a step or two and sank down onto a Queen Anne chair in a state of disrepair. She squeezed her eyes tightly shut and whispered a frantic prayer for the vision to disappear. When she opened her eyes, though, it was still there.

A wooded hillside. A curving road a short distance away. Water quiet and still in the evening. A cluster of small buildings on the far side of the road.

And the woman.

She lay on the wet ground with blood everywhere, soaking her clothing, seeping into the earth. She was unmoving, her head tilted to one side, her blond hair falling to hide her face. Her hand was frozen, stretched out, palm up, a beseeching gesture. The hand showed signs of terrible suffering—deep cuts caused by manicured nails, raw scrapes from clawing at the hard ground beneath her.

Crystal covered her eyes with her hands, rubbed fiercely as if she could make the scene disappear. She knew she couldn't, though. It would never disappear. Along with the other one, she would remember it forever.

When she took her hands away, the image was fading. The lake disappeared first, then the buildings, the road. The woman—not dead, Crystal realized, but dying—was the last to fade away, her outstretched hand the very last. The pleading, supplicating hand. *Help me, please help me.*

"I can't," Crystal whispered brokenly. Not again. The last time had almost destroyed her. She'd lost her job, her home, the man she loved, her parents. It had left her with *nothing*.

She couldn't lose what little she'd since regained. She couldn't risk her new life for someone who was already dead, who couldn't be helped. She couldn't do it!

When she thought her legs might support her, she got to her feet. With some trepidation, she picked up the book, half afraid that it had somehow triggered the vision, but her mind remained assault-free. Maybe this vision was different. Maybe she *could* put it out of her mind, ignore it, pretend it didn't exist, and in time, oh, please, maybe she could forget it.

If it would be ignored.

If she could forget.

If it didn't keep haunting her the way the last one had.

Giving her head a shake to clear it, she carried the book and its three companions to her desk. Her workspace in the back room of her great-aunt Winona's shop was filled to the rafters with boxes awaiting unpacking, items needing sorting, cleaning or repairs, items to be disposed of. The aisles were narrow and the desk was overflowing, but she managed to find the phone and the Rolodex card file.

She placed a call to a rare book dealer in Helena, a good friend of Winona's, and arranged to deliver the four volumes to him for appraisal. As she hung up the phone, her gaze caught on her hand. With a growing sense of horror, she watched as it shifted, changed, turning into someone else's hand—smaller, pampered, reaching, pleading.

"Leave me alone!" Crystal whispered angrily. "I can't help you! No one can!"

...Please help me...

"No!" Crystal jerked her hand back, clutched it in her other hand to make certain that it was hers. Though the fingers were unnaturally cold, it most definitely belonged to her.

It was her gold nugget ring on the index finger, her Red-brown Haze polish on the nails, her calluses and cuts.

Turning away from the desk, she almost bumped into Winona, gave a startled cry and took—jumped—a step back.

"Why, Crystal, you look as if you've seen a ghost!" her aunt said with a laugh. Her expression sobered, though, as she studied Crystal's face. "What's happened?"

"N-nothing. Really, Aunt Winona, it's…it's nothing."

When she would have pushed past, her aunt stopped her with one gentle hand and continued to study her. After a moment sympathy flashed through her eyes and her mouth flattened into a thin line. "You've had a vision," she said as if it were the most natural thing in the world. "Tell me about it."

Crystal wanted to refuse, but refusing Winona was easier said than done. Besides, in truth, some part of her wanted to confide in her aunt. She wanted to unload the whole burden onto Winona's far more capable shoulders. Having psychic powers of her own, Winona would never mock or scorn her, the way people back in Georgia had. She would never hush her in mid-telling, as her parents had, with warnings to keep her oddities to herself, lest she be shunned by the normal people around her.

"Tell me, child," Winona encouraged, "and together we'll deal with it."

Together. In twenty-six years, there'd never been a *together* for Crystal, except that one last, awful time. And what a disaster that had turned out to be. It had all been too much to bear—the humiliation. The hurt. The ostracism. Her parents, distancing themselves from their own daughter, coldly shaking their heads and muttering, "We warned you." Her fiancé, benefitting from her so-called gift, then breaking her heart because of it.

It had been the worst experience of her life. She'd thought running halfway across the country might save her, but now it was starting again.

But this time she had Winona. Her aunt who'd welcomed

her, loved her and never made her feel like a freak, would
help her this time.

Winona took Crystal's hands, holding them firmly in hers,
and waited without judgment, without fear. Gathering courage from her, Crystal haltingly answered. "I saw...a woman.
I think it was Christina Montgomery, and—and..." Drawing
a deep breath, she blurted out the rest.

"Aunt Winona, she was dying."

One

Deputy Sloan Ravencrest sat at a red light, tapping out an intricate rhythm on the steering wheel and thinking about the drive he was about to take out to Winona Cobbs's Stop-n-Swap outside town.

There were some, including most of the other officers assigned to the Montgomery case, who would say he was wasting his time and the taxpayers' money. Winona Cobbs was a flake, a crazy old woman who talked with spirits and ghosts. She was forever coming forward with some bit of information gleaned from the "other side." She was crazy, but harmless.

On the other hand, there were some, including his father, his grandfather and most of the more traditional Cheyenne on the reservation, who accepted that "other side" as a natural part of life. They had visions, too, or knew people who did. They believed in mysteries and spirits and things logic couldn't explain. They didn't discount anything merely for lack of proof.

Sloan wasn't sure which group he belonged in. He had some faith, but he also had his share of skepticism. That was thanks, his father claimed, to his white mother. He had a foot in both the Cheyenne and the white worlds, so why shouldn't he straddle the line on this, too?

All he knew for a fact was that Winona had come by the sheriff's office a few weeks ago to recount her latest vision to him, one in which she'd claimed to see Christina Montgomery dead. And that neither the sheriff's office nor the police department nor the state bureau of investigation had any better leads to follow up. And that the powerful Montgomery family wanted answers yesterday.

And one other thing, he acknowledged with a grin as the light changed and he eased away from the intersection. He knew that Winona Cobbs's niece Crystal was just about the prettiest little thing he ever did see.

His grandfather who'd helped raise him would tell him he should be ashamed of himself, using his job to get an introduction to a pretty woman. But, hell, he'd tried every other way. He'd managed to bump into her on a couple of her rare trips to town, but she'd been in too big a hurry for small talk. He'd tried to get one of her few friends to coax her into the bar where a fair number of Whitehorn's single folks hung out, but that had been a no-go. He'd even done a little unnecessary shopping at the Stop-n-Swap, but she'd hardly looked at him.

His grandmother, who had also helped raise him, would tell him he was foolish, expending effort to meet a white woman. Hadn't it been a white woman who'd broken his father's heart? Who had abandoned Sloan on his father's doorstep three days after he was born to save her parents the shame of knowing they had a half-Indian grandbaby? Why didn't he look closer to home? she would urge. Why not look for one of his own kind?

Because not one of his own kind had ever intrigued him the way Crystal Cobbs did. Maybe it was the way she looked—beautiful, with black hair, green eyes and pale china-doll skin. Fragile, with her defenses firmly in place whenever anyone came close.

Or maybe it was the way she talked—in a rich, lush Georgia drawl that put a man in mind of hot days, steamy nights and astounding women. Even curt brush-offs sounded incredibly sensual in her slow, honeyed voice.

Maybe it was the way she moved. Just last weekend he'd stood in the produce section at the grocery store and watched her select apples and tomatoes in a way that made his mouth go dry and his mind go blank. He couldn't have spoken to her to save his life, not after watching her long, slender fingers and their slow, enticing touches.

Maybe it was the look in her eyes when he did try to talk to her. Wary. Aloof. Distant. And, underneath all that, frightened. It was easy enough to guess that she'd been hurt. Why else would such an elegant Southern belle trade Georgia's gentility for Montana's rugged frontier?

It wasn't so easy to tamp down the protective feelings she roused in him. It wasn't at all easy when he watched her stroll through the market, touching this, damn near caressing that, to restrain the urge to wrap his arms around her and promise she would never be hurt again.

But he never made promises he couldn't keep. Since he hadn't yet managed to get beyond "Hi, how are you?" with her, the chances that he could protect her from anything were somewhere between slim and none.

Slowing down, he turned off the highway just outside of town onto the dirt-and-gravel parking lot that fronted the Stop-n-Swap. In weather warmer than this November day, Winona did much of her buying, selling and trading outside on a shaded patio, but the bulk of her goods were stashed in one giant room in a squat, concrete-block building. Much of it was junk, but if a person took the time to poke around, he could find some bargains. His grandmother's oak rocker had come from there, and half of Aunt Eula's Depression glass collection could be traced back there.

There was only one find Sloan was interested in. Maybe this third visit would be the charm.

He parked beside a battered pickup that belonged to one of the old Jefferson brothers and climbed out of his patrol unit. Considering that Montana was widely believed to be the finest of God's country, the landscape around the Stop-n-Swap wasn't particularly pretty, and the two-bedroom trailer off to the side where Winona and Crystal lived did nothing to enhance it. The mobile home was forty years old if it was a day, white with turquoise trim and skirt, with a wobbly deck serving as front porch and an array of faded plastic whirligigs in flowerbeds where, to the best he could recall, no flowers had ever grown.

It was easier by far to imagine Crystal living in a pre-Civil War mansion, some gracious, elegant place with eighteen-foot ceilings, three-story-high columns, verandas and servants.

He went inside the shop, removed his hat and sunglasses and took a quick look around. Winona was dusting a display of china, and Vern Jefferson was in a distant corner. As he'd expected, there was no sign of Crystal.

As soon as the bell over the door sounded, Winona put down the dusting cloth and approached him with both hands extended and a warm smile. "Deputy Ravencrest. How nice to see you."

She was as short as her niece was tall, as round as Crystal was slender. As did most of the elderly ladies he knew on the rez, she wore her iron-gray hair in a braid that wound around her head, and covered her all-purpose bright cotton dresses with shawls that sometimes matched but just as often didn't. There was no family resemblance between her and Crystal, but the word around town was that they were devoted to each other.

So if Winona liked him, would that win him any points with Crystal?

"Are you here to shop, Deputy, or is this official business?"

"It's business, ma'am. I'd like to ask you a few questions."

"I'll answer them if I can. Would you like something to drink?"

"No, thank you, ma'am." Not unless accepting would bring Crystal out of hiding.

She pursed her lips a moment, then called, "Vern, you find what you're looking for, I'll be outside." The volume went up a notch. "You hear that, Crystal?" Without waiting for a response from either one, she linked her arm through Sloan's. "We can talk on the patio."

There were two patios—one directly in front of the store, shaded by a faded awning that stretched out from the roof, and a smaller one between the store and the house trailer. This one was half open to the Montana sky, half covered by a trellis that supported honeysuckle vines. When they were in bloom in the spring, he imagined it was quite a place to sit.

They sat at the dining table under the trellis, with Winona facing the trailer, Sloan watching the shop.

"Is this about our last visit? About the vision?"

"Yes, ma'am. Have you had any other visions?" He'd already ridden into the woods up near the Crazy Mountains but had seen nothing. He needed more to go on.

"Not a one—at least, not about that. I did preminisce that a collector from Los Angeles would buy those books we got from the Fortier estate, and sure enough, he did. Paid more than I was planning to ask but less than they're valued at, so we were both happy."

She flashed a self-satisfied smile that Sloan couldn't help but return as he pulled his notebook from his pocket. "Have you remembered anything else about this vision?"

Her expression shifted slightly, became less open, more guarded. He wondered why. Was it as simple as the fact that visions of Christina dead made her uncomfortable? After all, Winona's premonitions were generally of the harmless guess-who's-coming-to-call variety. They rarely involved anything as serious as death.

"No," she said quietly. "Not another thing."

"You said the scene was a wooded area, with a road and a body of water in the distance. Can you tell me anything else about it? Was the water a lake, a river? Was there anything you might recognize?"

She shook her head. "None of it was familiar."

"Except Christina, and you didn't see her face. How could you be so sure it was her?"

"I just knew. You're a policeman. Sometimes you just *know*."

True. In his business they called them hunches, and he'd learned over the years to trust his. It was a hunch that made him go on. "You said she was lying on her back with her arm stretched out."

"That's right. She was covered with blood, and her head was bent like this—" she demonstrated "—and her left arm was stretched out."

"Could you see her hand? Was it palm up or down?"

She considered her own beringed hand a moment before deciding. "Down. I believe it was down."

Feeling a curious tickle on the back of his neck, Sloan flipped through his notes, found what he was looking for, then fixed his gaze on the old woman. "A few weeks ago you said it was her right arm that was stretched out and the palm was up."

Winona appeared startled for a moment, then gave a nervous chuckle. "Left, right...depends on your point of view, doesn't it? Your left is my right."

"Up and down don't change, though," he said mildly. "Were you looking at her palm or at the back of her hand?"

"Whatever I said last time is right. The details were fresh then. I hadn't had time to get confused."

"I've never known you to get your details confused," he pointed out patiently. "You predicted everything about my cousin Ruth's baby, right down to the birthmark and which cheek it was on." He hesitated, then politely, respectfully, asked, "*Was* there a vision, Ms. Cobbs? Did you really see Christina, or was this an attempt to gain a little attention?"

Winona's face flushed red. "Oh, no, not at all! Why, if it was attention she wanted—we—I mean I wanted..." Looking miserably flustered, she let the denial trail away.

...*if it was attention she wanted*... Who? Christina Montgomery? Had she planned her own disappearance to get her father's attention? While he wouldn't put it past her, based on what he knew of her, staying away for three months seemed excessive. Letting her family believe she might be dead for so long was cruel, and cruelty didn't appear to be one of Christina's shortcomings.

But she and Winona were the only females involved in this discussion, weren't they?

"Ms. Cobbs, *was* there a vision regarding Christina Montgomery's death?" he asked again.

She nodded grimly, worriedly.

"But you didn't have it."

After a moment's obvious indecision, she shook her head. "Who did?"

Her hands fluttered nervously. "I gave my word I wouldn't say. This gift has caused her nothing but distress, but the vision was too important to go unreported. I told her I would claim it as one of my own. I told her no one need ever know. I promised her... Oh, dear."

Movement near the shop caught Sloan's eye and he looked from Winona to her niece, standing just outside the open door, sending a cool, aloof stare his way. Just like that, he knew. Call it a hunch, call it instinct, but he knew who Winona was fronting for.

It was Crystal who'd had the vision, who'd seen Christina dead, who'd known nothing but distress.

Crystal, who shared her aunt's psychic gift.

For one moment he put business aside and considered that fact. How strong were her powers? Those few times he'd spoken to her, when she'd tersely brushed him off, had she known that his interest was more than neighborly friendliness? Had she had a clue what he was thinking that time he'd watched her in the market? Could that explain her aloofness, her indifference?

Grimly he turned back to her aunt. "Will she talk to me?"

"I don't think—"

He laid his hand over hers to still the trembling. "If Christina *is* dead, the killer and your niece are the only ones who know it. I need to know everything *she* knows. I need to talk to her, Ms. Cobbs."

"It's all been so unpleasant for her," the old lady said, sorrowfully shaking her head.

"I imagine dying alone on ground soaked with her own blood was much more unpleasant for Christina," he said dryly. "If it really happened. Tell Crystal I need to talk to her. Ask her if she'd rather do it now or at the sheriff's office."

"Oh, you can't take her in to the sheriff's office! I promised her no one would know. She's been through so much... It cost her so much..." She lifted her head, straightened her spine. "You'll have to make the same promise to me. You'll have to give me your word that no one will know your information came from her."

"I can't do that. This is a police investigation that will hopefully lead to a criminal trial. Everything has to be documented." Then he relented. "I can keep her name out of it for now. If the lead doesn't pan out, then I won't have to say anything. That's the best I can offer."

Winona considered it for a time, then reluctantly nodded. "Wait here. I'll talk to her."

He watched her follow the path from patio to shop, where she spoke with great animated movements for several minutes. Cool, contained Crystal was animated, too, refusing in every way possible to say no. Twice, she sent cold, stinging looks his way, then at last she made a stubborn gesture, spun around and disappeared inside.

Sloan met Winona halfway along the path. "I'm sorry, Deputy," she said, dignity in her bearing and her voice. "My niece chooses not to talk with you."

"Maybe you didn't try hard enough to convince her. Maybe she'll listen to me."

She looked as if she wanted to refuse and send him away. She also looked as if she couldn't bring herself to do it, either. "She's in the back room."

With a nod of thanks, he went inside the shop, letting his eyes adjust to the dimmer light as he made his way down the center aisle. The door to the back was closed, but there was no lock on it. The knob turned easily in his hand.

The room was crowded with inventory. Near the back windows, a space had been cleared for repairing and refinishing furniture before moving it up front to sell. There was a chair missing its seat, a dresser stripped down to bare wood and an oak table getting the sanding of its life. He stood in the shadows and watched as Crystal laid the sander aside, wiped the tabletop with a cloth, then ran her palm lightly across it. He'd already learned that he liked the way she touched things. If he wasn't careful, he could easily get turned on just watching her long, smooth strokes and imagining the same sure touches on him.

As if sensing that she was no longer alone, Crystal abruptly looked up and wariness came into her eyes. She grabbed a couple half sheets of sandpaper, knelt on the floor and went to work on the nearest leg.

He stepped out of the shadows and moved to lean against the dresser. He wanted to ask a dozen questions—what kind of psychic abilities did she have? Why did she hide them? Why had she asked Winona to lie for her? More, he wanted to say nothing at all and simply watch her try to ignore him. Judging by the intense concentration the table leg required, she wasn't finding it easy. He'd be flattered if he believed for a second that she was having trouble ignoring him as a man, but he knew too well it was his uniform and deputy sheriff's badge that bothered her.

He decided to wait her out. He was patient. He could sit for hours on surveillance, or on a riverbank with a line in the water. He knew the value of being still, of watching, waiting, listening.

Minute after minute passed. She finished with one leg and moved to the next. When the third leg was done, she stood, tossed the crumpled paper into a trash can, then glared at him.

Keeping his expression blank, Sloan met her gaze. He didn't speak, but waited for her to spit out whatever was on her mind. Clearly, she was angry. Hostile. Belligerent. So damn tense that she might shatter into a million pieces right there in front of him. She looked as if she'd come up with a lot of things to say, but not the right one. A moment later, that changed. "I don't have to talk to you."

"No, you don't," he mildly agreed.

She brushed her hands down her thighs, leaving a trail of dust on her jeans, then folded her arms and clenched her fists. "You can't make me answer any questions."

He shook his head.

"And if I ask you to leave the premises, you have to."

Again he shook his head, but this time to disagree, not confirm. "You're not the owner of these premises. I'm here with your aunt's blessing." That was stretching it a bit, but the old lady hadn't asked him to leave. She had let him come back here for the sole purpose of talking to her niece.

Crystal clenched both jaw and fists tighter. "Then *I* can leave."

He let her walk a dozen feet before speaking. "Unless I'm mistaken, Ms. Cobbs, you don't own any property in the State of Montana, so there's no place you can go that I can't follow, either with someone else's permission or no permission at all."

That stopped her in midstride. It also made her angrier. He could see the tension in her body, could hear it in her voice as she slowly turned. "I can't help you." Each word was icy, filled with conviction, and left no room for argument.

He argued, anyway. "You can't know that until you try."

"Aunt Winona told you everything."

"I want to hear it from you."

The look she flashed him was sarcastic, pained, scathing. "We can't always get what we want, can we?"

This was getting him nowhere and, more than likely, costing him ground. What he needed was to win her trust, or at least some measure of it. If she knew she could count on him to protect her, if she could be persuaded to think of him as on her side and not her enemy, then she might be more willing to help him. "Ms. Cobbs, I— Can I call you Crystal?"

She stared mutinously at him, giving him no response either way. He would take it as permission.

"I understand your need to protect your identity, Crystal. I know having psychic abilities isn't as easy for some people as it is for your aunt. But this is a serious case. A twenty-two-year-old woman is missing and quite possibly dead. Her family's worried sick. We have no clues. Right now you're the only lead I've got."

"Then you have nothing." With that deadly cold pronouncement, she returned to the table, picked up a new sheet of sandpaper and went to work on the last leg.

If he believed she was that cold and uncaring, he'd walk out the door and never give her another thought. But he didn't believe it, not for an instant. In fact, he would suspect that her problem was that she cared too much. What was it Winona had said? Her psychic gift had been so unpleasant for her, had caused her nothing but distress and had cost her so much.

"I can keep your identity secret for now," he promised. "I just want the chance to find out if there's anything to this vision. If we find something relevant to Christina's disappearance as a direct result of your involvement, then I'll have to include your name in my report, but if not... It's just between you and me."

If we find something relevant... Crystal mentally snorted. She had *seen* Christina's body and the place where she was murdered. In anyone's book, that was pretty damn relevant.

How had Deputy Ravencrest figured out that she'd had the vision and not Winona? Was her aunt a less capable liar than she'd imagined? Or was Ravencrest smarter than they'd given him credit for?

He looked smart, she acknowledged reluctantly. He looked like a man who paid great attention to detail, who learned more from a single glance than most people did from an endless stare.

He also looked, she admitted just as reluctantly, like her romance-novel fantasies come to life. The cowboy and the city girl. The cop and the psychic. The Indian warrior and the white captive. With his black hair, brown eyes and brown skin, and oh, so masculine aura, he could take the hero's role in any of them.

But she couldn't be the heroine.

After another moment or two of silence, he asked, "Have you ever been arrested, Ms. Cobbs?" His tone was mild, his manner friendly, and both were deceptive.

"No. Why do you ask?" So much for "Can I call you Crystal?" The first hint of suspicion entered his mind and he was all business again. Typical.

"I'm just trying to figure out why you're being so obstructive. Generally, people who don't want to cooperate with the police can be divided into three groups—those who have been treated badly by them, people who are protecting someone close to them, and people who have been in the system before. Now, I can't imagine any member of a well-off, old Southern family receiving anything less than respect from any well-trained Southern cop, and you haven't met enough people here to be protecting one of them, so that leaves a brush with the law."

He was right on the first two counts. Her family was comfortably well off, their name well established in Georgia's history books as well as its social structure, and they—if not Crystal herself—commanded respect from everyone in their town, including the police. And she didn't know anyone well enough in Whitehorn to feel the need to protect him.

She also didn't know anyone well enough to trust him.

"Or, gee, here's a fourth one—a desire to be left alone," she said sarcastically.

He went on as if she hadn't spoken. "Of course, there's always the possibility that your lack of cooperation has nothing to do with your feelings toward law enforcement and a lot to do with your feelings toward me."

"And what feelings do you suppose I might have toward

you?'' This time she went beyond sarcasm into pure snideness.

"I'm Cheyenne—well, half. To most folks, that's the half that counts.''

He was suggesting that her refusal to talk to him was based on her prejudice and his race. Racial bigotry was nothing new to her, but being accused of it herself *was* new. It was offensive, insulting, infuriating. Her first impulse was to tell him everything, just to prove to him how wrong he was. Her second impulse was to ignore the first.

A spasm in her hand, clenched tightly at her side, reminded her to flex her fingers. She worked out the cramp, then slowly got to her feet and faced him. "I've never been arrested. I've been boringly well behaved my entire life. I have my prejudices—we all do—but race isn't one of them. I've been cooperative. I had a vision that appeared to concern your case. My aunt passed the information along to you. There's nothing more I can tell you. Unless you want me to make up details, that's it. That's all there is.'' She paused to let that sink in, then quietly added, "And now I want to be left alone.''

Taking a tack cloth from the workbench, she crouched beside the table again, running the sticky fabric over the legs she'd just sanded. The piece had been a mess when it had been brought in—stained, painted, nicked, gouged, burned. It was old—not so old she had to concern herself with preserving any antique value—but it was good sturdy pine, with a lot of years' use left in it. In its original condition, they would have been lucky to get twenty dollars for it. By the time she finished with it, it would be worth ten times that.

If, she thought with a grimace as she felt the dark gaze centered on her back, she ever got a little peace to finish it.

"What are your prejudices?''

She considered pretending she hadn't heard him. Going to the trailer and locking the door on him. Ignoring him. Instead, she straightened, then began rubbing the tack cloth over the tabletop. Once she'd removed every speck of dust from the wood, she looked up and gave him a cool smile. "I don't like cops. Or deputies or prosecutors, or any of the so-called good guys." They'd harmed her in ways that, months later, still held the power to stun her.

"And what experience caused you to form this opinion?"

"That's none of your business."

"You tell me that you're prejudiced against deputies. I'm a deputy. I think that makes it my business."

"You think wrong." She returned the tack cloth to its plastic bag, then crossed to the wooden cubbyholes that filled one wall and held a wide selection of half-used stains and paints. She picked one, shook the can to judge how full it was, then grabbed a screwdriver, plastic refinishing gloves and a handful of old T-shirt remnants.

And the whole time he stood there and watched her. It was unnerving how still he could become, how narrowly he could focus his attention, as if she were the only thing in his world. She could imagine the situation in which such undivided attention could be flattering, even desirable, but right now it simply made her uncomfortable. She wanted to fidget, to hide out of his sight, but she'd be damned if she would let him have the satisfaction of knowing that he could intimidate her.

Finally, after long minutes had passed—ten? fifteen? no, probably fewer than five—he drew a breath. "I give you my word of honor, Crystal—"

"I don't know that you have any honor." The cops she knew personally didn't. They'd used her, then stood back and helped James destroy her. They'd taken her dignity, her pride, her honor, all to save their own. Maybe Deputy Ravencrest was different, better, but she didn't know that. She could only assume he was the same or even worse.

"I don't betray people," he said quietly, intensely.

She met his gaze one more time. He looked sincere, honest as hell. If she could trust her instincts, she would believe he *was* honest and honorable. But she couldn't trust her own judgment. Hadn't she believed James was honest and honorable, and that he loved her, to boot?

"I don't trust cops."

After another long look, he nodded once and started toward the door. Crystal didn't pretend to believe she'd won. She didn't think for an instant that she'd heard the last from him.

Halfway across the room, he turned back. "I don't like to give ultimatums, but you leave me no choice. I'll be back tomorrow. You can talk to me or not. That's up to you. But if you don't, I'm going to the Montgomery family. I'm going to tell them I have reason to believe that you know something about Christina's disappearance. Within hours everyone in town will know. You'll be the new prime topic of gossip in Whitehorn. Is that what you want?"

It was so far from what she wanted that she just might weep. She'd come to Whitehorn to escape all that, to be just a normal person living a normal life. Just a single woman working to make ends meet. Not the nut case or the poor delusional woman. Certainly not the freak.

She stared at him, all too aware of how stricken she looked. For the first time he didn't meet her gaze—couldn't, she thought, because he felt guilty for his threat.

But not guilty enough to keep him from carrying through.

He turned on his heel, his boots making hollow thuds on the concrete floor as he strode away. Once the door to the store had closed behind him, once she was sure he was gone, Crystal replaced the lid on the can of stain. She stripped off the gloves, let herself out the side door that provided a shortcut to the trailer and for a moment simply stood there, her face tilted back, her eyes closed. The sun touched her face with its brightness but offered little warmth. To find the degree of warmth she needed, she would have to head for a rain forest somewhere in the tropics.

When the door opened behind her, she didn't startle. She supposed it could be Ravencrest, come back to make some threat he'd forgotten, but in her bones she knew it wasn't. He lacked the warm, caring aura that surrounded the newcomer. He could make her feel many things, but never safe, not the way Winona made her feel safe.

"He's gone," Winona said unnecessarily as she wrapped her arms around Crystal from behind.

"But he'll be back."

"Yes. That boy's like a puppy with a bone. He's not going to let go until he's got what he wants."

Eyes still closed, Crystal tried to summon an image of Ravencrest as a cuddly, ornery little puppy. It wouldn't form. There was nothing the least bit cuddly about him, nothing cute or playful. Maybe as a full-blown dog—a Rottweiler or a Doberman, maybe an ill-tempered German shepherd. Something big and vicious and dangerous to someone as weak as she was.

When she opened her eyes again, nothing had changed. The sun was still shining, the air was still cool, and her world was still tilted askew. "He threatened me," she said softly.

"With what?" Winona demanded indignantly. "You've done nothing wrong!"

"If I don't cooperate with him, he's going to tell the Montgomerys and everyone else." Tears welling in her eyes, she turned to hide her face against her aunt's shoulder. "They'll say I'm crazy, Aunt Winona! They'll make fun of me and pretend they don't know me! It'll start all over again, and I can't bear it again! I can't go through it again!"

"There, there," Winona clucked soothingly. "It's all right, honey. Nothing's going to start all over again because you and I aren't going to let it. You're not alone anymore, Crystal. We'll handle it together."

You're not alone anymore. They were the sweetest words Crystal had ever heard. She clung to them as a drowning man might cling to a life preserver, and she hoped that this time they were true.

Because one more betrayal would be more than she could survive.

From a rise a few hundred yards away, Sloan lowered the binoculars to the truck seat and tried to rub the image of

Crystal in tears from his eyes. He didn't even try to erase the guilt. That would be impossible.

He'd made suspects cry before, but not innocent women. Not women with more secrets and sorrows than he might ever understand. Not beautiful women with wary eyes of emerald green and all the temerity of a doe caught in headlights.

Grimly he started the engine, shifted into gear and spun the rear tires in the dirt as he pulled onto the road. Unless he could find a puppy to kick or a kitten to run over, his job here was done.

At least for the day.

Two

Shortly before noon on Friday, Sloan parked in front of the Stop-n-Swap, radioed his location to the dispatcher, then went inside. There were a couple of customers, strangers to him, but he spared them little attention. His gaze was locked on the two women behind the counter.

Crystal noticed him first. Though she didn't look at him, he knew because one instant she was so fluid and animated, and the next she was rigid. What had some idiot Georgia cop done to earn her distrust for cops everywhere? Wrongly accuse her of a crime? Break her heart? Betray her?

He hated that kind of all-encompassing distrust. Some cop made a mistake, and so all cops were bad. Some man hurt her, and so all men would do the same. Or—a version he was intimately familiar with—some Indian somewhere was a drunk, lazy or a thief, and so all Indians were suspect.

He wanted to tell her that he wasn't like other cops, other men, other Native Americans. He was an individual, one person with his own unique traits. If she was going to dislike him, he had a right to be disliked for his own failings, not someone else's.

But he'd given her good reason to dislike him yesterday. He'd threatened to expose her to ridicule and gossip. He'd made her cry. The only thing keeping her from fleeing to the back of the room was fear. Of *him.*

He stopped at the counter and laid his gray Stetson and dark glasses on it. "Miz Winona," he said with a nod. "Crystal."

"Morning, Deputy." Winona glanced at her niece, then circled the counter. "I—I'll leave you two to talk."

Finally Crystal turned and looked not directly at him, but in his direction. It was a start. "What do you want to know?"

"Can we go outside? I know it's a little cool, but..."

She took a sweater from a hook on the wall and wordlessly led the way outside to the same patio where he'd sat with Winona the day before. She sat on one side of the table, holding the sweater front closed with her arms across her chest, and fixed her gaze somewhere off in the distance.

He sat across from her, pulled out his notebook and pen, then cleared his throat. Before he could speak, though, she did.

"You said you would keep my name out of it."

"As much as I can." Regretfully he added, "I don't want to give you a sense of false security, though. If your vision pans out and helps us in any way, then it and you will have to be part of my report. I can't avoid that."

The look that came over her delicate features was one of despair, followed almost immediately by resignation. "What do you want to know?" she asked again.

He studied her for a moment—the cold green eyes, the taut jaw, the defensive posture—before forcing his mind to the notes from his first conversation with Winona. Instead of a pertinent question, though, one born of curiosity popped out. "How long have you had these abilities?"

Her gaze darted suspiciously to him, then away. "What does that matter?"

"Background. Humor me." What he really wanted to say was, I'm interested. Trust me.

"All my life. And that's the first and last question that doesn't concern Christina Montgomery."

All her life. She was younger than him, and he was only twenty-nine, so "all" her life didn't add up to much in terms of numbers, yet she made it sound as if it were centuries.

Ignoring her comment, he pushed on. "Psychic abilities

must run in your family—you, your aunt. Is your father also psychic?''

She snorted derisively but didn't speak. That was answer enough. It told him there was a problem between Crystal and her father. Maybe he thought she was a flake, unbalanced or even cursed. Maybe he was part of the reason she'd left Georgia for Montana.

Oh, he'd heard the story. After Winona's heart attack last summer, she'd needed help and Crystal had been the only family member in a position to come. Supposedly she'd liked Whitehorn so much—and loved Winona so much—that she'd stayed.

Which was bull. Oh, not the love for Winona. That was obvious. But liking Whitehorn? Even now, months later, she hadn't seen enough of it to know if she liked it. She made rare trips into town and spent the rest of her time hiding out here.

She hadn't decided to stay in a new place that had captivated her. She'd decided to not return to an old place that had hurt her.

''Tell me about your vision.''

''There was a hillside—''

He stopped her with one up-raised hand. ''What were you doing when you had it? Where were you? Was it different from other visions you've had?''

She looked as if she wanted to squirm but couldn't allow herself to move so much as a muscle. He'd questioned people before who hadn't wanted to be questioned, but none who hadn't wanted it as much as she didn't.

Taking a shallow breath, she began speaking. ''I was in the back room, unpacking some items we'd purchased at an estate auction in Kalispell, including a set of rare books. When I opened one, the vision started.''

''Could it have been caused somehow by the book?''

She shook her head. ''If there was a trigger, don't you think I'd avoid it?'' After another shallow breath, she went on. ''After the first vision passed, a few minutes later I had a second one. As far as being different from other visions...I don't know. They seemed more intense, more vivid, but seeing someone dying *is* more intense than having a premonition about a letter or a phone call."

"'Seeing someone dying.' How do you know she wasn't already dead?"

"Because she spoke."

That was something Winona had left out. Because in a story that sounded completely unbelievable, that part somehow seemed even more unbelievable than the rest? "What did she...say?"

His hesitation was slight, but she caught it. It added another layer of tension to her jaw. "'Help me, please help me.'"

"Was she pleading with whoever had hurt her? Calling out in case someone was near enough to hear?"

Abruptly Crystal shuddered, as if an unbearable chill had passed through her, and for the first time that day, she looked directly at him. "I think...I believe she was speaking to me."

Disconcerted, he sat back. According to true believers, communication between the dead and the living was neither rare nor difficult. Sometimes the spirits of those who had passed on provided guidance to those who remained. Other times they offered nothing but trouble. His aunt Rita was such a believer. She insisted that her first husband Leon was too jealous to let her be happy with her second husband Frank, that he was more troublesome to her dead than he'd ever been alive.

His grandmother thought the only spirits threatening Rita's marriage to Frank were of the bottled variety. But Crystal didn't strike him as a woman fond of the drink.

"You don't believe me, do you? You're putting me through this for nothing, because you don't believe a word I've said."

"Honestly, I don't know what I believe. But I do know I don't know everything. I know there are things that can't be explained. And I know I'd be a bad cop if I ignored a lead because it didn't fit my preconceived notions of how the world is." He paused one beat, two, then added, "I'm *not* a bad cop, Crystal."

Her expression remained impassive.

The silence between them dragged on until he finally broke it. "Tell me about the vision. Everything you can remember, whether it seems important or not."

She spoke in a dull monotone, recounting the same scene Winona had described to him weeks ago. A hillside, a road, a body of water, buildings. Christina.

"If you close your eyes and concentrate, you can see the scene again, can't you?" he asked softly. He didn't know whether his theory was close to the mark or way out in left field, but after a moment, with her eyes open wide, she nodded. "Will you do that?"

She looked afraid. He didn't blame her. Murder scenes, if that was what this was, were difficult for anyone to examine closely. It must be even tougher for a Southern belle who'd lived a pampered, privileged life before coming to Montana.

"It can't hurt you, Crystal. It's just an image. It's the middle of the day. You're sitting in bright sunlight. I'll be right here in front of you."

"I'd be happier if you'd never come near me," she said with a thin, bitter smile. The sentiment stung, almost as much as that terrible little smile. Then she closed her eyes and summoned up the memory she'd no doubt spent the past few weeks trying to forget.

Sloan used his lowest, calmest voice, so it wouldn't be intrusive. "Do you see Christina?"

"Yes."

"What is she wearing?"

"A dress. Navy-blue, pleated, too big for her. It's covered with blood."

"What can you see where she's lying?"

"The ground is wet. There are a lot of trees, some boulders. The clearing's not very large."

"Are there any wildflowers? Can you see any traffic on

the road? Any lights on in the buildings? Is there anything remarkable about the clearing or the water or the woods?''

"No," she said impatiently, encompassing all four questions, then shrugged. "Yes. Lights outside the buildings. Yellow lights. And there's a flat rock in the clearing, set at a right angle to another rock, almost like a natural chair.''

"You mentioned a second vision. Same scene?''

She shook her head. ''It was just a flash. An image of her hand reaching for help.''

Sloan leaned back, hands folded over his stomach, and let his gaze turn thoughtfully to the mountains on the horizons. A small clearing surrounded by trees, not far from a curving roadway, with water in the distance. There were probably countless places in the county that matched that description. He could think of half a dozen off the top of his head. He'd already ridden up into the hills. How much time would he waste checking out every one of them?

But what else did he have to do? He, like everyone else on this case, was at a dead end. He couldn't sit back and do nothing while waiting for a legitimate lead to pop up.

Besides, she'd said something that had caught his attention. *The ground is wet.* They'd had heavy rains at the time of Christina's disappearance, so the ground would have been wet. It was possible that Crystal had simply remembered and inserted that one detail, but not many people could recall weather conditions for one particular day several months earlier unless they had some reason to.

Though faking a vision of a dying woman could be a good reason to go look up the weather on that particular date.

But he didn't believe Crystal was faking anything. The vision might not amount to anything, but he believed it was very real for her.

He also believed that Christina *was* dead. That part felt too right, had been too easy to accept. He felt a moment's regret for the Montgomery family, for Christina herself. He didn't really know her—he didn't exactly run in the same social circles as the very young, very spoiled daughter of the most influential family in town—but she'd been too young to die. But hell, who wasn't?

Slowly he became aware that he was under intense scrutiny. He moved his gaze to the right, to Crystal, who was staring at him as if he were as unwelcome a sight as the vision. How badly had he screwed things up with her? Was it likely that she would ever forget how he'd blackmailed her into cooperating with him? And what if she did? Was she ever going to overlook the fact that he was a cop and she didn't trust cops?

He smiled at her, his best, friendliest, nonthreatening smile. "Can I interest you in a back-roads tour of the county tomorrow?"

"No."

"I'd leave the uniform and the patrol unit at home. You could forget I'm a cop."

"Do *you* ever forget you're a cop?"

He shook his head.

"I didn't think so."

"Aw, come on. I'll bring lunch. I'll show you some of the prettiest places you've ever seen. There's a spot up on the river where the sunrises and sunsets are incredible, and the fishing's not half bad, either."

"And, of course, on the way to that spot up on the river, we'd be stopping at every small clearing you could find, wouldn't we?" Her chilly smile disappeared. "No, thank you."

With some regret, he closed his notebook and stood up. "Thank you for your time."

She remained where she was, gazing impassively at him.

He started to walk away, to return to the store to get his hat, then leave, but abruptly, before his nerve failed him, he turned back. "One more question," he said conversationally, as if that was really all it was. "Are you ever going to forgive me for this and give me a chance?"

Her already china-doll-pale skin turned even paler, then

gave way to two spots of crimson in her cheeks. "A chance to do what?" she asked warily.

Though he smiled, he didn't feel he had much reason. "To impress you. To flatter you. To take you out. Maybe to court you."

She looked as if the idea appalled her at least as much as being the main course for Whitehorn's gossip-hungry crowd. "I— You— No! Never!" Jumping to her feet, she rushed to the trailer and slammed herself inside.

He'd thought he knew all about rejection. Hadn't his own mother abandoned him because his skin was a few shades too dark to suit her bigoted family? He'd dated a lot of women, and had been turned down by his share. But he'd never seen a woman look so repulsed by the idea of going out with him. He'd never made a woman jump and run to get away from him.

And he'd never felt such intense regret.

"Have you ever wondered why I never married?"

Crystal looked up from her breakfast with a fierce scowl. Ever since Deputy Ravencrest had left the day before, Winona had been probing, gently prying, urging, encouraging. She'd made at least twenty comments about that nice Ravencrest boy who came from a good family, was respected both in town and on the reservation, and was a hardworking boy who never gave up.

Rather like her aunt on that last one. The old woman was curious about the outcome of yesterday's meeting. She'd already remarked that when Ravencrest had gone inside to reclaim his hat and glasses, he'd looked stricken. She'd also wondered out loud more than once why Crystal had retreated to her bedroom for much of the afternoon.

"What did you say to him?" Winona had asked at one point, and Crystal had wanted to protest her innocence. *He* was the one guilty of saying something, not her! But then Winona would want to know what he'd said that was so awful, and Crystal would have to tell her. He said he wanted to go out with me, to impress me, to court me.

And Winona would have proof then that her niece was crazy, and that her insanity had nothing to do with her psychic curse.

Crystal took a deep breath and forced herself to reply to her aunt's question. "I always thought you were having much too much fun being the belle of every ball to settle down with one man."

Winona gave her a loving smile and squeezed her hand tightly. "You can be so kind."

And so unkind, Crystal thought, remembering how rudely she'd run from the table yesterday.

"I *was* the belle of every ball," Winona said dreamily. "I may have been flaky, but I was also young, thin, and pretty, and my family was wealthy. I was a good catch. But finally I did fall in love, with a handsome young army officer from Mississippi. His family was wealthy, too, and he was as good a catch as I was. He was very proper, very duty-bound. The night before he shipped off to Europe, he gave me this ring—" the crystal around her neck caught the light as she pulled another chain from underneath her dress to display the gold signet ring dangling from it "—and he promised we would be married when he returned."

She smiled faintly at the ring before looking up at Crystal. "When he didn't return, I quit going to parties. I quit meeting young men. My one true love was dead. My life was over. There was nothing left but endless mourning."

"Aunt Winona, I never knew. That's so sad—"

With purpose, Winona dropped the ring back into place. "It is sad. And it's poppycock. Regardless of what I thought at the time, Henry Dumaine was *not* my one true love, and my life was not over. Heavens, if he'd actually come back to keep his promise, I probably would have run the other way. He was so stiff and straitlaced, and I was impulsive and capricious. Our whole affair was so romantic—the brave, noble soldier heading off to war, the pretty young girl waiting at home and praying for his safety. But if he'd come home, if we'd been forced to go through with the marriage, we would have been at each other's throats in no time. He would have hated the real me, and I would have learned to hate the real him."

She laid her hand on top of Crystal's. "My point, Crystal, is I let that experience close me off to all other possibilities. All those years I was mourning Henry, I could have met someone I might really love, someone who might have really loved me. I missed all those prospective Mr. Rights because of one man. I don't want to see you do the same."

Pulling her hand free, Crystal took her cereal bowl to the sink, rinsed it, then scowled at her aunt. "I'm not looking for Mr. Right."

"Why? Because of what happened back home? Let me tell you this, young lady. James Rich-man Johnson the Third isn't half the man Sloan Ravencrest is. He didn't love you, Crystal! He loved the woman your parents tried to force you to be, but that's not the real you. The first time he got a glimpse of the real you, he turned his back. He betrayed you. He didn't love you!"

"But I loved him!" Crystal angrily dashed a tear from her eye. "I *loved* him, Aunt Winona, and he used me, and he betrayed me."

"So blame him for it! Hate him! But don't take it out on someone you didn't even know at the time. Don't judge Sloan by James's shortcomings. Don't condemn yourself to growing old alone, to never having children, to never having your own family, because you'd rather mourn what you've lost than find something to replace it."

"I'm not mourning James," Crystal said defensively.

"Right. You've had long conversations with Sloan for two days in a row. Can you even tell me what color his eyes are?"

"Brown." There was a note of triumph in Crystal's voice. She ruined the moment, though, when the next words tumbled out, heedless of her desire to stop them. "Dark, intelligent, sensitive brown."

Winona's brows arched toward her hairline and she came out of her chair with a big smile to catch Crystal around the waist and waltz her around the kitchen. "Oh-ho. Maybe young Crystal's not as grief-stricken as she once was. Have you also noticed that he's one of the best-looking men in the county? That his smile could be lethal to a susceptible woman? Have you noticed that he's just the slightest bit sweet on you?"

Sweet on you. It was an old-fashioned phrase and too easily reminded her of another one. *Maybe to court you.*

What would it be like to be courted by Sloan Ravencrest? No doubt, totally different from any time she'd ever spent with James. James had taken her to the finest restaurants their small city had to offer, to parties with the county's and even the state's movers and shakers, to political dinners and debutante balls. Sloan's idea of a good time was probably a picnic lunch on the riverbank, burgers and dancing at the Branding Iron or watching the sun set, then making love under the stars.

A tingle stirred low in her stomach—a tingle of lust, desire, sexual awareness. She'd thought that part of her had died, but it wasn't dead, merely dormant, and Deputy Ravencrest was the wake-up call it had needed to return to life.

Not that she was ever going to do anything about it, she assured herself. A cop who'd already shown himself not averse to blackmail to get what he wanted was *not* deserving of her trust.

Even if he did have incredible eyes and a lethal smile. Even if he did appear to be endearingly, old-fashionedly sweet on her.

Pushing the thoughts away until she had time to strengthen her defenses, she gently disentangled herself from Winona's embrace. "If you don't still love Henry," she began as she wrung out a dishcloth to wipe the dining table, "then why do you still wear his ring?"

Winona's head bobbed in the direction of Crystal's left hand. "For the same reason you still wear James's ring. To remind myself of what my foolishness cost me. But our purposes are different. You want to make certain that you never risk any part of yourself again. I want to be certain that a day doesn't go by when I don't risk every part of myself. Life is short, Crystal, and too precious to waste. I don't want to find myself old someday and regretting what might have been if only I'd been brave enough, bold enough, foolish enough."

After her experience with James, Crystal knew she would never be brave or bold, and she'd been foolish enough to last a lifetime. Not wanting to repeat her mistakes didn't make her somehow less than Winona. It just meant their goals were different. Winona wanted a full, rich life with every chance taken, every path explored.

And Crystal wanted to be safe.

Before she could be forced to acknowledge what a pathetic goal she'd set for herself, the sound of a slamming door outside caught her attention. "We have an early customer," she remarked with a glance at the clock. "Do you want to open up, or should I?"

Winona lifted the curtain to peer out, then flushed crimson. "Oh, dear. I talked too long about Henry and lethal smiles and rings and purposes, and never got to the real point of it all."

Feeling a mild dread dancing up her spine, Crystal placed her hands on her hips and squarely faced her aunt. "What point?"

Outside, footsteps echoed up the steps and across the porch. Winona smiled nervously, clutched the ends of her shawl together and blocked the door while hastily explaining, "I called Sloan last night and in the course of the conversation he mentioned that he had offered to show you around today and you had refused, and so I told him that you'd changed your mind and would like to go, after all."

The knock was perfectly timed, punctuating her last rushed

word. Throwing a helpless, flustered, pleading smile Crystal's way, Winona opened the door and effusively greeted their guest in the same rushed manner even as she pushed past him. "Why, Sloan, it's a pleasure to see you this morning. I do wish I could stay and chat, but someone's got to open up the store this morning. Do have a good time and take good care of my niece."

Once Winona was outside, she gave Sloan a none-too-gentle shove inside, then closed the door. In her mind's eye, Crystal could easily see her scurrying away as if the more distance she put between them, the likelier her plan was to work.

Well, she was wrong. It *wasn't* going to work. She was going to expose Winona for the meddling busybody she was, tell Deputy Ravencrest that she hadn't changed her mind at all and wasn't setting foot outside this trailer with him, and then she would spend the day the way she'd intended to spend it—working in the back room. Alone. Safe.

And pathetic.

She was grinding her teeth in an effort not to shriek her dismay and frustration to the heavens when he spoke. "I would plead total innocence, but I knew when she called last night that you hadn't changed your mind."

"And yet you came, anyway."

"It would have been rude to not show up when she was expecting me."

She finally allowed herself to look at him and wished she hadn't. Instead of his black-and-gray uniform, he wore faded jeans and a snug black T-shirt under a denim jacket. His cowboy hat this morning, cradled in his hands, was black, and his boots were well worn. He looked handsome and sexy and so damn *male*.

She tried to speak, but her mouth had gone impossibly dry. Tried to walk away, but her feet were rooted to the floor. Desperately she reminded herself that this was the man who'd blackmailed her, who'd threatened to expose her to ridicule, and that helped. It didn't cool her blood, but it helped her find her voice. "I'm sorry you drove all the way out here for nothing."

"I've seen you. That's not 'nothing.'"

She silently scoffed at the notion that merely seeing her was worth anything to anyone as he turned to leave. With the door open, he turned back to face her. "You know, if you don't go with me, the old lady's going to pester you all day long. She's going to tell you that you're too young to live cooped up out here the way you do, that you have to learn to take a chance now and then, and she'll be right."

"I don't take chances," she said flatly.

"Sure, you do. You left your home, your job, your family, everything familiar, and came here to live."

"With my elderly great-aunt."

"But you hardly knew her. She told me she hadn't seen you ten times in your entire life."

Crystal acknowledged that with a cool smile. "She left Georgia nearly sixty years ago. She found too much family closeness stifling—at least, with our particular family."

"So you took a chance coming to live in a new place with a virtual stranger. Take another one. Spend the day with me."

"I don't trust you."

"I'm not asking you to…yet."

"You blackmailed and threatened me."

He came a few steps closer. "That was a bluff. I never would have told the Montgomerys about you."

"Easy enough to claim now that you've gotten what you wanted."

His eyes darkening, he closed the distance between them and lowered his voice, made it thick and dark and husky with promise. "Oh, Crystal, that's not all I wanted. Not by a long shot." He punctuated his words with the light touch of one fingertip on her arm, warm pressure starting at her elbow and sliding up the back of her arm, underneath the short sleeve of her T-shirt, up to the sensitive place just below the shoulder, where his touch was a tickle, a heated sensation. Her first impulse was to jerk away from him. Her second was to move in closer, to silently plead for more. She settled for doing neither, but merely holding herself rigid, and he withdrew soon enough—too soon—on his own.

"Take a chance, Crystal."

"I don't trust you," she repeated with less certainty than before.

"So live dangerously. Just once." He grinned, reminding her for all the world of an abundantly good-natured kid. For that moment there was no hint of danger around him, no overwhelming aura of intense sexuality—and believing for even one moment that he was neither dangerous to her nor sexy as hell was the biggest danger of all.

That was why she opened her mouth to refuse him once again and send him on his way. And for some reason, that was also why the words that came out of her mouth didn't have a "no" in the bunch. "All right. I'll need to change clothes first."

Because wanting nothing more from life than to be safe was sad. Because life *was* too precious to waste. Because she was twenty-six and had nothing to look back on but regrets.

Because she desperately wanted more than regrets.

She left him standing by the door and went down the hall to her bedroom. The room was typical of a decades-old mobile home—small, square, cramped. When she'd first come to visit, it had been furnished with a full-size bed, but once she'd decided to stay, she'd traded it for a twin bed from the shop. She was never indulging in sex again, never sharing her bed with anyone ever again, so why give up valuable floor space for unused bed space? she'd reasoned.

Still breathing deeply for control, she kicked off her skirt and stepped into a pair of indigo blues. Over her short-sleeved T-shirt, she added a sweatshirt bearing the logo of her alma mater, then sat on the bed to lace up her tennis shoes. That done, she checked her appearance in the mirror over the built-in dresser in the corner, then realized what she was doing with chagrin.

This *wasn't* a date, or even anything she *wanted* to do, and

Sloan Ravencrest absolutely, positively, was *not* a potential Mr. Right. As long as she was clean and neat, that was all that mattered.

Yeah, right, her inner voice retorted as she touched up her lipstick. She tucked the tube in her pocket, returned to the kitchen, got her keys and a jacket and waited pointedly for Sloan to leave first so she could lock up. Once that was done, they walked together but apart across the yard to the parking lot.

Left at home with the deputy's uniform was the deputy's truck. Instead he was driving his own vehicle, a fairly new, wholeheartedly red pickup that required a high step into the cab. She climbed in before he could offer assistance, fastened her seat belt and directed her gaze straight ahead.

What in the world are you doing? her common sense demanded. Going off to spend much of the day alone with a man she didn't know—a man who, so far, had infuriated her, frightened her, intimidated her and aroused her. A man who made her think too much about things she wanted to forget, who threatened the new life she'd made for herself, who was dangerous and appealing and boyishly charming. Was she crazy? Was she out of her mind?

Or was she coming back to it?

Three

By noon, they'd checked out four clearings on hillsides without any luck. Though she didn't say so, Sloan knew Crystal thought they were searching for a needle in a field full of haystacks, and though he didn't say so, he more or less agreed. Still, they might get lucky. In fact, he already had. He was spending the day with her, wasn't he?

He'd planned their route to bring them around lunchtime to that place on the river he'd told her about the day before—his place. They were too late for the sunrise and way too early for sunset, but it was still the prettiest place in the county, and he still wanted to show it to her.

Not that she was likely to be impressed. So far, judging from the unchanging flat expression she'd worn all morning, nothing had impressed her, least of all him.

But he hadn't even seriously started trying.

When he turned off the highway onto a dirt road, she glanced at him but didn't say anything. Three miles later, when he turned off the dirt road onto what was little more than a faint trail, she finally spoke up. "Where are we going?"

"It's lunchtime. I know a place up here."

"A restaurant? All the way out here?"

"A place," he repeated. "I told you yesterday that I would provide lunch." With a jerk of his head, he indicated the ice chest secured in the back of the truck. "I'm not much of a cook, but I do all right with sandwiches."

"Isn't it a little chilly for a picnic?"

"In Montana, we call this unseasonably warm," he said

with a grin, though she was right. It was cool, but in the sun with their jackets on, they'd be comfortable. And if she needed more heat than her jacket could provide, he'd be generous. He would help her generate it.

The trail snaked through the woods, over ground rough enough in places to jar his teeth, before finally emerging in a meadow. He parked in his usual spot, then circled the truck to walk with Crystal to the bank of the stream. "This is the Little Blue River."

"With emphasis on 'little.' Back home we'd call this a creek."

He couldn't argue that with her. The river was no more than forty feet at its widest point, with a depth ranging from one foot to fifteen or so, but it was clear, clean and cold, and the fishing was good.

"Those are the Crazy Mountains," he went on, gesturing to the jagged-peaked mountains to the west. "Whitehorn is that way, and the rez is over there."

"What's it like?"

"The reservation? It's…a place," he said with a shrug. "There are houses, people, cattle, horses. A general store, a gas station, a post office, some tribal buildings. Lots of empty land."

"Do you live there?"

As far as he could recall, that was the first personal question she'd asked him. Since most of the time in their brief association he would have sworn that she hadn't experienced a moment's curiosity about him, he was pleasantly surprised…and pleased. "I grew up there, but a few years ago I decided to get a place in town. It was easier for the job."

"Do you have family there?"

He laughed. "It would be easier to count the people on the rez who aren't connected to my father's family than the ones who are. My dad is one of thirteen kids, and most of them still live out there."

"What about your mother's family?"

"I've never met them," he said, then casually added, "Never met her, either."

That made her look at him, with a mix of surprise and sympathy darkening her eyes. "Is she dead?"

"I don't know." He turned back to the truck, intending to get the quilt he'd stuffed behind the seat and the ice chest. She walked alongside. "My father met her when they were in college. He thought they would get married after graduation and come back here to raise a family, like his father and his older brothers. He didn't realize that, for her, sleeping with an Indian was…I don't know. Daring. Exciting. Forbidden fruit, and all that garbage. But marrying him was out of the question. So was raising his child."

"I'm sorry."

He reached inside the truck for the quilt, handed it to her, then lifted the ice chest out. She chose a spot near the river to spread the blanket, then gracefully lowered herself to sit cross-legged in one corner.

"It was for the best," he said as he sat opposite her. "She minded that I was half Cheyenne, while my father couldn't care less that I'm half white. She was afraid to even let her family know she was pregnant. My father's family raised me, and they treated me no differently than all the other kids."

"Aren't you the least bit curious about her?"

He leaned toward her to emphasize his answer. "She gave me away when I was a couple days old because she didn't like the color of my skin. What more do I need to know?"

"I can't imagine…" With a shake of her head, she let the words trail away. As if it were the most natural thing in the world, she opened the ice chest and began unpacking their meal. It probably did come naturally to her. The well-bred Southern belle, raised to be the perfect wife, the perfect hostess, gracious in all situations, was a stereotype, he knew well. But stereotypes had to come from somewhere. If there hadn't been generations of lovely young Southern women raised in just that way, the stereotype would never have come into being.

She removed plates and cloth napkins wrapped around silverware from the tray balanced across the top of the chest. "Are you an environmentalist?" she asked, her long fingers unrolling the cloth, catching the silverware before it tumbled, folding the napkin with a flourish. He was so caught up in watching her hands that her question barely registered.

Realizing that she was waiting for an answer, he blinked, then lifted his gaze to her face. "Why do you ask?"

"Most people use paper and plastic. But most people care more about convenience than the earth's resources or its garbage dumps overflowing with non-decomposing products."

"Would it make you think better of me if I said I care a great deal about the earth and the way we take care of it?" He grinned at the flush that tinged her cheeks pink. "Truth is, I was running late and I didn't have time to stop at the store. It was either real plates and cloth napkins or paper towels and...well, paper towels. I do recycle, though, and I do believe we should take better care of our environment than we do. Our kids deserve a place as beautiful as this to visit, don't they?"

She glanced around before unwrapping the foil that held their sandwich. "Who owns this property?"

"I do. I'm going to build a house here when I get married."

"It'll be a long drive to work."

"But worth it to come home to this every evening." And maybe to her. She could belong here, could belong to him, if she wanted. If she would trust him. If his instincts were right—and his instincts were almost always right. "We're on the back porch right now. This is the view I want from the living room and from our bedroom. The kids' bedrooms will be upstairs, and the front porch will face east, so we can watch the sun rise with our morning coffee."

"You have a lot of plans. Don't you think your prospective wife will want a say in things?"

"I'm sure she will. And she can do whatever she wants with the rest of it. Those are my only requirements."

After fishing out canned drinks, a bag of chips and a bag of cookies, she closed the ice chest lid, then positioned it between them for a table. The sandwich—meats, cheeses and vegetables, all thinly sliced—filled a wide loaf of French bread slathered with creamy dressing. He'd cut it into small sections before he wrapped it. Now he watched as she helped herself to the smallest portion.

They ate in silence for a few minutes, until she reached for the next smallest portion. "This is good, and the bread is wonderful. Where did you buy it?"

"I picked it up at Arlen's kitchen." When she looked puzzled, he went on. "That's my dad. He's the best baker in the state."

"Is that what he does for a living?"

"Nope. He raises cattle, horses and kids. The baking is for fun."

"So you're not an only child."

"I was when it counted. I was in college before Dad married Amy. I've got four half brothers under the age of ten." Since he hadn't asked her a personal question all morning, he decided he was due. "Are you an only child?"

"To my disappointment and my parents' great dismay."

"They wanted a big family?"

"No. They intended to have only one child. They just didn't intend for her to be such an embarrassment." Realizing that she'd said more than she'd meant to, she made a brittle, apologetic gesture. Then, as if she figured she might as well get it over with now rather than later, she explained. "They thought they had the perfect daughter who would grow up to make the perfect marriage, provide them with perfect grandchildren and make them perfectly proud. Instead they had me." Her voice was unsteady there at the end, and her hand trembled when she reached for her soda. Leaving it alone, she laced her fingers together and hid her hands in her lap.

If he knew her better, he would put his arms around her, hold her tight, soothe her without words. But he didn't, so words were all he had. "What did they think was so wrong with you?" he asked quietly.

She looked up, tried to smile as if it didn't matter, but the smile was really a grimace, and her voice was taut with anger and deep hurt. "I was different. I saw things no one else saw, heard voices no one else heard. All they wanted was a pretty little girl, and all they got was a pretty little freak."

Abruptly she pushed her plate away, jumped to her feet and walked away. Restlessness lengthened her stride, and embarrassment, he suspected, made her shoulders hunch and her head bow.

His appetite gone, Sloan repacked everything but the cookies. Taking the bag along, he walked upriver a hundred feet to where Crystal had finally settled on a boulder at the water's edge. Though space was tight, leaving only inches between them, he sat beside her and offered a cookie. When she hesitated, he gently nudged her with one elbow. "I have it on good authority that cookies are always good for what ails you."

She took the cookie, then delicately bit a chunk of chocolate from the edge. "Whose authority?"

"My grandmother's. I'll take you to meet her sometime. She's eighty years old, four-foot-nothin', and can still keep us all in line with nothing more than a look. I think you'd like her. But I have to warn you. She thinks Ravencrest men lose their wits around pretty white women."

Taking a bigger nibble of the cookie, she glanced sidelong at him. "Is that true?"

"I think it might be. My mother certainly made a fool of my father, and I'm feeling a bit foolish right now." He felt her glance skim across him again, but this time he was looking out toward the mountains. "I really wouldn't have told the Montgomery family anything about you. I knew you weren't cooperating because you were afraid. I knew you'd been hurt. I was just trying—"

"To use it to your advantage."

The truth sounded uglier from her point of view in her

honeyed drawl. Even though he believed he'd done what was necessary, even though he would do it again if he had to, he felt himself flush with the heat of embarrassment. "To do my job," he corrected.

"No matter what." Though there was no inflection in her voice, that sounded ugly, too.

"Put yourself in the family's place. What if Christina were your daughter, your sister, and someone out there knew something about her? Wouldn't you want to know, no matter what?"

"Yes," she admitted readily. "But I'm not in their place. I can't feel their fear and sorrow. I can only feel my own."

She finished the cookie, then took another when he offered. When it was gone, she pulled her knees up, rested her chin on them and stared off into the distance with him. After several long minutes had passed, she finally spoke again. "What I said back there... Just forget it, will you?"

Just forget that her parents had made her feel like a freak. That they'd blamed her for something she'd had no control over. That because they were narrow-minded bigots, she felt fear and sorrow.

Oh, yeah. And while he was at it, why didn't he also just forget how much he wanted to get to know her, how much time he'd spent thinking about her, how much effort he'd expended to meet her?

"Just forgetting" was impossible. But if she wanted to pretend it wasn't, he could play along. "All right," he agreed. "I'll forget."

And because he was willing to lie, she pretended to believe him.

After a time she asked, "Why are they called Crazy Mountains?"

"Some people say it's because the peaks are so jagged. Some say it's because they're geologically different from the other ranges around here. Most people prefer the story that a woman whose family died and left her alone on the prairie went crazy and wandered off into the mountains to die."

"Why do they call the reservation Laughing Horse?"

"I don't have a clue. But give me a minute and I'll come up with something."

She smiled then. It was small and fleeting, but it was a real smile, and it made him feel as if he'd accomplished something. But before his ego could swell too much, she stood up and dusted her jeans. "We'd better go. We've still got places to look at."

The decided lack of enthusiasm in her voice chased away some of his pleasure. He caught up with her halfway back to their picnic blanket. "We don't have to do that."

"I don't mind."

"What happens if we find the place?"

Wariness stole over her again. "You're the deputy. You tell me."

"I mean, to you. For you. Will it affect you?"

"I don't know."

"Are you concerned that it might?"

"I don't know," she repeated, the words subdued. He knew the vision had been powerfully disturbing to her in the relative safety of the Stop-n-Swap's back room. How much more disturbing could those sensations be if she was right in the middle of the clearing?

"I'll be right there," he assured her.

She gave no response.

Back at their picnic site, he carried the ice chest to the truck, then turned to watch as she shook out the quilt. At first, she started to fold it, but, with a noticeable shiver, she wrapped it around her shoulders instead. The blanket covered her clothing except where the edges flipped back around her ankles, and the vivid reds, blues and greens flattered her.

In that moment, as she made her way slowly across the meadow to him, he wanted her with an intensity he'd never felt before. His skin grew warm, his body hard, and every breath he took was shallow, raw. He should turn away, before she noticed. Or maybe he should take hold of that quilt when she was close enough and haul her against him for the hardest, greediest, neediest kiss either of them had ever known. Maybe he should seduce her right there, right then, and overlook the fact that she didn't trust him, was pretty sure she didn't like him, and for damn sure didn't want him around.

In the end, he didn't turn away, and he didn't grab her, kiss her, seduce her. He simply looked at her, wrapped in that quilt of bright colors his grandmother had made for him, and said in a perfectly normal voice, "You should have told me you were cold."

Perfectly normal...for a man who was incredibly aroused.

"I'm not cold," she denied, then nonsensically explained, "I'm just admiring your quilt. Did someone make it for you?"

"My grandmother."

"It looks new."

"Not new. Just not used." She'd pieced the intricate star pattern by hand and had spent countless hours quilting it by hand, too. All that work, all that love, in a quilt intended for use by one of her favorites among her grandsons and the woman he chose to marry. She'd warned him to choose well, but in the four years since she'd presented it to him, he hadn't chosen at all.

Or maybe he had.

His fingers were itching to reach out and touch the fabric— to touch Crystal. It was only through greater self-control than he'd known he possessed that he was able to stop himself.

"It's beautiful," she said as she shrugged it off her shoulders, then began folding it. "Too beautiful to be using on the ground."

On the contrary, laying it on the ground, and laying her down on top of it, was just about the best use he could think of.

She returned the quilt to its place behind the seat, then climbed inside the pickup. After taking a couple of deep, calming breaths, he joined her.

Crystal stared out the side window as they left the meadow. Part of her was glad to escape the intimacy of the place, but part wanted to stay there, to spend the rest of the afternoon right there next to the river and watch the sun go down. She wanted to avoid all other clearings, to keep that little knot in her stomach from growing, to keep for-the-most-part pleasant memories of a Saturday afternoon picnic from turning into her worst nightmare.

But she didn't suggest a longer stay. She simply shuddered with foreboding as they followed the trail out of the meadow, as the forest closed heavily around them again.

Sensing movement behind her, she smiled faintly. "Don't bother. I'm warm enough."

After a moment's unnatural stillness, Sloan asked, "How did you know?"

"Madame Crystal knows all, sees all," she said in a spooky voice. Turning to face him, she watched him withdraw his hand from the quilt behind her seat and return it to the steering wheel. He had good hands—strong, capable, nails neat and trimmed, palms nicely callused from years of work. James's hands had been weak, pampered. He'd visited his manicurist far more often than she had, and he'd never partaken in any activity that might leave calluses, not without protective gloves.

James had never taken her on a picnic, either, and he'd never, ever, fixed her something to eat with his own hands. She doubted he'd ever fixed himself a meal with his own hands.

What was the point, she wondered, in comparing Sloan to her former fiancé? Making note of all the ways they were different didn't change the ways in which they were alike. James had been, as Sloan now was, in a position to use her, betray her, destroy her. She had trusted James with her life and her heart, and he'd done just that. Could she risk trusting Sloan?

Today was an incredibly ambivalent day for her. Part of her wanted one thing, part wanted another. She wanted to trust Sloan, and to keep him at a distance—to never see him again, and to hold tight to him and never let go. Back in the meadow, when he'd assured her he would be with her if finding the clearing triggered anything, she'd wanted to say something scathingly sarcastic, and to quietly, sincerely thank him.

They *would* find the clearing. That was what the knot in her stomach was about. She didn't know if it would be the next place he took her to or if they would examine twenty other clearings first, but they would find the place where Christina Montgomery had suffered so terribly.

The idea of standing in the spot which she had seen in her violent vision filled Crystal with apprehension. She'd had only one such vision before, and there had been no reason to visit that site. Would the psychic energy that had given life to the vision in the first place remain in the area? Would it—Christina, her spirit, her essence—understand that Crystal was trying to help, or would it fill her mind even more vividly than before?

"Are you okay?"

She glanced at Sloan. "I'm fine. Why do you ask?"

"You're pale, and the tension is all but radiating off you." Reaching across the truck cab, he fumbled for her left hand—fumbled, because at some point, without realizing it, she'd crossed her arms tightly and tucked her hands between her arms and body. "Your hand is like ice."

His was warm when it closed around hers, so warm and strong. The heat seeped into her body, along with a vague sense of comfort and security. It allowed her to take a deep breath, to relax her posture and find some small bit of courage. "I'm all right," she murmured. "Just…afraid."

"You've never had a vision like this."

She thought of the other time, the other girl, and felt a wave of sorrow as she lied. "No. Not like this."

"Maybe we won't find the clearing."

A fresh stab of tension swept through her, curling her fingers tightly around his. "We will."

He gave her a long, steady look but said nothing.

After a few minutes of silence he pulled over to the side

of the road, released her hand and got out of the truck to come around to her side. There were several faint trails leading up the hillside, as if people used the wide shoulder as a jumping-off point for a day hike. Maybe some family lived in isolation on the other side of the hill, she thought whimsically, and their teenage daughter used the trails to meet secretly with the boyfriend her parents didn't approve of.

Whatever the purpose of the trails, she didn't think they were in the right place. She would feel more distress if they were so close to the place where Christina had died. Still, she followed Sloan up the hill, past boulders and dry washes, into woods that offered shade and trapped the earth's rich scents close to the ground.

When they reached their goal, she glanced around, confirming what she already knew, then shook her head. "Do you know every clearing in the county?"

Sloan grinned. "Maybe. We roamed all over the countryside when we were kids—my cousins and me. I've hiked most of the county, I've probably fished every body of water, and what I haven't covered on foot, I have on horseback."

"Your father gave you a lot of freedom."

"Yes," he simply agreed, then asked, "Did your parents give you any?"

"Not that I noticed. We lived in town. Even if I'd had room to wander like that, it wouldn't have been allowed. Not much was."

"So what did you do with your summers?"

"Took piano lessons. And ballet. Won the library's award for reading the most books during summer vacation six years in a row. Learned to swim and ride horses and play tennis, and went to mother-daughter luncheons at the country club once a week."

"Sounds like you were prissy as all hell."

The good-natured insult surprised her. So did the laugh that escaped her. "I was, I suppose. And look at me now. Working in a junk store and living in a trailer in the godforsaken wilderness."

"And traipsing around the countryside with a wild Indian," he added. "Which part of that would upset your parents the most?"

"Everything about me upsets my parents." Though true, her answer was evasive, because there was no doubt about it, the "Indian" would disturb her mother most. Marabeth Cobbs could turn the junk store into an antique shop, and describe the trailer in such a way one would never guess it was on wheels. She could even make Montana seem the most sophisticated place west of the Mississippi, but there wasn't much she could do to transform Sloan.

"He's not our kind," she would stress in her best hypercritical-mother's voice, which meant many things. Not a Southerner in general or an old-moneyed, illustrious-historied Southerner in particular. Not of their social prominence. Not of their financial status. If the occasion called for it, not of their religion or their political persuasion. Definitely not of their race.

Marabeth would look at Sloan and see a minority, a lowercaste civil servant, a commoner working at a common job and living a common life—and generations of inbred selfcenteredness enabled her to turn the word "common" into an insult. He lacked Southern roots, a fortune of his own or claim to someone else's, power and influence and the ambition to gain more power and more influence, and that would make him unacceptable in her eyes.

While in Crystal's eyes, he was... Handsome. Kind. Appealing. Sexy as hell. Dangerous.

A man who could make her forget everything.

A man who could cost her everything.

"There's another place, up and around that way." Sloan gestured with one hand. "Want to check it out?"

"Is there access from the road without coming this way?"

He shook his head, and so did she. "Christina wasn't here."

"You can tell that."

"I can't explain how. I just know..." If Christina had

come this way, she was convinced she would somehow *feel* it. She wouldn't be able to stand here with nothing more pressing on her mind than childhood pastimes and her parents' prejudices.

"Okay. Then let's head back."

The downhill trip was easier than going up. As soon as they were buckled into their seats, he pulled onto the highway, driving north. "You still play the piano?"

"Not if I can avoid it." She loved music, but hated making it herself.

"Tennis?"

"No." That had been James's game—that, and golf. She'd joined him at the country club at least twice a month to play one or the other, and hated it.

"Ride horses?"

She stopped her automatic no before it escaped. "I liked riding, but when I was…oh, sixteen or so, my mother made me stop. All that was necessary, she said, was that I know *how* to ride. It wasn't proper that I keep proving it."

"I keep a horse at my dad's place. We can borrow one of his for you and go for a ride sometime if you want."

She was supposed to be on her guard with him, she reminded herself, enduring this time together because it was the easiest way to get him out of her life. She was supposed to be satisfied with the life she'd made for herself since coming to Whitehorn—the all-work, no-play, very-few-friends-and-absolutely-no-men life that she'd sworn she would live until she died.

But she wanted to go riding with him.

She looked at him and saw nothing to be wary of. Just a nice guy asking her to go for a ride, not trying to take her for one. "Maybe," she agreed shyly. If her common sense didn't regain control before then.

After a few miles the road came to an end and Sloan shut off the engine. This area, she was sure, served as a trail head for hikers. Instead of just the shoulder, there was an actual parking lot—primitive, no markers, room for about six cars.

Crystal climbed out of the truck and shivered, certain that the temperature had dropped ten degrees in the last ten minutes.

That was silly, she told herself. The sun had merely gone behind a cloud, though she made the claim while staring at her own shadow. The elevation here was a little higher than the other places they'd been to, even if she hadn't been aware of the change. She'd just caught a bit of wind blowing down from the north, though everything was still.

But there was nothing silly about the knot in her stomach. It made her feel queasy, made her feet leaden. And there was nothing silly about her increased heart rate, or the tightness in her chest.

This was the place. Christina had come here one evening three months ago, and she had died here.

Just as he had at every other site, Sloan started along one path. After a moment, she forced herself to follow, though she wanted nothing more than to crawl back into his truck, curl up inside his quilt and hide from the world, from her visions, from herself.

The trail required nothing more than an easy stroll at the start, but gradually began to incline. Crystal kept her gaze locked on the ground ahead of her, not noticing the view, not looking to see the road curve out of sight, or the lake—for now she knew that was what it was—shimmering in the afternoon sun.

As the trail grew steeper, she heard the rustle of skittering stones, cascading dirt. Sloan had taken a big step up and the dirt had given way beneath his weight. After catching himself, he leaned against a boulder as tall as he was and bent forward to give her a hand. Once she stood beside him, he kept hold of her hand and took the other hand, too, and she felt his intense gaze lock onto her face.

"You can wait at the truck," he said at last. "You've told me what to look for."

Without looking at him, she shook her head. "I need to be sure."

He didn't argue, didn't insist she leave the task to the bigger, braver, stronger man. He simply squeezed her hands reassuringly, let go, and resumed the climb.

The part of her that wanted to be as independent and capable as Winona was grateful he didn't argue. The part that was scared senseless wished he'd made the suggestion one more time. Pride had demanded she refuse once. Self-preservation would have let her flee a second time.

The higher they climbed, the more difficult breathing became for Crystal, but not because of the physical demands. Except for the place by the boulder where Sloan had helped her, it was a fairly easy trail. It was the dark aura that surrounded the area, and the knowledge that in another few minutes she would be stepping right into the scene of her worst vision.

Thanks to Sloan's broad shoulders and her own refusal to look around, she didn't see the clearing until they were at the edge. He stopped, then stepped to one side and reached for her hand, pulling her forward.

First she raised her gaze to the vista beyond—the road, the lake, the cluster of buildings on the far side, exactly where she'd known they would be. She skimmed over the two slabs of stone set at a right angle among a tumble of other boulders, and the pines and, finally, the place where Christina had lain.

Seeing only dirt covered with pine needles, she gave a tiny sigh of relief. Somewhere deep inside, she had feared they would find Christina's body, or whatever remained. Instead there was nothing.

Nothing but the feelings. The fear, the terrible pain, the other woman's certainty she was dying.

Letting go of Sloan required effort, but she managed, and walked slowly to the place where Christina had lain. Nothing had survived the last three months—no stains that could be blood, no scratches in the dirt where she'd clawed, no tracks, nothing. Gathering courage, Crystal knelt, reached out one hand and stopped, her fingertips centimeters above the ground, struck by sensations so powerful that she nearly lost herself in them. Incredible pain, paralyzing fear, sadness, sorrow, panic. She tried to catch her breath but couldn't, tried to move, but the pain was too intense, and the hand, the slender, dirty, bloodied hand, reached for her, pleaded with her. *Help me, please help me.*

With a great cry, Crystal wrenched free of the image. Her breath came in terrible gasps, in heartbroken sobs, as she jumped to her feet and ran blindly back the way she'd come.

"Crystal!"

She shoved past Sloan and raced down the trail, slipping, stumbling. The small part of her mind that remained rational knew she should slow down or risk breaking a limb, but emotion drove her recklessly on. Somewhere she lost the trail, but she couldn't slow down, couldn't backtrack to find it again. She simply pushed on through the brush, praying it would lead her back to the parking lot and safety, and thankfully, when her legs were fatigued and her lungs bursting, when her whole body was consumed with shaking, it did. She broke free of the woods and saw the bright red truck ahead.

She was leaning against the locked passenger door, struggling for air and control, when pounding footsteps slowed behind her. "Crystal." Sloan's voice was short of breath but quiet and steady, and his hand, when he laid it on her shoulder, was solid and warm. When she didn't pull away, he slid his arms around her and stood there in silence and held her.

Gasps gave way to sobs which, after a time, gave way to relatively normal breathing. The trembling slowly stopped, and somewhere along the way she traded leaning against the truck for leaning against Sloan. He didn't seem to mind in the least.

She couldn't guess how long they stood that way. Long enough for her chills to go away, for her breathing to return to normal, for her fear to become manageable. Long enough to start feeling silly. She released her grip on his arm, subtly tried to pull away, but he was slow to let her go. She faced him, but couldn't get her gaze higher than his middle. "I—I'm sor—"

Hushing her, he lifted her chin, gently untangled a twig from her hair, brushed his palm soothingly over her short hair to her shoulder. "Are you all right?" He didn't sound the least bit annoyed, impatient or put out with her emotional display.

James had always gotten annoyed, impatient or put out.

To her dismay, tears welled and overflowed, though whether she was crying for Christina, whom she'd never even met, or herself, she couldn't say. "It wasn't fair," she murmured as he pulled her close again. It wasn't fair that Christina's last minutes of life had been so traumatic, that she'd suffered so greatly before her death. And it wasn't fair that Crystal's own life had gotten so traumatic, that she'd been abandoned by people who'd claimed to love her, that something beyond her control should cause her such sorrow.

It wasn't fair, damn it! It just wasn't fair.

Four

She felt so small and fragile in his arms, Sloan thought as he stroked her hair with one hand and rubbed her back in small circles with the other. Even her tears were delicate and small. No great gasps, no heaving sobs. Just delicate little heartrending tears.

He shouldn't have made her come. He knew nothing about parapsychology. He had no clue what effect such things would have on the person involved, but he did know that Crystal wasn't the strongest woman around. Her so-called psychic gift had caused her a great deal of pain before, and he'd had no right to demand that she put herself in a position where it could do so again.

No right...but he'd do it again if it would help locate Christina or her killer.

Before long she quieted. After a time, she raised her head, sniffled, then dabbed ineffectively at the damp spot she'd left on his jacket. She didn't try to offer another apology. Instead she smiled unsteadily and said, "Thank you. I needed that."

"Any time. I've got two shoulders, no waiting."

She dried her cheeks with her fingers, then took a deep breath. "I don't normally cry."

Not normally. But this made twice in three days, and he was responsible both times. It stirred his guilt. "Maybe you should. Crying is good for the soul."

"Not when you cry alone." She pulled out of his arms, then backed up to put space between them. "I—I'd like to go home now."

He unlocked the doors, then walked around to the other

side. By the time he'd settled in his seat, she looked for all the world as if she were in control again. But he didn't miss the slight tremble in her hands, the occasional quiver of her bottom lip or the tiny catch in her breath.

"Who left you to cry alone back in Georgia? Who, besides your parents, wasn't there for you?" He asked the questions in a casual, conversational tone as he pulled back onto the road, though he expected no answer. Regaining control for Crystal, he suspected, meant shutting off her emotions, blocking out old hurts and disappointments, living only in the moment. But he didn't want her shutting off her emotions. He wanted her to open up to him, to trust him with those hurts, to trust him with who she really was, with what she really felt.

After a mile or so had passed, she surprised him with an answer. "His name was James. James Richmond Johnson the Third. Aunt Winona calls him Rich-man."

Rich-man. Of course. What other kind of man would the marriageable daughter of a prestigious, old-money Georgia family be attracted to?

Not someone who made little more than a living wage. Not an illegitimate nobody who'd grown up poor and was never going to have much. Not someone who'd barely squeaked through his second year of college before chucking it all and coming home to pin on a badge.

"Doctor, lawyer or banker?" he asked dryly.

"Lawyer. How did you know?"

"Call it a lucky guess." Rich and smart, and probably ambitious, too.

Then she added one more thing that sent his insecurities on their way and roused his curiosity in their place. "He's an assistant district attorney in the county where I grew up."

I don't like cops, she'd told him on Thursday. *Or deputies or prosecutors, or any of the so-called good guys.* Good ol' James was a prosecutor, and he'd let her down. How?

"What was James to you?" Friend, boyfriend, lover or—

"My fiancé." There was that little catch in her voice again.

"If things hadn't fallen apart, we would have been married in June in a quiet little intimate service for six hundred."

He pretended to concentrate on driving while he envisioned the sort of wedding she was talking about. It probably would have taken place in the garden of some incredible Southern mansion, with Crystal in a one-of-a-kind gown with a train so heavy and long that she would have needed assistance to walk down the aisle. She would have had a dozen or more attendants, a string quartet, exotic flowers from the other side of the world, food and drink to impress the impossible-to-impress. She would have been registered at the finest stores, would have raked in a fortune in gifts, and the whole production probably would have equaled Whitehorn's budget for the year.

When he got married, it would probably be in front of the preacher at the Baptist church in town, with a backyard party at his folks' place afterward. His dad would butcher a cow and fire up the smoker, the music would come from the boom box in the kitchen window, and the whole thing would cost practically nothing.

But he had no doubt which ceremony would be more fun. He also had no doubt which marriage would be happier and last longer.

"So you were in love with Rich-man."

"Yes."

"Are you still?"

When she didn't answer, he looked at her. She was gazing at her hands, where the fingers of her right hand anxiously twisted the gold nugget ring on her left hand. He didn't have to be psychic to know the ring belonged to James. The man had let her down when she needed him, had hurt her so deeply that she'd fled all the way to Montana, and yet she still wore his ring. That was answer enough, wasn't it?

The knowledge created an uncomfortable emptiness in the pit of his stomach. She wasn't supposed to be in love with another man. Sloan had enough problems to overcome without adding that to the mix.

After a moment she pulled the ring off and held it up to catch the late-afternoon sunlight that slanted in the window. She turned it this way and that, sending prisms dancing across the dashboard, then slowly returned it to her finger. "No," she said quietly, confidently. "I'm not in love with him."

"Then why are you wearing his ring?"

"To remind me."

"Of what?"

"Of what I had. What I lost. And why."

So the ring was a daily reminder of James's betrayal, a reminder to not trust anyone, to not give her heart, to never give anyone the chance to hurt her again. He would have almost preferred that she still love the bastard. It seemed an easier task to win her love from someone else than to overcome her defenses, distrust and hurt.

He would have liked to pursue the conversation further but the Stop-n-Swap came into sight ahead. He wanted to pass it by, to keep driving until the road ran out, and then to set off cross-country to see where they ended up. Instead he pulled into the parking lot, taking a space at the end nearest the trailer, and shutting off the engine. "Thank you," he said in the ensuing silence.

She looked uncomfortable. "For what? You didn't find anything."

"We found the clearing."

"With no proof that Christina had ever been there."

He believed she had. He believed those emotions he'd seen cross Crystal's face back there had been Christina's emotions. "I didn't get a chance to look around. I'm going back now."

"And if you find something?"

"Then I'll have to write a report."

The wariness was joined by a tight, pinched look. "With my name in it. My vision."

"I'll do everything I can to keep it between me and the sheriff."

But that wasn't a strong enough reassurance. She expected the worst from him, because that was what she'd gotten from James. He managed a smile. "Hey, look, there may not be anything there to write a report about."

"No, I may just be crazy."

"I didn't mean—"

"I have to go." Quickly she opened the door, slid out, then started toward the trailer, her long legs eating up the ground. She was at the steps before he caught up with her.

"Crystal, I didn't say that. I just meant that it's been a long time. The area's exposed to the elements. Whatever evidence there was might have disappeared."

"Well, who knows? Maybe you'll get lucky." With a brittle shrug, she unlocked the door and swung it open.

He caught her arm before she could cross the threshold. "Don't do this, Crystal. What do you think is going to happen if people around here find out you're psychic? Do you think they're going to cringe from you in horror? Do you think they'll snicker and smirk and call you Crazy Crys—"

Just like people snickered and called her aunt "Crazy Cobbs." He broke off, but it was too late.

"Crazy Crystal, just like her crazy old aunt. Those loony Cobbses. Maybe they *are* harmless, but, just in case, shouldn't they be locked up for their own good?" She gave him a thin, coldly lonely smile. "Go back out to the clearing and look, Deputy, and if you find something, write your report. But don't bother coming here again. I'll be too busy packing to say goodbye."

Pulling her arm free, she went inside, closed the door and secured the lock.

Rankled by her use of his title, and more shaken than he wanted to admit by her threat to leave Whitehorn, he considered shouting through the door or going to the shop to get Winona's key and letting himself in. But in the end, he did neither. He returned to his truck and drove back to the clearing.

Nothing had changed. There was nothing to indicate that

Christina had ever been there, nothing at all to suggest that she might have died there. He knelt where Crystal had knelt, reached out his hand just as she had, but he felt nothing. No otherworldly connection, no fear, no foreboding.

Maybe he was too pragmatic, too much an unbeliever. Maybe the spirit, the energy, the memory, whatever the hell it was, was accessible only to someone who believed.

Crystal believed, but he couldn't ask her to come here again. It was too cruel. But what about Winona? She was a believer, too, and embraced the whole idea far more willingly than Crystal did. If there was some psychic energy here, surely she could detect it.

Deciding he would ask the old lady to come out with him the next morning, he straightened and began a serious survey of the site. He was looking for anything to suggest that he and Crystal weren't the first people to set foot in the clearing in ages—a gum wrapper, a footprint, a broken twig. He searched the clearing, then the ten feet beyond, then another ten feet, and found nothing.

That should make Crystal happy, he thought as he returned to the clearing. No clues meant no report, and no report meant her secret was safe. He should be happy, too, because as long as he kept her secret, she had no reason to leave Whitehorn.

Besides, it wasn't even logical that Christina would come here. She hadn't been the outdoors type. Her idea of a good time had been shopping, spending Daddy's money and partying. A nighttime hike wasn't in keeping with what he knew of her, especially if the rumors that she'd been pregnant were true.

But Crystal had seemed so certain that Christina had come here, so convinced that something terrible had happened to her here.

After a moment Sloan realized that his gaze was fixed on yellow lights on the far side of the lake. Dusk had settled, and tiny pin-dots of light scattered across the darkness indicated that friends and neighbors were home safe for the night.

It would be in his best interests to head home, too, before it got so dark that he tripped on the trail and broke his fool neck.

He made it back to his truck without incident, but instead of turning toward town and his apartment, he went the opposite direction. It was only a few miles to the reservation, only three miles farther to the house where he grew up. He tapped the horn once, an old signal to let his father know he was there, then headed for the pasture north of the house.

There were more than a dozen horses in the field, everything from quarter horses to paints to Arabians, plus Amy's Appaloosa. Leaning on the board fence, he whistled and half of them wandered over, expecting feed, a treat or at the least a good scratching. His paint separated from the others and walked right up to him, stretching his neck across the fence for Sloan's attention.

"I'd ask how things are going, but the fact that you're out here with your horse on a Saturday night tells me all I need to know."

Sloan glanced at the man who came to stand beside him. His father was two inches taller, ten pounds leaner, and his skin a few shades darker, but other than that, the resemblance between them was strong. So was the bond between them.

"How are things going out here?" Sloan asked.

Arlen smiled. "I can't complain, and I shouldn't brag. What about you?"

Sloan could tell him about work or catch him up on everything happening in town, but he chose a different topic. "I met a woman. She's white. Doesn't care much for me. Doesn't want to see me again. But I think I'm going to marry her."

His father was silent for a time, taking all that in. They'd discussed the women in each other's lives quite often, but this was the first time marriage had come into the conversation since his dad had announced ten years ago that he was marrying Amy. Clearly, it had thrown him for a loop.

After a while Arlen cleared his throat, then said, "Well,

hell, son, why settle for something so easy? Why don't you find yourself a real challenge?" Then, "Tell me about her."

"Her name is Crystal Cobbs. She's from Georgia. She's Winona Cobbs's great-niece, and she's...delicate as hell." Distracted by the image of her, he forgot about scratching until the horse butted him. He absentmindedly started again. "Remember that mare you got from Uncle Delbert years ago?"

"Thoroughbred so skittish even her own shadow spooked her?"

"That's Crystal. She got her heart broken by some idiot fiancé and she's determined not to ever risk it again."

His father chuckled. "Spoken like a man who's never had his heart broke before. Take it from one who has, son, it's not an easy thing to risk again."

Sloan glanced at him. After the experience with Sloan's mother, it had taken his father almost twenty years to get serious about another woman. Back then, if he'd given it any thought, he would have guessed that Arlen had no need of a regular woman in his life, or that he'd enjoyed dating multiple women too much to settle for just one, or even that he hadn't been able to find a woman who wanted him *and* the reservation *and* his illegitimate, half white kid.

He had never thought residual feelings for his mother could have played a role in Arlen's choice to remain single. He had to admit, he wasn't totally comfortable with the idea.

"What did this idiot fiancé do to break her heart, besides not marrying her?"

"I'm not sure. I know it involved betraying her trust."

"That can be worse than breaking a heart."

And harder to forgive, especially for Crystal, who, he suspected, was already woefully low on forgiveness.

"Does she have any notion that you're planning to marry her?"

Sloan leaned back against the fence, his elbows hooked over the top rail. "I doubt it. She still hasn't gotten past the fact that I'm a cop—she doesn't trust cops—or that I know something about her that she wanted to keep secret.''

"You'd better tread carefully, son,'' Arlen warned, "or you may convince her that you're no better than the idiot fiancé.''

Sloan didn't tell him that he'd already used her secret to blackmail her into cooperating with him. It wasn't something he was proud of. "I got her to consider coming out here to ride some weekend. Is that all right with you?''

"Of course. You can stay for dinner. Let the family meet her.''

"Family,'' Sloan knew, included his grandparents, whose house was just a quarter mile down the road, and any aunts, uncles or cousins who happened to come calling. They were all good-humored, good-natured, passionate people, and he tried without success to imagine Crystal in their midst. She was no doubt much more accustomed to quiet, formal dinners than loud, rowdy parties—and every meeting of the Raven-crest clan was a party.

"She's an only child who spent a lot of time at country club dinners. Could we restrict dinner invitations the first time to the grandparents?''

"Next you'll be asking that you get the chance to propose to her before Amy and your grandmother start planning the wedding,'' his father teased, then relented. "All right. I suppose this one time we can do that.''

Silence settled between them, the companionable kind that a man could be comfortable with. Sloan had never known an easier man to be quiet with than his father. For as long as he could remember, they'd shared these times, where neither had to talk if he didn't want to, but where nothing was off limits for discussion if he did want to. For the first time in longer than he could remember, he chose to broach the one subject that was closest to off limits. "*Did* she break your heart?''

Arlen glanced his way, but in the dim light it was impossible to read anything in his expression. "Your mother? She surely did."

Your mother. It was a foreign phrase to Sloan. In twenty-nine years he'd never really thought of himself as having a mother. There was merely the woman who'd given birth to him. Who hadn't wanted him. Who'd given him away without regret.

He knew more about her, of course. Her name was Elizabeth, Betsy for short. She'd had blue eyes and blond hair, and she'd grown up in northern Wyoming. She'd majored in business in college, had wanted a career and *hadn't* wanted him.

"Do you ever hear anything about her?"

His father shook his head, then asked, "Do you?"

Sloan echoed his father's no. He certainly had the resources to locate her, if he chose, but what would he say to her? There was nothing he wanted to know, except maybe if she'd ever regretted it. If she'd ever had suitable kids—white kids—did she ever look at them and wonder about him? Did she ever think that, in putting him out of her life, she might have lost someone who was worth knowing?

"If…" Arlen cleared his throat. "If you ever wanted to look her up and maybe go see her, Amy and I wouldn't mind."

"Why would I want to do that?"

"It would be natural if you did. She is your mother, after all, and every kid needs a mother."

"That sounds like Amy talking," Sloan said with a grin. His stepmother was a peacemaker—with four rowdy sons, she needed to be. She looked for the good in everyone, preached compromise and encouraged forgiveness. Sloan believed in treating the people in your life with respect and not worrying about the ones who weren't there. "Tell her not to worry. I had a grandmother, eight to ten aunts, and a dozen older female cousins all mothering me. I didn't grow up deprived in that department."

"All the same, if you ever want to meet your real mother, it's all right with us."

"I'll keep that in mind." And he would, even though he couldn't imagine the situation in which he would want to meet the woman. "I'd better head back to town."

"Let us know when we get to meet your girl. We'll make sure your brothers are on their best behavior."

"Forget the boys. Make sure Grandma and Granddad are on *their* best behavior. No comments about her being white, history repeating itself, or sticking to my own kind."

His father laughed as they walked to the truck. "Maybe we'd better restrict this to only the immediate family. You might better get a ring on her finger before you introduce her to the rest."

After giving him a hug, Sloan climbed in and backed out. *A ring on her finger.* That was damned optimistic, considering that the last time he'd seen Crystal, she'd called him Deputy and told him not to come around again.

But he was nothing if not optimistic.

And with Crystal, he needed all the optimism he could muster.

After one long, lousy night in bed, Crystal woke up Sunday morning feeling as cranky as a teething baby. Her all-night tossing and turning had been interrupted only infrequently by restless naps and bad dreams. She would have been better off staying awake all night, she decided, and waiting for sheer exhaustion to put her to sleep. Then maybe she wouldn't look so puffy and feel so fatigued. Then her head wouldn't be hurting, and her heart—

Well, her heart always hurt. It had ever since she'd realized that James was going to betray her, her parents were going to abandon her, her friends were going to ignore her and her employer was going to fire her. It had especially hurt ever since Sloan Ravencrest had walked into the back room at the shop. But it had stopped hurting completely in odd moments since then. She'd gotten too caught up in him a few times to remember to suffer... When she'd first seen him in the kitchen yesterday, looking impossibly handsome and sexy. Or when he'd drawn his fingertip up the length of her arm, making her want to rub against him and purr like a kitten. Or when she'd asked him to forget all that garbage about her parents, and he'd said sure, no problem.

Or when he'd held her while she cried.

When was the last time a man had held her while she cried? Never, that she could recall. James had hated tears. On the rare occasion that she'd shed them around him, he'd reacted with scathing remarks about overemotional women. Her father hated tears, too, and, on those even rarer occasions, had called to her mother to do something with her daughter.

But Sloan had held her, soothed her, told her it was good to cry.

And she had called him "deputy" in that scornful tone and told him not to bother coming back.

Scowling, she left the bedroom for the bathroom, then the kitchen. A glance in the bathroom mirror had warned her that she looked every bit as bad as she felt—downright scary, in fact, with her short hair standing on end and shadows under her eyes—but there was no one to see her but Winona, who had some pretty scary mornings, too.

She was rounding the corner into the kitchen when she became aware of voices at the small table—Winona's and the deep rumble of a man's. When she saw Sloan sitting in her usual place, cradling a cup of coffee in his hands, she came to a sudden stop. Feminine vanity demanded that she flee back down the hall, but her bad mood was equally insistent that she hold her ground. Before either could win, Winona inadvertently directed all attention her way.

"Oh, my." Her aunt smiled anxiously. "Have a bit of a bad night, did you, dear?"

Sloan's gaze shifted to her, so potent she could physically feel it, so compelling she couldn't move to save her life. His look started at the top of her head, then moved slowly down

over her face and the startled expression frozen there, down
her throat to the thin, snug tank top she still wore for sleep
despite the November chill, over her breasts and stomach to
the matching boxers that left way too much thigh exposed.
It went all the way down to her feet, then just as slowly
started back up again. She wanted to fold her arms across
her breasts but couldn't, wanted to casually stroll farther into
the room, but couldn't do that, either. All she could do was
stand there, feeling exposed and hot and incredibly aroused—
and knowing that he was, too. He was thinking about undressing her, seducing her, about removing her top and stroking her breasts, about the contrast between his dark hands
and her pale skin, an image that made her bite back a groan.

Slowly he smiled, a smile different from all his other
smiles she'd seen. There was nothing charming about this
one, or friendly or boyish or regretful. It was the satisfied
smile of a man who knew he'd aroused her with no more
than a look—and how could he not know? Her breathing had
gone shallow and ragged, and her breasts had drawn up tight,
her nipples forming hard crests obvious under the thin shirt.

"Good morning." His voice was low, husky. It sounded
erotic as hell to Crystal, but her aunt didn't seem to notice a
thing.

"Perhaps you'd like to grab your robe and join us for
breakfast," Winona suggested pointedly from her position in
front of the stove.

Murmuring an excuse, she spun and returned to her room.
There she caught sight of herself once more in the mirror
and didn't know whether to laugh or cry. She looked a
fright—bad enough to make James groan and turn away.

But Sloan hadn't turned away. He'd been turned on, too.
She'd seen the look on his face.

She considered getting dressed, brushing her teeth, combing her hair and walking into the kitchen once more. She
wasn't sure she had the nerve. Maybe with makeup and her
most modest outfit. And after a cold shower. With a stiff
drink for courage.

She also considered crawling back into bed, pulling the covers over her head and pretending sleep when Winona eventually came looking for her. She was trying to decide between the two when a knock sounded at the door.

"Crystal?"

It was Sloan. She went to the door, well aware there was no lock on it, and leaned against it. "What?"

"Breakfast is ready."

Breakfast, eaten across the table from Sloan when he'd just...when she'd just...

"I'm not hungry," she murmured against the door. She didn't hear him leave, though. Instead he tapped on the door again, a little knock created with one fingertip, possibly the same fingertip he'd trailed along her arm yesterday morning and made her—

"Open the door, Crystal."

She swore she could feel his heat through the hollow-core door, reaching in, warming her already-too-warm body. "I can't," she replied in little more than a whisper. "I'm not dressed."

There was a thunk on the other side of the door, followed by a chagrined chuckle. "Oh, hell, just go ahead and shoot me. Put me out of my misery."

She eased the door open a few inches. The thunk, she realized, had been his forehead hitting the door, while the chagrin came from a most impressive complication. "You don't look miserable." Oh, no. He looked sinful, sensual, sexual, sensuous—all those wonderfully bad S words used to great effect in the romances she read.

Gripping the door in one hand, he pushed it open a few inches farther, until she blocked it. "Let me look at you a few seconds more..." Then, in an instant, he changed, became serious, intense. "Are you still mad at me?"

Heat flushed her face, from embarrassment this time instead of arousal. "I wasn't mad. I mean, I was, but not at you. Jobs come first. They're important. Sometimes I forget that." James's career, both in the D.A.'s office and the political office he aspired to, was of utmost importance. It dictated everything he did—the way he dressed, the clubs he belonged to, the people he was friends with, the woman he would marry.

And when she had become a liability instead of an asset, it had dictated that he dump her and ruin her life.

"Jobs aren't that important," he disagreed. "Doing the right thing is. Being able to live with what you've done is. People are very important."

He sounded as if he believed what he was saying a hundred percent. Too bad she couldn't be as sure. She wanted to believe him. She wanted to believe *in* him. But James had taught her better.

"I didn't find anything last night."

"So am I crazy, deluded, or an outright liar?"

Taut lines formed at the corners of his mouth. "I'm beginning to think you might be deluded. Just because James and your parents let you down doesn't mean everyone else will. I'm not like him, Crystal. I told you that."

"All I have is your word. I have no proof." She folded her arms across her chest. "You know what? If you asked James to describe himself, he'd swear he's honorable. 'A man of integrity. A man who understands the meaning of a promise.' That's part of his campaign material. But I know from firsthand experience that he has no honor, no integrity."

For a moment he simply looked at her, then slowly he grinned. "Go out to my dad's with me today and he'll tell you what kind of man I am. So will my stepmother and my brothers and about a hundred other Ravencrests." After another moment, his grin faded and the intensity returned. "What did he do to you?"

Her throat tightened, and her voice grew thick with unshed tears. "He destroyed me."

"You're not destroyed. You have a new home, a new life, an aunt who loves you dearly. People who want to be friends with you. People—one, at least—who want a whole lot more. You're destroyed, Crystal, only if you let him win. If you let him force you into a miserable little existence, afraid to trust anyone, even yourself, *then* you've lost."

Nice sentiment…if she could embrace it. She wasn't sure she ever could.

To avoid responding, she asked, "What are you doing here?"

"I'm going back out to the clearing this morning. I thought I could use a little company."

Disappointment streaked through her, settling like a rock in her stomach. When would she learn? Just because he acted concerned and held her when she'd cried and was sexually attracted to her, didn't mean he was any different from James. He wanted something from her, and he would use whatever means necessary to get it—blackmail, coercion, seduction. He would say all the pretty words, do all the right things, but in the end, he would hurt her the same way James had.

Stiffly, she walked away from him, going to the closet, staring at the garments there as if picking exactly the right one was a matter of life or death. "Sorry," she said stiffly. "I'm not going back there again."

She wasn't aware he had crossed the room until he reached over her shoulder and took a lavender sweater from its hanger. "Wear this. I like the color." Then, without missing a beat, he went on. "For the record, Crystal, I wasn't planning to invite you. I came to ask Winona to go with me."

Embarrassment warmed her face again. She felt bad that she'd automatically expected the worst, but at the same time she was disappointed that it wasn't a desire for *her* company that had brought him back.

Almost as if he'd read her mind, he said, "Don't get me wrong. If I were going anyplace else, doing anything else, I would be more than happy to invite you along. But not to the clearing. Not after yesterday."

She took a pair of jeans from a hanger, then turned, clasping the clothes to her chest. "What makes you think I would go anyplace else with you?"

His grin came slowly. "Because you're attracted to me,

even if I am one of the 'so-called good guys.' I am, you know. One of the good guys.''

She didn't know. That was part of the problem.

"I'll make you a promise, Crystal. I won't ask you to go back to that clearing or to have anything further to do with the Montgomery case. If you have another vision, or if you come to me, fine, but *I* won't ask *you*. I promise.''

Her gaze shifted from his face to the hand he'd offered, then back to his face. He looked so sincere… But she'd witnessed James's sincerity when he'd looked into the television cameras and said she was unstable, bitter and vindictive. He'd been so damned sincere that she'd practically believed him herself. People who knew her well *had* believed him.

But James was a snake, a politician, a natural-born liar. Could Sloan match his talents?

Warily she placed her hand in his. "If you're lying…''

His callused palm rubbed against hers as his fingers tightened. "It's easy enough to keep track. If I ask for your help, then I've broken my promise. If I don't, then I haven't. Simple.'' Slowly he released her hand and headed for the door. "Get dressed. Come have breakfast with us.''

Oh, yeah, Crystal thought as the door closed behind him, his plan was simple. Only time would tell—time in which she could become even more attracted to him. Time in which he could become important to her. If he broke his promise then, it would hurt so much more.

If he broke his promise then, he might finish what James had started. He might destroy her.

And if he didn't? If she could trust him? If she could count on him to be honest and honorable? He might undo the damage James had done.

He just might save her.

Five

Tuesday afternoon found Sloan sitting at one of several desks available for deputies' use in the sheriff's department, doing his least favorite part of the job—writing reports. The computer made the process easier—he remembered the days of two-fingered, correction-tape typing—but he'd still rather be doing anything else.

Sheriff Rafe Rawlings rapped on the corner of the desk on his way to his office. "Come on back when you get a chance."

Sloan answered affirmatively without taking his eyes off the screen. He'd investigated two burglaries that day, as well as one case of vandalism, had transported a prisoner a hundred and fifty miles to Helena and another seventy miles farther to the state mental hospital in Warm Springs for observation—and this had been a light day compared to yesterday. Last night he'd gone home three hours late, too tired to even think straight.

But not too tired to think about Crystal. She'd been on his mind nonstop for the past week. He'd been thinking a lot about her skittishness, about how badly she'd been hurt before, how vulnerable it had made her, how easily she could be hurt again. After a stern warning from Winona on Sunday—"That girl's delicate and she's been betrayed by everyone she ever trusted, so don't you go adding to her pain"—he'd examined his feelings and motives for wanting to get close to her. He'd decided on the way back from Warm Springs this afternoon that his motives were pure.

Well, he clarified with a grin, not exactly pure. One glance at her in that thin cotton top and shorts last Sunday morning had filled him with all kinds of impure thoughts—and he'd gotten a whole lot more than one glance.

His intentions were honorable, he rephrased it. Unlike James Rich-man, he wasn't ambitious enough to plot ways to use her to further his career. He wished to God she'd never had that vision of Christina so it wouldn't be between them now. He just wanted *her*. To spend time with her, make love to her, have kids with her, grow old with her.

It sounded silly, he knew. There was so much about her he still didn't know, so much about him she'd shown no curiosity about. But his instincts said this was the woman he'd been waiting for, and he always trusted his instincts.

Finishing up the last report, he filed it, then went to Rafe's office. Though they'd been friends all their lives, he knocked and waited for a response before entering. "Friendship" ended the moment he put on his badge and wouldn't come into play until he took it off at the end of the day. During those hours, their relationship was purely professional.

"Have a seat," Rafe said, nodding toward the battered chair in front of his desk. He continued to fiddle with his computer for a moment before shoving the keyboard away in disgust. "Damn thing's acting up again. You can say what you want about 'em, but at least a typewriter never ate my reports. So…how's it going?"

"Okay. I found most of the stuff stolen from the Smiths' house in the woods about a quarter mile down the road. I set up out there for a while to see if anyone came back for it, but I got called away, so I took it with me. Mr. Smith will be in soon, if he hasn't come already, to make a complaint because I wouldn't give the stuff back to him then."

"It's only because you're Cheyenne. A white deputy would have done the right thing," Rafe said dryly. Like Sloan, Rafe was half Cheyenne. He'd experienced his share of bigotry.

"And caught the burglar while he was at it," Sloan agreed. "Anything new on the break-in at the church?"

Sloan shook his head.

"How about the Montgomery case?"

For a moment Sloan debated how to answer. He had nothing concrete to offer, so he wouldn't be out of line to brush off the question, but that wasn't the way he worked. Still, he'd made a promise to Crystal, and he would do his best to keep it without being out-and-out dishonest. "Winona Cobbs came to see me a while back, to tell me about a vision involving Christina. I'm trying to check it out, but so far I haven't found anything to support it."

"What kind of vision?" Rafe's expression was unreadable. Whether he believed in ESP and premonitions was anyone's guess. On most subjects, he kept his opinions to himself.

Sloan related the bare bones of the vision, then added, "Winona thinks it has something to do with Christina giving birth." The old lady had said so at the clearing yesterday, and it had made sense to Sloan. The blood-soaked dress, the agonizing pain, the fear she was dying—childbirth could account for all three. When his cousin Roy's wife was in labor with their third kid last year, she'd threatened to remove vital parts of his anatomy, and she'd been in a hospital, under a doctor's care, and knew what to expect. How much worse would it be for a first-time mother alone in the woods?

Winona had also said that Christina, if dead, hadn't died in the clearing. When Sloan had asked why her impressions were so different from Crystal's, she'd merely shrugged. Parapsychology wasn't an exact science, she'd said. How could it be, when it dealt with the mind, with spirits and auras and otherworldly mysteries?

"What do you think happened to her?" Sloan asked. He'd heard theories from everyone but Rafe. Most people thought Christina had run away. Some thought she'd been taken against her will; a few believed she was punishing her family for their lack of attention.

"I don't know," Rafe replied. "At first I thought it was a play for attention. She got so needy after her mother died, and Ellis refused to take time away from business to take care of her. Now, though…" He shrugged, then glanced at his watch. "Hey, Raeanne told me to invite you for dinner Friday. She said for you to bring Becky."

Sloan had been so preoccupied with Crystal that he needed an instant to remember the last woman he'd dated. Becky Masters was nice enough, but he'd known from their first date that nothing would come of it. She'd been looking for a husband, and he'd been looking for a distraction from Crystal, whom he hadn't even managed to meet yet. Neither of them had found what they'd wanted.

"I don't think Becky's new boyfriend would appreciate me borrowing her for the night. But if the invitation stands without her, I'll be there. I might even be able to round up a date somewhere."

"You'd better. If you don't, Raeanne will feel it's her duty as a happily married woman to set you up with someone, and being a public defender, most of the women she knows are cops, lawyers and/or criminals."

Since none of the three held any interest for him, Sloan dryly replied, "I'll see what I can do."

"Seven o'clock, our house."

Sloan nodded in acknowledgment as he left the office. Maybe he could sweet-talk Crystal into going on the pretext that, if she was going to live in Whitehorn, she needed to meet some people. Of course, the fact that one of those people was the sheriff might not sit well with her, but what better way to prove that she was wrong in her blanket distrust of law-enforcement types than to introduce her to some of them?

With his shift long over, he clocked out and headed home. His apartment complex was on the west side of town and bore the improbable name of The Chalet. Other than a few faux architectural details on the building that housed the office and clubhouse, there was nothing to set it apart from every other apartment complex he'd ever seen. The buildings were typical construction, two stories painted dark brown, with doors opening onto breezeways both upstairs and down. The pool was kidney-shaped and too small to actually swim in, the grounds were planted with the standard low-maintenance shrubs and trees all the other complexes used, and the parking lots were too crowded.

But it was home, he thought as he let himself in. It was a good place for having an early dinner, watching a little TV, then getting to bed early to make up for all those long miles behind the wheel.

He tossed the mail onto the counter, then went into the bedroom, hitting the play button on the answering machine as he began undressing. There was a call from Amy, confirming his father's dinner invitation, and another from his cousin Shelley asking if he was available to provide a fourth on a double date with her boyfriend's aunt who was visiting in town. He was wondering just how old her boyfriend was, or how young the aunt was, when the next message started.

"Deputy Ravencrest," Winona Cobbs said cheerfully. "We were wondering if you might be available to join us for dinner this evening. I'm sorry for the short notice, but the idea just now occurred to me—I mean, us. There's no need to call back. If you can make it, just show up sometime between six and seven. And if you can't...well, maybe next time."

As the machine clicked to a stop, he removed his gun belt, left his pistol on the bed and hung the belt over the back of a chair. His badge went on the dresser, his uniform into the dry-clean pile on the closet floor. It was amazing how quickly a man's mood could change. Sixty seconds ago he'd really wanted to be in bed by nine; the past two days had been exhausting. Now, faced with that choice or dinner with Crystal.... Well, hell, who needed sleep?

Not that he kidded himself for a minute that Crystal was part of, or even aware of, Winona's invitation. He thought about calling the old woman back and telling her he would accept on the condition that she tell Crystal first. So far, she'd sprung him on her niece twice without warning, and neither time had Crystal been the least bit prepared.

But if she was prepared, she might do something Crystal-like, such as choose tonight to venture into Whitehorn and sample the nightlife. Much as he liked Winona, he didn't want to have dinner alone with her while Crystal was out attracting other men.

By the time he'd showered and dressed, it was coming up on six. He slipped his .45 into a holster, which he clipped onto his belt at the small of his back, then shrugged into a shearling jacket, grabbed his Stetson and left.

Though the Stop-n-Swap was closed for the day, there were lights on inside and Crystal was visible through the plate-glass windows, tallying the day's receipts. He ignored the Closed sign and tried the door. As he feared, it readily swung open.

Neither the bell nor his footsteps distracted her from her counting, but she was aware of him. Without glancing his way, she said, "Hello, Deputy."

"Miz Cobbs. You should keep that door locked after hours. You never know who might wander in."

She made a notation on the bank form, then looked up. "Speak for yourself. I knew it was you."

"Winona decided to not surprise you this time?"

"Aunt Winona hasn't said a word about you. I *knew*. You know..." Waggling her fingers, she did a fair imitation of spooky movie music, then swept stacks of bills, coins and checks into the vinyl bank bag, zipped it and deposited it in the small safe under the counter. When she was done, she leaned on the counter. "Does that make you uneasy?"

He mimicked her position, lacing his fingers together so they were almost touching hers. "I don't know. Do you know what I'm thinking right now?" Deliberately he called up the real image that had tormented him for three days, her wearing those thin cotton nightclothes, and the fantasy image it had inspired of him removing those thin cotton nightclothes. She was so slender, so delicate, in his image, with perfect breasts and narrow waist and long legs, with her hair tousled and her eyes smoky.

Her cheeks reddened, and she couldn't meet his gaze any longer. She tried to sound carelessly scornful. "What single, attractive man doesn't think about sex? If you want to test me, try something a little less clichéd."

"That wasn't sex, sweetheart. It was *you*." Before she could argue, he covered her hands with his and quickly went on. "You think I'm attractive?"

"What? Does the ego need a little stroking?"

"Oh, darlin', if you're going to stroke, I can think of something that needs it far more than my ego."

She tugged her hands free, straightened and gave him an annoyed look, but he knew, as surely as she had known it was he who'd walked through the door, that she wasn't really put out. "What did you mean when you asked if Winona had decided not to surprise me?"

He straightened, too. "She invited me for dinner. But I won't stay if you don't want me to."

"It's her house. She can invite anyone she wants." With a burst of energy, she yanked the bag from the trash can next to the safe, tied up its top, then picked up another bag and came around the end of the counter.

He sidestepped to block her way. "I mean it. I'll leave now. Just tell me to go."

She stood there, wearing faded jeans and an ivory sweater that was comfortably too big, looking as if she knew she should say one thing when she really wanted to say the opposite. He didn't know which was which, though. Was she going to ask him to stay when she really wanted him to go, or would her defenses send him away when some part of her wanted him to stay?

At least, he hoped some part of her did.

One minute stretched into two, then three. He was considering making the choice for her and leaving when she sighed loudly. "Want to come over to the trailer and have dinner with us?"

"Gee, what a gracious invitation."

Looking up, she batted her lashes and, dropping the trash bags, laid her hand gently on his forearm. The words that followed were syrupy and drawn out into extra syllables in a voice that was pure Southern belle. "Why, Deputy Ravencrest, would you be so kind as to come by the house and share the evenin' meal with us? I would so enjoy your company, and Aunt Winona, I'm sure, would be absolutely delighted. We're havin' baked Virginia ham, mashed potatoes and gravy, succotash and biscuits with honey butter, with the best pecan pie you ever imagined. I baked it myself, from an old family recipe." She gave him an oh-so-feminine flutter of her lashes. "Please do say you'll come, Deputy."

When had it gotten too warm in the room to breathe? When she'd fixed her green gaze on him? When she'd touched him? Or when that incredible sultry voice had wrapped around him? He didn't know and didn't care. He just…wanted.

Aware of the tension in the air, Crystal swallowed hard. She removed her hand from his arm and folded both her arms across her chest. "Was that gracious enough for you?" she asked, trying her best to sound combative when, really, all she felt was awkward.

Sloan slowly grinned. "Would you come over here a little closer and whisper that whole speech in my ear? Because if you do, I guarantee you, I will come."

She acknowledged his double entendre with a smirk—after all, she'd inadvertently set herself up for it—then ignored it. Instead, she picked up the trash bags and gestured toward the door. He held the door for her, then took the bags while she locked up.

"Do all well-bred Southern belles have that effect on a man?" he asked as they headed for the Dumpster around the corner.

"That was Crystal in training to be the governor's wife someday, maybe even the president's. Of course, that was before James found out I was more than he expected."

"What did he expect?"

"The perfect wife. The perfect hostess. The perfect help-mate." While he tossed the bags into the Dumpster, she tilted her head back to stare up into the night sky. The feeble lights that shone on the parking lot all night and the few lights coming from the trailer couldn't make a dent in the night's darkness, couldn't begin to compete with the breathtaking light of the stars. She turned in a slow circle, just looking, feeling incredibly small and insignificant and, for one moment, incredibly peaceful. Under a sky so vast, what could her problems two thousand miles away in Georgia possibly matter?

Sloan walked away a few steps, noticed she wasn't coming, and came back to stand behind her. "It's an amazing sight, isn't it?" His voice was quiet, only centimeters from her ear. "When I was a kid, my dad and I used to camp out over in the Crazy Mountains. He slept in the tent, but I put my sleeping bag next to the campfire, so I could fall asleep looking at the stars. They always made me feel..."

"Safe," she finished for him, then hesitantly offered a memory of her own. "After things ended between James and me, I moved to Atlanta for a while, to a tiny apartment with a tinier balcony. At night I would go out to look at the stars, and sometimes I couldn't even see them. Between the haze and the smog and the glow of millions of city lights, the stars got lost somewhere up there. It made me feel lost."

"And how do you feel tonight?"

She risked a glance at him. He was standing too close, so close that she could smell his cologne and the clean fragrance of soap on his skin, so close that his murmur raised goose bumps on her neck. So close that all she had to do was turn and she could be in his arms. She knew instinctively it would be a comfortable place to be. She wanted to believe it would also be safe, but she was afraid.

"Vulnerable," she whispered in response to his question. That was how she felt tonight.

He raised one hand and touched her cheek as gently as a

whisper. "I would never intentionally hurt you, Crystal. Can't you believe that?"

"I believe you believe it."

"But *you* can't believe it because you don't trust me."

The faint undertone of bitterness in his voice stung her. "It's not a matter of my trusting you, Sloan. I can't trust myself. My judgment has been proven to be so flawed that I'm afraid to believe in it anymore. It tells me you're not like James or my parents or my friends in the ways that count, but I don't know if that's true, or if it's wishful thinking, or if it's just lust." She blinked once to clear the moisture blurring her vision. "I let myself down, even more than they did. I found out how incredibly wrong I can be about people. The worst thing that ever happened in my life was my fault, and that's a really hard lesson to recover from."

"Well, at least you called me Sloan. And you admitted you want me. That's a start," he said with a gently teasing grin. His fingertips brushed her cheek again, then his palm flattened against it, warming her skin, as he brought his other hand to her other cheek. "You're wrong, Crystal. The worst thing that happened, happened because you loved those people, and loving someone is never wrong. It's not always wise, but it's never wrong. The fact that they betrayed your love is *their* fault, *their* flaw. Never take the blame for other people's shortcomings. And never assume that because one man hurt you, the next one will, too. And never—" he bent closer "—ever think you can casually mention lusting for me and walk away without this…"

His mouth covered hers, sending a powerful wave of heat through her, and his tongue slipped between her teeth. Some feeble, fearful part of her thought she should push him away and run screaming for the safety of her bedroom, but her stronger side—a side she'd seen pitifully little of in recent months—refused to even consider such cowardice. She'd been wanting this kiss, this connection, since… Heavens, since she was old enough to want.

She wrapped her arms around his neck, and he slid his

hands to the middle of her back, pulling her close against his hard body. She pressed against him, frustrated by layers of thick clothing, wanting to touch him, to feel him, to see him the way he'd envisioned them both earlier. She wanted to see in reality how her pale skin looked against his darker skin, wanted to learn the differences in their bodies, to figure out where and how he liked to be touched. She wanted him to make her feel womanly and beautiful and desired and safe. He *could* make her feel safe. If only she could let him.

He broke the kiss, though she wordlessly protested, and held her tighter to still her body's unconscious movements against his. For a time, she pressed her face against the suede of his jacket, breathing in deeply of leather, cologne and Sloan. When she thought her voice might sound reasonably steady, she ventured an offer that terrified her on two levels— if he accepted and if he didn't. "We could forget about dinner and go someplace and…"

"Finish what we started?" He sounded aroused, overloaded with sensation and faintly regretful. "You don't know how much I'd like that."

"But…?" She knew there was a "but" coming. She could feel it in the suddenly hollow place in her stomach.

"Call me a fool. I'm sure I'll be coming up with worse insults about three in the morning," he said wryly. "But I want more from you, Crystal, than just sex." She moved against him, and he caught his breath, then regretfully added, "More than just great sex. I want you to trust me. I want you to know in your heart that I'm nothing like James, that I would never do to you what he did. I want you to admit that we have a future. I want it all, Crystal, or at least a fair shot at it."

It was on the tip of her tongue to flippantly ask him to define "all," to snidely point out that he was probably the only unmarried man in the state of Montana who would turn down great sex with a reasonably attractive woman, to pridefully mention that she could make the same offer in any of the local bars and get takers in every one.

Instead she clumsily pulled out of his embrace. "I guess you're just an old-fashioned guy at heart," she said, aiming for sarcasm but sounding wistful instead.

"I guess I am."

Abruptly she shivered and remembered that while he was appropriately dressed for a November Montana night, she'd left her coat at home. "We'd better get inside. It's cold."

She got a head start and was halfway to the trailer before he moved. He caught up with her at the porch, though, taking her hand to stop her. "It'll work out."

The look she gave him was doubtful. She was too afraid. The risks were too great. Already he was becoming too important. "I don't know."

"Aw, come on, have a little faith," he cajoled, then faked a grimace. "Sorry. I forgot. You're fresh out. But I'm not. I'll believe for you, until you're able to believe yourself. Fair?"

"Foolish."

"Sweetheart, I turned down the chance to have incredible sex with you tonight. I think we've already established that I'm a fool."

Or maybe just a really decent guy. An old-fashioned guy. A forever sort of guy. Exactly the kind of guy she'd always wanted.

So who was really the fool here?

Dinner was over, the dishes done and Winona had retired to her room, leaving Sloan and Crystal alone in the living room. Despite his best efforts, he was too tired to contain his yawns anymore.

Catching one of them, Crystal smiled faintly. "Have a long day?"

"Two of 'em. I think I've put about eight hundred miles on my unit the last two days."

"Then you should have stayed home and rested."

"And miss dinner with you?"

"I have dinner every night."

"But you don't invite me every night." He didn't mention that she hadn't invited him tonight, either. He'd been there. That was what counted.

But the time would come when she *would* invite him. He was counting on it.

She rose from the rocker with such grace and went to the coat tree near the door, taking his jacket from the hook there. "Come on. It's time to go home."

For a moment he remained on the sofa, watching her as she walked halfway back, as her hands smoothed over the suede, then brushed the shearling. Someday she would touch him that way, with gentle, comfortable, pleasurable touches, and then he might never need sleep again.

But that day wasn't here yet, and he really was exhausted, so he pushed himself to his feet, took the jacket from her and put it on. She walked to the door with him, but, barefoot and coatless, it was obvious she was going no further.

"I enjoyed dinner."

"I'll tell Aunt Winona."

"I enjoyed kissing you, too."

She had no answer to that except a faint blush.

"I've been invited to a friend's house for dinner Friday. I'd appreciate it if you'd go with me."

"Why?"

"Besides the obvious? Raeanne—that's Rafe's wife—fancies herself a matchmaker. If I show up without a date, she's going to nag me all night about one friend or another." He moved a step closer to her. "If you say yes, then I'll owe you a favor. It's not a bad thing to have a cop in your debt."

"I don't like favors," she murmured.

Of course not, he thought, remembering too late her comment about James wanting to be governor. Politics cast the practice of trading favors in an ugly light. "All right. No favors. Will you go to dinner with me Friday night? Just a date, plain and simple. You'll meet some people, have a good dinner and a good time, and I'll get to kiss you good-night when it's over."

She pretended to consider it a moment before agreeing. "I suppose it couldn't hurt."

"My kisses never hurt. Would you like a demonstration?"

Her gaze turned smoky and her breath seemed to catch in her chest. "I don't think that would be wise," she said huskily. "Not now. Not here."

Not wise, maybe, but definitely right. But he didn't try to persuade her. After clamping his hat on his head, he opened the door, and a blast of cold air blew in on the northwest wind. "I'll pick you up at six-thirty on Friday."

She nodded, then hugged herself as she stepped out onto the porch after him. "Hey. Are you okay to drive?"

It was the first real concern she'd shown him. Turning back, he acknowledged it with a grin. "I'm fine. But thanks for asking."

The scowl she sent his way was almost as fierce as a real one. "Don't let it go to your head."

"Oh, sweetheart, you went to my head the first time I ever saw you. See you Friday."

If not before.

One corner of the back room at the Stop-n-Swap held all the remnants of Crystal's previous life. She'd directed the movers to leave the cartons and crates there the day they'd arrived in Whitehorn, and she had never gone near them since.

Friday afternoon, she was more than near them. She was right in the middle of them with a box cutter, opening wardrobe cartons, thumbing through the clothes that had filled two large closets in her Boonesville apartment. There were the modest, sensible outfits she'd worn to her teaching job, the slacks and sweaters and summer dresses that had made up her casual wardrobe and, of course, the dressy clothes that had been required for life with James. Ten cartons, and not a pair of jeans or a simple shirt in the bunch.

In the carton she'd just opened was the black dress she'd worn to too many boring dinners. The red-sequined number for last year's debutante ball. Oh, yes... The iridescent beaded dress bought just for the Johnsons' New Year's bash two years ago; the pale peach silk worn to her engagement party; the rich green satin for Christmas dinner with James's grandparents, and the royal blue eye-popper used to court financial support for James's campaign from Boonesville's old money and newly rich alike.

All the outfits held a memory, most of them bad. She should give them away to someone who could put them to good use. There were a couple she should burn over an open flame, offered as sacrifices to the powers-that-be that had saved her from that life, those people, that marriage.

Whatever their fate, she wanted the clothes out of the Stop-n-Swap and out of her life. She would never need them again, would never be that desperate-to-please woman again.

With a sigh, she moved on to the final carton, slicing the tape, unfolding the flaps. If that carton wasn't hiding something suitable, she would have no choice but to borrow Aunt Winona's truck and go into town. She hated to go shopping—she, who had been raised a blue-ribbon shopper—but if the occasion demanded it, and tonight's dinner with Sloan's friends did, she would bite the bullet and go.

In that box, though, she struck gold...or silver, at least, with a pair of gray wool trousers, a delicate gray cardigan and a camisole woven of gray with an occasional shot of metallic silver. She pulled the garments from the overstuffed box, sniffed them and found only faint hints of the herbal moth repellent, then went digging for black shoes and a handbag.

With her arms loaded, she went into the main part of the store where Winona was chatting with her friend, Homer Gilmore. The gossips in town said the old man was crazy, but, having heard the same thing said about herself, Crystal wasn't quick to believe them. He might be a little odd—after all, he did believe he'd had numerous encounters with UFOs—but he was harmless and sweet, and Winona considered him a dear friend. That was a good enough endorsement for Crystal.

"Oh, how lovely," Winona remarked when she spied the outfit Crystal had unearthed. "I was wondering just how casual you were going to be about this date tonight."

"Hello, Mr. Gilmore," Crystal greeted him politely before turning to her aunt for at least the tenth denial since telling Winona her plans. "It's not a date. It's just dinner with friends." Of course, Sloan had used those exact words. *Just a date, plain and simple.* But she could split hairs if she felt like it, and at the moment, she did.

"Dinner with *your* friends might be just dinner," Winona pointed out. "Dinner with *his* friends is a date. Isn't that right, Homer?"

The old man murmured something that might have been agreement, but didn't jump into the conversation. Crystal had seen him probably two dozen times, but she'd never really talked to him. He seemed shy around her, and she'd been too wrapped up in her own problems to try drawing him out.

Whatever he said, Winona took it as support for her side. "See? We both think it's a date, and I'll bet if I ask Sloan, he'll agree. That makes it three against one."

"Yes, but since I'm the one, I don't have to change my opinion unless I want to," Crystal said in a triumphant so-there tone. "Do you mind if I take off early and get these ready?"

"Of course not, child. Go on. Make yourself beautiful for your beau."

Crystal rolled her eyes but didn't let herself get drawn back into that argument. Besides, honesty forced her to admit as she stepped out into the sunny, cold afternoon, she kind of liked the idea of having a beau. It sounded so much better than friend, boyfriend or gentleman friend, and was so much more accurate than lover—though maybe not for long. It was sweet, steeped in the innocence and grace of an earlier time. It was old-fashioned. Like Sloan.

By six-fifteen she was ready. The silver-and-gray set was

soft, feminine, not too dressy but not too casual, either. Her makeup was perfect, her perfume on long enough to be subtle instead of too much, and she'd even done her nails. She'd settled on a pair of silver earrings and a simple silver chain around her neck. Her hair—well, it was too short to do anything with, but it looked fine.

The only discordant note was the chunky gold ring on her index finger. She'd pulled it off a half dozen times and put it back on every time. Mixing gold and silver jewelry was a definite taboo in Marabeth Cobbs's world, and that alone was reason enough for Crystal to do it. But tonight, on this, her first date—there, she'd admitted it!—since James broke her heart, she needed the reminder of the ring.

When Sloan arrived at precisely six-thirty, she was glad she'd gone to a little extra effort. Instead of his usual jeans, he wore navy-blue trousers with a creamy-hued pullover. He looked even more incredibly handsome than usual, and he looked at her as if she'd accomplished Winona's recommendation and made herself beautiful.

Had James ever looked at her that way? Maybe the day he'd found out her godfather was a fishing buddy to the current governor, whose support he would need if he was going to hold that office according to the schedule by which he lived his life.

Was that before or after he proposed to her? At the moment, she couldn't recall.

They said their goodbyes, settled in the truck and headed back toward town. Before they'd gone a mile, Crystal asked, "Who are these friends we're having dinner with?"

"Rafe and Raeanne Rawlings. She's a public defender in town."

"So she tries to keep out of jail the people you try to send there. Interesting. What does he do?"

"He, uh, he's the sheriff."

The sheriff. She twisted the gold ring around her finger. She'd told him she didn't like cops, deputies or prosecutors, so what was his plan for their first date? Dinner with the sheriff. "You like to live dangerously, don't you?"

He flashed her a charming grin. "You'll like Rafe, honest."

"And if I like him, then I might have to admit that my prejudice against cops is unfounded, right?"

"Well, the thought never occurred to me, but now that you mention it..."

She gave an amused shake of her head. "You're a lousy liar, Ravencrest."

"That's because I've never had much practice at it." He reached across the console to claim her hand, settling it on his thigh, settling his own hand over it. "Keep that in mind."

She thought the gesture a little too intimate for a first date, and wondered if he might hope to get a lot more intimate before the night was over. She doubted it, though. He'd made it clear that he wanted more than sex, and she was fairly sure that was all she was offering. Maybe someday down the line, when she knew him better, when he'd proven himself, she could give him the trust he wanted. But someday could be a long time coming, and he very well might decide that she wasn't worth the wait.

A sudden surge of anger welled inside her. Damn James for making her so fearful because she didn't measure up to his ridiculous standards. Damn her parents for failing to give her the things every child deserved—confidence, courage and the certainty that she was loved. And damn fate for bringing a man like Sloan Ravencrest into her life when she was least capable of doing something about it.

There was a time—before James—when she would have grabbed hold of him with both hands and never let go. He knew her worst secret and wanted her anyway. What more could a woman like her want?

Now she was afraid to trust. Afraid of being used, hurt, betrayed. Afraid that she would always be afraid. She didn't know if she had the strength to put her past behind her, or the courage to face her future, and she couldn't even begin to guess whether Sloan had the patience to help her.

"You've gotten awfully quiet—and tense." He rubbed his hand back and forth over hers, uncurling her fingers and flattening them once again against his leg. "Are you worried about meeting Rafe and Raeanne? 'Cause you don't need to be. They'll like you."

"What makes you so sure?"

"Because I like you. That'll be enough for them."

She took a few deep breaths, pushed the anger and frustration to the back of her mind and deliberately refocused her attention. "You must be good friends."

"We are. Rafe's part of the reason I'm working for the sheriff's department."

"He recruited you?"

"Nope. I've known him all my life. He was abandoned as a baby by his white mother, too, but not with his family. She left him in the woods to die."

Crystal was appalled. If she were fortunate enough to have a baby, she would love him, treasure him, sacrifice her life for him if necessary, no matter what she felt for the father. But these two women had had no problem turning their backs and walking away from their babies. It was so cold, and so sad.

"Fortunately, he was found and adopted by the Rawlings family. They live near my dad, so Rafe was kind of a big brother growing up. Whatever he did, I wanted to do, too. I hadn't outgrown it by the time he went to work for the sheriff's department. I was in college and not too happy there, so I figured why not give the sheriff's department a try. Luckily, I like the job, and I'm good at it. I'm not as ambitious as Rafe, though. I have no desire to take on the headaches of running the department. I like being a field deputy."

"What did your father think about you becoming a deputy?"

He gave her a puzzled glance. "I don't know that he

thought anything. He told me to be careful, to always wear my bulletproof vest and to give it my best.''

The smile reflected back at her in the window was humorless. ''My parents knew before I was born what private school I would go to, what college I would attend and what degree I would earn, and they had my job lined up for me before the ink on my diploma was dry.''

''And what if you didn't want to go to that college or accept that job?''

''What I wanted didn't matter. It's never mattered.''

He pulled into a driveway behind a black-and-white sheriff's vehicle and shut off the engine, then turned to look at her. ''Until now. Now you don't have to please anyone but yourself. You don't have to *be* anyone but yourself. And if you think about it, Crystal—'' he left the sentence hanging while he got out, then came around the truck to open her door ''—James Rich-man and your folks did you and me both a hell of a favor when they got out of your life.''

Six

Before the peal of the doorbell faded away, the door was flung open and four-year-old Skye launched herself into Sloan's arms. He caught her, and she wrapped her arms around his neck, pressing a loud, smacking kiss to his cheek. "Hi, Sloan, guess what? Daddy said I could have a puppy!"

"I said we would talk about it," her father corrected from around the corner. His interruption left Skye unfazed.

"I'm gonna get a red one, like Grandma's got. Or maybe a black one. My friend April Ann has a black one, and he's wiggly and likes to kiss my face."

"Sounds like you," Sloan teased, tickling her enough to make her wiggle. "What're you gonna name him?"

"Not Spot or Red or Blackie. Maybe Harold."

"Harold?" her mother echoed, also out of sight around the corner.

"Harold's a good name," Skye said decisively, then immediately switched her attention to Crystal. "Who're you?"

"This is Crystal Cobbs," Sloan introduced her. "Crystal, this is Skye Rawlings."

Skye grinned, showing dimples. "I'm Sloan's best girl. Ain't that right, Sloan?"

"Yes, ma'am, it is." He gestured for Crystal to go in, then followed her, closing the door. Still clinging to his neck, Skye scampered around so she was hanging on his back. "Hold on, monkey," he advised, giving her a ride into the kitchen where Rafe and Raeanne were finishing the dinner preparations.

Switching the salad bowl to his other hand, Rafe lifted

Skye to the floor, then offered his hand as Sloan performed the introductions. Raeanne left the stove long enough to say hello, then directed them to move on to the dining table so she could serve the meal.

Crystal looked uncomfortably shy as she took the seat across from Rafe and next to Sloan. He'd expected to see the well-bred, poised-in-every-situation Crystal, the gracious, charming, groomed-to-be-the-governor's-wife Crystal. Some part of him was pleased that she hadn't made an appearance. That Crystal, he thought, was part phony, with the real woman overshadowed by the Cobbses' idea of the perfect daughter and Rich-man's idea of the perfect fiancée.

But her shyness this evening was genuine. Endearing. Sweet.

Raeanne brought platters of roast beef, vegetables and hot rolls fresh from the oven before taking her seat beside Rafe. They took a moment for Skye to say the blessing, then the conversation started in earnest.

"Crystal, I understand you're from Georgia," Raeanne began. "What part?"

"Boonesville. It's an hour or so south of Atlanta."

"And you've come to Whitehorn to stay. It must be quite a change. Do you miss Georgia at all?"

"No. I was ready for a change of scenery."

"What did you do there?"

"I taught third grade at Chatham Preparatory Academy."

"Sounds like a very exclusive place. Are you interested in teaching here?"

A cautious look came into Crystal's eyes, and she suddenly found the food on her plate worthy of closer attention. "No. It wasn't the job for me."

Sloan wondered who'd made that decision—Crystal or someone else? He could easily imagine her as a natural in the classroom, surrounded by kids who called her Miss Crystal and clamored for her attention. They all would have adored her, and probably at least one would have wished she was his mother and not his teacher, because then he wouldn't be hurt, ignored, abused or abandoned.

Raeanne was in the process of asking yet another question when Rafe stopped her. "Sweetheart, you invited her for dinner, not for interrogation. Let her enjoy her meal, and maybe you can grill her again over dessert."

"I'm not—" Raeanne's denial ended midsentence. Sheepishly she smiled. "You're right. Sorry, Crystal. I spend so much time questioning people that sometimes I forget how to carry on a normal conversation."

"It's an occupational hazard," Crystal said with a shrug as if she hadn't minded. "I used to go home from school and talk to people as if they were eight years old."

One of those people being James, Sloan thought with a scowl, who'd treated her with all the maturity and sensitivity of an eight-year-old.

By the time the evening ended, Crystal's wariness had disappeared. She was fairly friendly with Raeanne, even making plans to meet for lunch the next week, and she seemed to like Rafe, too. Sloan would call the evening a success...though, of course, the good-night kiss was yet to come.

On the drive back to Winona's, he casually asked, "Is the Chatham Preparatory Academy as snooty as it sounds?"

"Snootier. And, yes, I'm a Chatham grad."

"Did you really discover that teaching wasn't right for you, or was that decision somehow connected to your breakup with James?"

She was quiet for so long that he thought she'd decided she had answered enough questions for one evening. Then, with a sigh, she replied, "James was a powerful man from a powerful family. People had no choice but to take sides."

No choice but to take *his* side. That was what she meant. "So because James decided not to marry you, your snooty prep school could no longer employ you?"

"More or less."

"Why didn't you sue them for wrongful termination?"

"I couldn't win. The best thing for me to do was accept it quietly and get out of Boonesville."

"So you ran away. And you're still running."

"No." She looked at him, her gaze direct and steady. "If I were still running, I wouldn't be with you this evening."

With you. He liked the idea of Crystal being with him, and not just for the evening. For all time. Physically, emotionally, socially, legally, spiritually—in every way two people could possibly be.

But he didn't say so. Instead he kept to the subject. "I bet your students loved you."

"They did. Almost as much as Skye loves you. You're very good with her."

The simple remark pleased him. "I have a kid brother about her age. In another five years or so, I hope to have a kid of my own about her age."

"You planning to get married?"

"You bet."

"Picked someone out already?"

If he told her the truth, she would probably panic and retreat into her shell and he would never coax her out again. Instead he shrugged. "I'm counting on fate to do that."

She turned away again to look out the side window. "Then I hope fate is kinder to you than it's been to me."

"I don't know. Fate saved you from marrying James Richman. You never would have been happy with him."

"And how do you figure that?"

"Because you're not the perfect-wife, perfect-hostess, perfect-helpmate type. You're a real person who needs a real life, not some phony, socially correct, public-eye political existence."

"You're wrong. I loved James."

"Did you? Or did you love the idea of finally doing something that made your parents proud? I bet they picked him out for you, didn't they? Just like they picked out your college and your career and your job."

She turned so that all he could see was the black of her

coat and her hair. All he could feel was the iciness radiating from her. He'd made her angry—again. But that was all right. Being angry was better than being hurt, and she'd spent too damn much of her life hurting.

"There's one other thing," he said as if she hadn't shut him out. "If you had really, truly loved James, the way you're capable of loving, you never could have kissed me like you did the other night."

She gave no sign of hearing him.

So much for tonight's kiss, he thought regretfully as the silence between them grew. He doubted she would even let him bring the truck to a stop at Winona's before she jumped out and stalked off into the house, locking him out. But he would make up for it with two next time—and there *would* be a next time. He was nothing if not an optimistic fool.

But she surprised him. When he parked in the Stop-n-Swap lot next to Winona's old truck, she didn't flee. After taking off her seat belt, she slowly turned to face him. "You are so damn smug."

He certainly didn't feel it as he searched her face in the dim illumination provided by the parking lot lights for some clue to her mood. He couldn't find any.

"Yes, my parents picked James out. They got together with his parents and hatched this plan, and we thought how lucky everyone was that we fell in love with each other in spite of them. And, yes, I was incredibly happy to finally be doing something right for once, something normal that pleased my parents. For the first time in my life, they weren't wishing they had any other daughter in the world but me. For the first time, they were proud of *me*. And for the record, I didn't kiss you. *You* kissed me."

He gave a silent sigh of relief before gently teasing her. "Ah, but you kissed me back." Reaching across the cab, he brushed the backs of his fingers across her cheek. "When you're ready, when you trust me as well as want me, I will be more than happy to do anything you want."

For a long time she simply gazed at him, managing to look

confused and hopeful, fearful and aroused, curious and thoughtful and tempted, all at the same time. Then she caught his hand and brushed the faintest of kisses to it before twining her fingers through his. "I had a really nice time."

"We'll do it again."

"I'd like that."

"How about tomorrow? Riding horses at my dad's and dinner with my family?"

"I have to work tomorrow. Aunt Winona's going to an estate sale in Billings. I'll be minding the store."

"Maybe next weekend."

They fell silent then, just looking at each other, until finally she opened the door and slid to the ground. He met her at the front of the truck and walked at her side across the yard and up the steps. At the door, he pulled her into his arms, and she came willingly, accepting his kiss as naturally as if she'd been doing so for years.

It was a slow, lazy, all-the-time-in-the-world kiss. It didn't matter that it was ten-thirty at night, or that the temperature had slipped into the low twenties, or that she didn't trust him, or that her past was still between them. Nothing mattered at all, except the two of them and this kiss.

She leaned back against the cold aluminum siding of the trailer, and he followed her, his body instinctively moving to press against hers. Opening his coat, she slid her arms around his middle and clung to him while he explored her mouth, tasting, stroking, filling her, making her tremble.

When he raised his head just an inch to catch his breath, she smiled dreamily, eyes still closed. In the moonlight she looked ethereal, angelic, so incredibly beautiful. "I hear bells…"

"Like a doorbell?" he murmured, brushing kisses to her cheeks, her eyes, her forehead before his words penetrated and she abruptly jerked her head up.

A tap at the door made them both look that way. The curtain over the small rectangular window there was lifted, and inside Winona was grinning ear to ear. She gave them both a wave, then dropped the curtain.

Crystal gave the doorbell an offended look when she moved away from it. "Well, there's nothing like having an audience, is there?"

"Winona's had her share of good-night kisses. She's not surprised."

"No, I'm sure she's not. She told me you were one of the best-looking men in the county. And that your smile could be lethal." Her own smile was pretty damn deadly, teasing and smug and sexy as hell. "And that you're sweet on me."

"And here I thought that was our secret...and Rafe and Raeanne's...and my dad's..." He punctuated each pause with another kiss, then backed away a few steps. "I'd better head home, and you'd better get inside before you freeze."

He was at the top of the steps when she called, "Sweet dreams."

He looked back with a wicked grin. "You'd better believe it, darlin'."

The noon rush was in full swing at the Hip Hop Café on Tuesday when Crystal arrived in town for her lunch with Raeanne Rawlings. She found a parking space down the street and passed several sheriff's department vehicles on her walk to the diner. Was one of them Sloan's? She wasn't embarrassed to admit that she'd taken a little extra care with her appearance this morning on the chance that she might run into him—though she certainly wouldn't admit it to *him* if she did. He was already a bit too sure of her.

After the way she'd responded to his kisses last week, how could he not be?

The bell over the door dinged as she walked into the café. She immediately stepped aside to allow three big cowboys to leave, then scanned the room until Raeanne's wild wave caught her attention. "I hope I'm not late," she said, shrugging out of her jacket before sliding into the booth. "I had to park a few blocks away."

"You're fine. I just got here a minute ago myself. The specials are always good, the burgers are nice and greasy, and the salads are decent for winter." Raeanne gave her only a moment to scan the menu before jumping right into the conversation. "So…how long has this been going on between you and Sloan?"

Crystal gave her a wary look that made her laugh.

"I'm sorry. Rafe says I became a lawyer so I'd have a more or less legitimate reason to stick my nose into other people's business. But we love Sloan to death, and he's going to make some lucky woman the best husband, and I just want to see it done. So pardon my nosiness."

"No problem."

"So…how long has it been?"

She seemed so good-natured about it that Crystal couldn't help but laugh. "Friday was our first official date."

"But you've spent time with him."

"A little."

"Are you going to marry him?"

Crystal wasn't sure marriage would ever happen for her. If her life had worked out according to her parents' plan, she would be five months into marriage to James now. She would never dare leave her house looking less than her absolute best, and she would spend her time going to luncheons and to fund-raisers, listening to boring speeches and pretending that she gave a damn whether he was the next governor. Instead of her parents running her life, his advisors would, and every move she made would be to his political benefit. Even having children, James had warned her, wouldn't happen until the time was right, meaning politically advantageous.

Sloan was right. James had done her a hell of a favor in dumping her.

What would marriage to Sloan be like? Incredible, she thought dreamily. Building their house in the meadow by the river. Watching sunrises and sunsets. Making fantastic love on the spur of the moment. Loving, admiring, respecting, supporting. Having babies with no regard for polls or voter opinion. Saving their time for each other, for family and friends, instead of strategists and proponents. Having a real life, with real problems, real solutions and real happiness, and not some phony, socially correct, public-eye existence.

It sounded almost too good to be true, she thought wistfully. And the possibility that she could have it, all her wildest dreams, with Sloan Ravencrest... It hurt somewhere around her heart to even think about it. What she'd lost in losing James was nothing compared to all she could lose if she had Sloan, then lost him.

"Earth to Crystal," Raeanne softly called. "I lost you somewhere, didn't I? In all those thoughts of how wonderful being married to Sloan could be?"

Crystal focused her gaze on the other woman. "Not long before I came here, my fiancé and I went through a very public and very contentious breakup. I need more time..." She finished with a shrug.

"I'm sorry. But, you know, time isn't always the healer. Sometimes it's love. What better way to get over a man who hurt you than to take up with a man who thinks you hung the stars?"

Before Crystal could respond, a young waitress came to take their orders. After she walked away, Raeanne sighed. "I could probably repeat that same speech to her. That's Emma Stover. She showed up in town not too long ago—no family, no friends. Most folks think she's run away from a broken heart, too. It's too bad. She's a sweet kid."

Crystal gazed after the pretty, auburn-haired woman for a moment, then was turning back to Raeanne when a group seated at the far end of the counter caught her attention. There were five men, all wearing the gray-and-black uniforms of the sheriff's department, seated on bar stools. Right in their middle was Sloan, and standing beside him, with his hand clasped firmly in both of hers, was a drop-dead gorgeous black-haired woman. She was smiling up at him in a teasing, wheedling sort of way, and he was smiling back, that lethal smile that could make any woman weak.

That lethal smile that she'd somehow foolishly thought might be reserved for her.

Stunned, Crystal forced her gaze away. She had no claim on him. So he'd kissed her a few times, taken her to dinner, spent a little time with her. He'd never hinted she was the only woman he was seeing. She didn't have the right to expect to be the only woman, not after only one date and a few kisses.

Not even after a few incredible, curl-her-toes, make-her-weak kisses.

She certainly had no right to feel betrayed.

Raeanne gave her a concerned look, then twisted around to see what had caused her to freeze up. When she turned back, she was smiling sympathetically. "Man, you have it bad, don't you? Let me tell you right up front that that woman hanging on Sloan is Shelley Walksalong. She's his cousin. He comes from a very large family, and they're all very close, and you're bound to see him with some of them from time to time. Let me also tell you that, with the exception of my husband, Sloan is the least likely man in the state of Montana to two-time you. When he commits to a woman, he's committed until it ends."

Crystal stared at her hands on the tabletop. On the one hand, her relief at finding out the woman was a relative was embarrassingly intense. On the other, the power he already had to hurt her was immense, and that scared her. If he was already so important to her, how could she possibly protect herself? How would she survive if he let her down the way everyone else had?

Hoping to salvage some small bit of her pride, she forced a smile for Raeanne. "He's not committed to me."

"Oh, yes, he is. Maybe you don't see it that way, but, trust me, Sloan does. As long as he's seeing you, I promise, he won't be seeing anyone else."

"How do you know that?"

"Because I know him." Raeanne said it simply, confidently. There was no doubt in her mind that she could possibly be wrong.

Crystal envied her confidence. She'd lost hers, along with her faith, her trust and her belief in the common decency of people.

She didn't get a chance to regain her equilibrium. Sloan's cousin returned to her own table, and the deputies were headed her way on their way to the door. She wished she could slide under the table, or huddle down in the corner of the booth, until they were gone, but she couldn't, and even if she could, Raeanne had no intention of letting her go unnoticed.

"Well, well, if it's not Blue River County's finest," she said when the first two deputies came even with their table.

They greeted her with the respect accorded the sheriff's wife. Sloan was the last to say hello to her, though his gaze was locked on Crystal. She could feel it, even though she hadn't found the nerve yet to look up.

"You guys go on," he said to the waiting deputies. "I'll catch up with you later." His long, dark fingers working the brim of his black Stetson, he waited until they were gone to speak again. "Crystal. Mind if I join you for a minute?"

When she didn't answer, Raeanne did. "By all means, have a seat."

The bench shifted as he slid in beside her. "You can look at me, you know," he said softly. "The uniform's not that bad."

The uniform wasn't bad at all. The gray pants with a black stripe down the outer seam fitted snugly, and the gray shirt was equally snug. The telltale outline of his bulletproof vest was visible underneath the crisply pressed cotton.

"If you don't like the uniform, you can imagine him naked," Raeanne teased. "I hear it's quite a sight."

Sloan actually blushed, Crystal saw from the corner of her eye. She found something endearing about a wickedly handsome, sexy man who could blush like an adolescent boy.

"Oh, hey, there's someone I know over there," Raeanne went on. "I need to go say hi. Keep her company while I'm gone, Sloan."

When she was gone, he turned in the narrow space to face Crystal. "She was kidding."

She would have said the last thing she wanted to do at that moment was smile, but when she looked up at him, it just happened naturally. "How do you know? Women talk about this kind of thing, you know. And I imagine it *is* quite a sight."

"All you have to do is say the word, and you can see for yourself."

"The word," she knew, was actually three words. I trust you. Three small words that sometimes felt impossible. That rivaled those other three small words—I love you—in importance. That could make or break them.

"I saw you with that woman." The instant the words were out, she wished she could call them back. She didn't even know where they'd come from. Some deep need to hear Raeanne's reassurances from him?

For a moment he remained silent, then he casually said, "Shelley's my aunt Betty's oldest girl. That makes her my cousin. Unlike you Southerners, we don't go in much for kissin' cousins up here."

"I never kissed a cousin," she denied with a laugh.

"I imagine kissing James must have been about like that. Because if you kissed him the way you kiss me, he never would have let you go." He leaned a bit closer and lowered his voice. "I don't intend to let you go, Crystal."

Warmth welled inside her, spreading out to her fingers and toes, giving her an all-over comfortable feeling. "I was jealous," she admitted. "And afraid."

"Afraid because you were jealous? Because you're starting to care about me? That shouldn't be scary. It should be sweet. Exciting. Fun."

Her smile trembled. "Hey, that's me—never could do anything right. It comes from being different, you know."

For an instant the gentleness disappeared and his voice turned stern. "Don't say that, Crystal. Different isn't better or worse. It's just different—and we all are, you know, in one way or another."

He said the words as if he believed them. Of course, she reminded herself, he'd experienced his own share of prejudice over something that he had no more control over than she did her psychic abilities. At least she was able to keep her differences secret. His was right there, in his dark skin, black hair, dark eyes and strong features, for all the world to see. People had to get to know her to find out about hers. All they had to do was look at him. They could judge him without ever speaking a word to him.

"Aunt Winona says the French have the right attitude. *Vive la différence.*"

The smile he gave her was meant for her and her alone. "That's not the only good idea they've had. There's the French fry. The French door. The French kiss…"

Heat curled in her belly as his gaze dropped to her mouth. She'd never imagined that a simple look in a crowded café could be so potent, but she suddenly found herself in need of a blast of cold air, or maybe just a few minutes' privacy with Sloan.

The radio attached to his belt crackled, and he reached to adjust the volume. "I've got to get back to work. I'll call you." He touched her discreetly, then slid to his feet.

Taking a long draft of ice water, Crystal tracked his progress to the door by the farewells the other diners offered with genuine affection in their voices. Clearly, he was well thought of, at least by the lunch crowd. That counted for something, didn't it?

Raeanne returned to her seat as Emma served their meals, hot-off-the-grill burgers. "I swear, steam was rising off you and Sloan like that," Raeanne teased. "I could hear the sizzle all the way across the room."

Now it was Crystal's turn to blush. Deliberately she changed the subject. "Tell me how a public defender wound up married to a sheriff. That must lead to some interesting moments in the Rawlings household."

"Actually, it doesn't, except that we aren't often able to discuss work. We never know when I might be assigned to defend someone his department has arrested. But that's okay. We have other, more important things in our lives to talk about." She hesitated a moment. "Does it bother you that Sloan's a deputy?"

Did it bother her? She would never again make the mistake of thinking that the simple act of putting on a uniform or clipping a badge to a belt automatically made a person honest or trustworthy. But would she change Sloan's profession if she could? Would she be any more at ease with him if he was a cowboy, an accountant or an insurance agent? Was she any less likely to fall for him simply because he was a deputy?

Maybe. At least a cowboy, an accountant or an insurance agent wouldn't be in a position to benefit from her visions— or to betray her because of them.

"It's not a dangerous job," Raeanne said, assuming that was the source of Crystal's bias. "Well, it can be. But Sloan's careful. He always wears his vest, he's an expert shot and he knows when to wait for backup. He never rushes into anything without being well aware of the risks. All the deputies are like that. They're cautious, and they look out for each other."

Great. Crystal hadn't considered the danger inherent to the job. Now she would have more to worry about than whether he was going to break her heart.

Once again needing a change of subject, she smiled at Raeanne and asked a question that was virtually guaranteed to redirect the woman's thoughts. "How's the shopping around here?"

"Oh, honey, have you come to the right woman. Let me tell you…"

As customers began returning to work, business at the Hip Hop slowly tapered off, finally giving Emma Stover a break from her waitressing. It hadn't been an unusually busy lunch, but she was glad it was over. Her feet hurt, her back hurt, and she had the beginnings of a bad headache. She just wanted to go home, soak in a tub of hot, fragrant bubbles and let her aches seep away down the drain.

But she wasn't sure there were enough hot, fragrant bubbles in the world to ease all her aches.

After pouring herself a cup of coffee to go with a slice of the cook's best pie, she went to an empty booth. She methodically prepared herself—sugar and cream in the coffee, a bite of pie—then pulled the official white envelope from her pocket. The return address was the Montana Women's Prison in Billings. She'd found it stuffed in the mailbox on her way to work, but she'd been running late, so she hadn't opened it yet.

Running late...or running scared?

Using the knife rolled with her napkin, she slit the envelope flap and removed the contents. "Dear Ms. Stover," it began innocently enough. "With regard to your request for information concerning making arrangements to visit an inmate at our facility..." It went on, listing visiting days and hours, personal items visitors could bring for the inmate as well as items that were prohibited. If she wanted to provide the inmate with money to use in the facility's commissary, she was welcome to make arrangements while there to deposit such funds in the inmate's account. Lastly, it included directions to the prison.

The prison. The very thought of getting into her car and driving off eighty miles to a prison for an afternoon visit was enough to send shivers down her spine. She'd never been in trouble in her life, had never even seen the inside of a jail, and here she was debating whether she wanted to see her birth mother badly enough to do it in a prison setting. High fences, thick concrete walls, armed guards, maximum security.... It was hardly the reunion she'd envisioned when she'd started her search.

She'd considered a lot of possibilities when she'd started. That she would never find her mother, no matter how she looked. That she would find her and the woman would want nothing to do with her. And, of course, her favorite, that she would find her and her mother would be elated and welcome her into her happy, loving family. But she had *never* considered the possibility that her mother—the woman who had brought her into this world—was a murderer who had destroyed other lives.

One dream down. Not many left to go.

Folding the letter, she returned it to its envelope, then stuck it back in her pocket. She picked up the fork and cut a sliver of pie, but left it uneaten on the plate. Instead, she cupped her coffee in her hands and gazed out the window. Whitehorn was a nice town, not too terribly different from Clear Brook, the small South Dakota town where, after bouncing from one foster home to the next, she'd finished growing up. Her search for her birth mother had brought her here.

Now fear was keeping her here. Fear of returning home to South Dakota with her search unfinished. Fear of driving those eighty miles to the prison for the worst reunion she could have imagined. Fear of not having the courage to face her disappointment, and of shattering her dreams forever.

Luckily, she didn't have to decide today, she thought as the bell over the door signaled the arrival of customers. She'd waited twenty-three years to meet her birth mother.

She would wait a while longer.

Sloan reported to the sheriff's office a half hour before shift change and joined most of the department, as well as most of the Whitehorn Police Department, in the conference room. He claimed a space against the wall as the doors at the opposite end opened. The police chief came in first, with Mayor Ellis Montgomery, Christina's father, and her brother Max. Rafe brought up the rear.

They'd been having these conferences ever since Christina had been reported missing, though with less frequency lately.

Other than making it easier to disseminate information through the ranks, there wasn't much reason for the meetings. They had no clues, no new theories, no breaks. They recovered familiar ground, revealed their own frustration, and fostered frustration in everyone else. They were pointless.

But the sheriff had mandated his presence, and so he was there.

As the chief began talking, Sloan's gaze settled on the Montgomerys. Ellis looked pretty ragged. First his wife's death, then this. He'd aged years in the past few months.

As for Max, Sloan didn't know him well and doubted that anyone in Whitehorn did, including Ellis. He'd graduated from high school about the time Sloan had entered junior high, had gone on to college and then traveled around the world overseeing his father's business interests. Four years ago he'd settled in town once again, taking over the presidency of the Whitehorn Savings and Loan when Ellis was elected mayor. Whether he was happy with the change was anyone's guess. What he'd done besides work in those four years was also, as far as Sloan knew, anyone's guess. If there was one thing Max Montgomery did well, it was keep to himself.

He certainly hadn't bothered himself with his troubled sister. Neither had his father or his other sister Rachel, who'd come home from Chicago to be with the family through the crisis. Maybe if one of them had shown this much concern for Christina six months ago, she wouldn't be missing now.

But it wasn't Sloan's place to judge. People made mistakes—the Montgomerys, Crystal's parents, his own mother. Hopefully, they learned from them. Hopefully, some people—like James—suffered for them.

There was a lot of talk at the meeting, but not much was said. Terry Wilkins and Mark Blakely, the two detectives who were primarily in charge of the police department's side of the case, were checking out leads. Officially, so were the two investigators handling it for the sheriff's department, though Sloan knew for a fact they had no leads. He suspected the detectives's leads were nonexistent, as well. Just so much talk for the benefit of the mayor and his son.

"All we need is for one of those 'leads' to lead to the rez," Eugene Elkshoulder, a young Cheyenne deputy, murmured. "Then the BIA police and/or the FBI can come in, and we'll see just how many people can B.S. at these conferences."

Sloan responded with a nod, but he didn't think that was a remote possibility. The Bureau of Indian Affairs police had jurisdiction over the reservation, and the FBI could come in at their invitation, but he didn't think Christina had made it to the rez that night. If Crystal and Winona were right, and she had given birth in the clearing, she would have had to walk miles through the forest to reach the reservation boundary, and then where would she go? The nearest house was several more miles, and Christina was neither physically active nor accustomed to hardship. She never would have had the strength of spirit to make it.

So where *had* she gone? Deeper into the woods? Back down the trail to the parking lot? And how had she gotten to the woods in the first place? Why? To meet someone? To get away from someone?

This was his least favorite kind of case. Too many questions and not enough answers.

Once the meeting broke up, Sloan waited where he was for the crowd to clear the doors. Elkshoulder had the same idea. "I hear the Montgomerys are putting pressure on the sheriff and the chief to make an arrest."

"Can't make an arrest without a suspect and probable cause, and we don't have either," Sloan replied.

"I think Christina's living in luxury someplace laughing at all the trouble she's caused."

"Her bank accounts haven't been touched, and her credit cards haven't been used. How is she paying for this luxury?"

Elkshoulder needed a moment to find an answer to support his theory. "The baby. She sold it to some black-market adoption ring. Rich folks will pay fifty thousand and up for a healthy infant these days.''

For a healthy *white* infant, Sloan thought. Considering the makeup of the county's population, there was a good chance Christina's baby wasn't as white as its pretty chestnut-haired, blue-eyed mother.

But Elkshoulder's theory was as viable as anyone else's. Stranger things had happened. And selling an unwanted baby was a definite step up from abandoning it.

Abruptly shifting gears, the deputy grinned. ''Hey, was that Crazy Cobbs's niece at the Hip Hop?''

Sloan had heard the nickname before, but this time it rankled. ''Winona Cobbs is a whole lot saner than you and me, son. And seeing that she's one of the citizens who pay your salary, it might be a good idea for you to refer to her as Ms. Cobbs.''

''Aw, I didn't mean nothing by it. But you gotta admit, the old woman is a little shy of a full load. She sees things that aren't there and thinks she can tell fortunes, for Pete's sake. Anyway, about her niece—''

''She's taken.''

Elkshoulder's look was both rueful and admiring. ''How the hell'd you do that? Jeez, today's only the second time I've even seen her.''

Seeing that the exit was clear, Sloan pushed away from the wall, then gave the deputy a pat on the shoulder. ''You can see her all you want—from a distance. But don't get too close. I'm a mite territorial these days.''

He left the conference room and headed through the crowd toward the front doors. They were blocked, though, by the police chief and his two detectives. ''And what would be his reason for this?'' the chief was asking as Sloan waited for officers coming into the building to pass so he could go around the ones talking.

''When has he ever needed a reason for anything?'' Wilkins asked impatiently. ''He's nuts. Isn't that reason enough?'' He broke off and glared at Sloan when he finally managed to get around him. Sloan didn't care. He didn't like the detective, anyway, and he wasn't the least bit interested in his business.

He did wonder, though, as he walked to his truck, who they'd been discussing. Blue River County's list of people considered to be nuts was a long one, and varied depending on who you asked. Obviously, Deputy Elkshoulder thought Winona was off her rocker, and Crystal feared that everyone would think she was delusional if word of her vision got out.

Maybe she was right. Maybe foolish people like Elkshoulder would give her her own nickname, or maybe they would just stick with Crazy Cobbs, One and Two. Elder and Junior.

He'd be damned if he would let that happen. Even if her vision had to become a part of his report, he would make sure there was no name-calling. She deserved that much.

But he intended to give her so much more.

Seven

It was late Friday afternoon when Crystal hung the picture on her bedroom wall, then stepped back, her head cocked to one side, to study it. It was a bit crooked, but she didn't bother straightening it. When you lived in a forty-year-old trailer house, things hung on the walls tended to wind up crooked. She was just getting a jump on it by starting out that way.

Of all the photographs she'd found in the moving carton she'd brought over from the back room, this, a hauntingly lovely shot of a giant live oak, was the only one she wanted to hang. She'd picked it up at an arts and crafts festival in Atlanta for ten bucks, then spent another hundred framing it. With its branches draped with Spanish moss and the cascading purple blooms of an ancient wisteria vine, the tree reminded her of what was good about home.

The rest of the photographs in the box reminded her of what was bad.

As a knock rattled the closed door, she nudged the carton aside with her knee so the door could open. "Come on in," she called, and he did.

Sloan.

He stood in the doorway, looking from her face to the hammer in her hand, then back again. "I think my pistol beats your hammer," he teased.

"My hammer's bigger."

"My pistol's deadlier."

She set the hammer down, then swept up an armful of

frames to drop into—to hide inside—the box. "What are you doing out this way?"

"I had a call a few miles from here. Since I've already put in an hour overtime, I thought I'd stop by and see my favorite girl."

"Sorry, Skye's not here," she said flippantly, even as she wondered if she had ever been anyone's favorite girl before. Not that she could recall. It had a nice, old-fashioned ring to it, and she was developing a new appreciation for the old-fashioned.

He gave her a smirk before glancing around the room. "Doing a little redecorating?"

She glanced around, too, though she already knew how bad the mess was. Boxes and their contents covered all the floor space and most of the furniture, too. She would have to clear a path to the bed tonight and another to the closet in the morning. "I'm unpacking a few things," she said, stating the obvious.

That brought his gaze back to her, with a decidedly pleased look in his eyes. "Decided to stay awhile, did you?"

"Yeah. Have a seat, if you can find a place." She perched on the end of a primitive pine bench, weathered to silvery gray, that she'd claimed from the shop for her own as he cleared a few inches of space on the bed.

"I thought I'd see if I could persuade you to have dinner with me."

"You mean, like a date?"

"The first one went well enough. Why not try a second?"

With another good-night kiss? The mere thought was enough to curl her toes, but all the wrapping paper and bubble wrap on the floor hid the reaction from his view. "Where I come from," she said primly, "dates are usually scheduled in advance."

"Is that what Rich-man did? Of course it is. And what else did he pencil into his schedule? Asking you to marry him? Making love to you? Breaking your heart?"

"As a matter of fact, yes, yes and yes." Her tone was

cooler than she meant it to be. She honestly wasn't offended or upset or hurt. She had just realized how right he was. Everything she and James had ever done together had been scheduled—by him, by their parents, by his campaign advisors. Everyone had had a say in her life except her. She'd wanted to keep the peace, to keep her parents happy with her, and so she had gone along. She'd been the most docile little fiancée in the whole state of Georgia.

"I'm sorry. I didn't mean to sound so…"

"Right?" she supplied dryly. "You are, I'm sorry to say."

"Then you're not mad? You're still considering dinner with me tonight?"

"Yes. I would like to have dinner with you." The satisfaction in his grin warmed her as she got to her feet. "Give me five minutes to change, and I'll be ready."

As he stood, the top picture in the carton chose that moment to slide over the side and onto the floor. Well aware exactly which photo it was, Crystal held her breath as he bent to pick it up. It would be human nature for him to turn it over—would she pass up the chance to examine the pictures of his life?—but she fervently hoped he would resist, just this once.

He didn't. Looking at the picture, he slowly sat back on the bed. For a long time he studied it in silence before making one quiet comment. "You don't look like a woman in love."

She sat beside him, pulling the elaborate frame from his hands. The photograph had been taken at her engagement party. The day had been hot and muggy, but a person would never guess it to look at all the cool, collected faces. The grounds of James's grandparents' plantation home had been filled with beautiful people in beautiful clothes, beautiful flowers, beautiful food and beautiful music.

She had worn a peach silk dress, and James had worn a cream-colored suit. Peach and cream had been her colors—too precious, she'd thought then and now—chosen for her by her mother and his. The dress had been chosen for her, too, and the party planned around her, the wedding planned without her.

James had never been more handsome than he was that day—or more smug, or overbearing. And why not? The ring—*the* ring, the ostentatious Johnson-family-heirloom rock—was on her finger, and their engagement was officially announced. He'd known that Marabeth would move heaven and earth to ensure that the marriage went off without a hitch.

He'd known that Crystal didn't have the backbone to call it off.

"Whose house?"

She didn't glance at Sloan. "His grandparents'. When they die, it will be James's. That's why he wanted our engagement party there."

"Are these your parents?"

"Marabeth and Andrew Cobbs, in their proudest moment."

"And his parents?"

She nodded.

"And James."

He was as fair as Sloan was dark, as overtly white as Sloan was Indian. Blond hair, blue eyes, country-club tan. Elegant and sophisticated, the result of two hundred years of selective breeding. Handsome, intelligent, ambitious, charming, and, not surprisingly, self-centered. And not *real*.

Sloan was real.

"And you…" he said quietly, then repeated with just as much conviction, "you don't look like a woman in love."

She didn't, she admitted. She looked…desperate. Desperate to please, to do the right thing, to not disappoint. Desperate to make their engagement work, to make the marriage work, to never let on to anyone, not even herself, that it was a mistake. That she wasn't in love with James. That she didn't want to marry Georgia's next governor.

She'd been so damn desperate, and afraid, and powerless.

Brushing her fingertip lightly over her own image, she whispered, "The things we do for love." For her parents' love, she would have gone through with it. She would have lived the rest of her life, deceiving everyone and most especially herself. She would have sacrificed herself, her future, everything, for her parents' love and acceptance.

And it all would have been an illusion.

After a few seconds, or a few minutes, he took the frame from her, turned it facedown again and returned it to the box. Then he pulled her to her feet and turned her in the direction of the closet. "Find a way over there, get changed and let's go."

Dinner, she remembered. "Dressy or jeans?"

"Whatever you want, darlin'."

He closed the door behind him, and she sorted through the clothes in her closet, settling on a green sweater, black jeans and black boots. She changed quickly, ran a comb through her hair and touched up her makeup before joining Sloan at the front door. "Does Aunt Winona know I'm leaving?"

"Not unless she preminisced it. I stopped in, looking for you, and she sent me on over here. By the way, what are you doing in your bedroom with the door closed and the front door unlocked? Anyone could have come in without you hearing."

"Someone did," she said with a grin as he helped her with her coat. "I'll lock the door next time. Scout's honor."

"Aw, you were never a Scout, were you?"

"No. But I would have liked to have been." She locked up, then they hurried across the yard to the shop. According to the thermometer mounted outside the Stop-n-Swap, it was thirty-four degrees, but the northwest wind made it feel much colder. She wondered when they would get their first snow and hoped she was up to the challenge of dealing with it. Georgia's worst winter on record couldn't begin to compete with Montana's average.

But this was her home now. She would adapt.

Before the bell above the door echoed into silence, Winona asked, "Where are you going for dinner?"

Crystal felt Sloan's glance. He was being a good sport

about it, but their foreknowledge still took him by surprise. It wasn't an easy thing to get used to. She'd been trying for twenty-six years.

He cleared his throat—and probably his mind—before answering. "I thought we'd check out Neela's, if it's not too crowded."

"It won't be, at least not until later. Have a good time." With a big smile, Winona winked at them. "I won't wait up."

"Good night, Aunt Winona." Crystal leaned across the counter to hug her before following Sloan out again. "Who or what is Neela's?" she asked as they settled out of the wind again in his sheriff's department Jeep.

"It's both a who and a what. Neela Tallbear came off the rez and went to Paris to cooking school. She worked in New York, San Francisco and St. Thomas, then got homesick and came back to Whitehorn. She opened her own restaurant about five years ago, serving local beef, and it's doing well."

"So a French-trained chef can find happiness running a steakhouse in the wilds of Montana," Crystal said with a chuckle.

"Why not? A snooty Chatham Prep grad is learning to find happiness working in a junk store and living in a trailer in the wilds of Montana."

And dating a Cheyenne deputy sheriff, she silently added. Before him, she'd been satisfied, more or less. Since getting involved with him, she'd realized she *could* be happy. She could make friends, make a life, fit in. She could be accepted, liked, wanted, and maybe even loved exactly the way she was. No pretending, no phoniness, no hiding her abilities. She could be just Crystal, and that was enough for him.

And *that* was more than enough for her.

Their first stop in town was the sheriff's department, where they traded the Jeep for his own truck. Next they went to his apartment so he could change out of his uniform. It wasn't much different from her own apartment back in Atlanta—a little bigger, definitely neater. Either he was a better house-

Get 2 Books FREE!

MIRA® BOOKS, The Brightest Stars in Fiction, presents

The Best of the Best™

Superb collector's editions of the very best novels by the world's best-known authors!

FREE BOOKS!
To introduce you to "The Best of the Best" we'll send you 2 books ABSOLUTELY FREE!"

FREE GIFT!
Get an exciting mystery gift absolutely free!

BEST BOOKS!
"The Best of the Best" brings you the best books by the world's hottest authors!

2 FREE BOOKS!

▲ To get your 2 free books, affix this peel-off sticker to the reply card and mail it today!

HOW TO GET YOUR
2 FREE BOOKS AND FREE GIFT

1. Peel off the 2 FREE BOOKS seal from the front cover. Place it in the space provided at right. This automatically entitles you to receive two free books and an exciting mystery gift.

2. Send back this card and you'll get 2 "The Best of the Best™" novels. These books have a combined cover price of $11.00 or more in the U.S. and $13.00 or more in Canada, but they are yours to keep absolutely FREE!

3. There's <u>no</u> catch. You're under <u>no</u> obligation to buy anything. We charge nothing – ZERO – for your first shipment. And you don't have to make any minimum number of purchases – not even one!

4. We call this line "The Best of the Best" because each month you'll receive the best books by the world's hottest authors. These authors show up time and time again on all the major bestseller lists and their books sell out as soon as they hit the stores. You'll like the convenience of getting them delivered to your home at our discount prices…and you'll love your subscriber newsletter featuring author news, horoscopes, recipes, book reviews and much more!

5. We hope that after receiving your free books you'll want to remain a subscriber. But the choice is yours – to continue or cancel, anytime at all! So why not take us up on our invitation, with no risk of any kind. You'll be glad you did!

6. And remember…we'll send you a mystery gift ABSOLUTELY FREE just for giving "The Best of the Best" a try!

MIRA ®

SPECIAL FREE GIFT!

We'll send you a fabulous mystery gift, absolutely FREE, simply for accepting our no-risk offer!

Books FREE!

HURRY! Return this card promptly to get **2 FREE Books** and a **FREE Gift!**

The Best of the Best™

YES! Please send me the 2 FREE "The Best of the Best" novels and FREE gift for which I qualify. I understand that I am under no obligation to purchase anything further, as explained on the opposite page.

Affix
peel-off
2 FREE BOOKS
sticker here.

P-BB1-00
385 MDL CY2W   **185 MDL CY2X**

| | | | | | | | | | | | | | | | | | | | |
NAME   (PLEASE PRINT CLEARLY)

| | | | | | | | | | | | | | | | | | | | |
ADDRESS

| | | | | | | | | | | | | | | | | | | | |
APT.#   CITY

| | | | | | | | | | | | | | | | | | | | |
STATE/PROV.   ZIP/POSTAL CODE

Offer limited to one per household and not valid to current subscribers of "The Best of the Best." All orders subject to approval. Books received may vary.

The Best of the Best™—Here's How it Works

Accepting your 2 free books and gift places you under no obligation to buy anything. You may keep the books and gift and return the shipping statement marked "cancel." If you do not cancel, about a month later we will send you 4 additional novels and bill you just $4.24 each in the U.S., or $4.74 each in Canada, plus 25¢ delivery per book and applicable sales tax, if any.* That's the complete price, and — compared to cover prices of $5.50 or more each in the U.S. and $6.50 or more each in Canada — it's quite a bargain! You may cancel at any time, but if you choose to continue, every month we'll send you 4 more books, which you may either purchase at the discount price…or return to us and cancel your subscription.

*Terms and prices subject to change without notice. Sales tax applicable in N.Y. Canadian residents will be charged applicable provincial taxes and GST.

If offer card is missing write to: The Best of the Best, 3010 Walden Ave., P.O. Box 1867, Buffalo, NY 14240-1867

BUSINESS REPLY MAIL

FIRST-CLASS MAIL   PERMIT NO. 717   BUFFALO NY

POSTAGE WILL BE PAID BY ADDRESSEE

THE BEST OF THE BEST
3010 WALDEN AVE
PO BOX 1867
BUFFALO NY 14240-9952

NO POSTAGE
NECESSARY
IF MAILED
IN THE
UNITED STATES

keeper, someone took care of it for him, or he spent little time in the place.

She waited in the living room with its balcony that provided a nice view of the Crazy Mountains, barely a shadow now in the darkening evening. There was a sofa and chair made for sprawling, a rocker with its share of dings, a television and compact stereo and one entire wall of bookcases filled with—surprise—books. She scanned the titles, ranging from old college texts to works about the Cheyenne people, from biographies and histories to fiction. The fiction was diverse, as well—blockbuster bestsellers, mystery, science fiction, Westerns and obscure literature.

"What do you know?" His teasing voice came from behind her as she browsed the shelves. "He's charming, he's handsome, he kisses like the devil, and, hey, he can read, too."

When she turned to face him, if she hadn't already been smiling, she would have smiled then. He'd changed into jeans faded a soft, comfortable blue and worn to a soft, comfortable, body-hugging fit. His button-down shirt was scarlet and tucked in to reveal an intricately tooled leather belt. "Nice belt."

"Thanks. My cousin Billy Knows-His-Gun makes belts, boots, saddles."

"Knows-His-Gun knows his leather, too." At his exaggerated wince, her smile turned into a grin. "Hardly an original remark, I take it."

"I've heard it a time or two before." He gestured toward the bookcases. "Do we have any similar tastes?"

"I've read a lot of these. The only thing you're missing is my favorite—romance."

"Twelve years of schooling at Chatham Prep—"

"Thirteen," she corrected. "Don't forget kindergarten."

"—didn't root out your ability to appreciate something so hopelessly common and universally appealing as romance novels? I'm surprised they ever deemed you suitable to teach there." Catching a handful of her wool coat, he pulled her close and nuzzled her neck. "I prefer my romance living and breathing and in my arms. But I'd be happy to clear off a few shelves for you."

And then he kissed her—nothing toe-curling, not breath-stealing, but a sweet, achy taste of what she was sure to get later. It lasted only seconds—thirty, maybe sixty. It left her feeling needy, greedy, wanting.

"Are you ready for dinner?"

She didn't want to go to dinner or anywhere else besides his bedroom. All she wanted was to take off those clothes he'd just put on, to strip off her own clothes and spend the rest of the night exploring how incredible the sex between them could be. He would agree, she was sure of that. All she had to do was say the words.

I trust you.

But did she?

She could say the words and make him believe them, and then they could seduce each other, but it wouldn't be fair. She would be taking something he clearly didn't want to give until he was getting something specific in return. She would be cheating him, and cheating herself, and their relationship might not survive. Way too much to risk just because her libido had come back to life with a vengeance.

"Sure," she said with an unsteady smile. "I'm ready."

Contrary to Winona's prediction, Neela's had been busy, with a fifteen-minute wait for a table. Sloan hadn't minded, though, since it had prolonged his time with Crystal by that much. He hadn't minded that he knew everyone in the place, too, or that half of them had spent their evening watching Crystal. *She* hadn't been too thrilled to be the center of attention, but she was so damn beautiful. How could he blame them, when all *he* wanted was to sit and watch her?

Now it was approaching ten o'clock and they were in the meadow on his land. He'd offered her several choices—dancing and a drink or two at one of Whitehorn's bars, a return to his apartment, a return to her house. She had suggested this, the site of their picnic in what was certainly not picnic weather. She didn't seem to mind the cold, though, and he didn't even notice it. Just looking at her was enough to make him hot. Thinking about kissing her was enough to keep him that way.

They were sitting on a boulder at the river's edge. The sky was filled with stars and a half moon, and the world seemed a million miles away. Everything was peaceful...except for one small part of his conscience.

He brought his feet up, rested his arms on his knees, let his hands dangle free. "That picture of you at your engagement party..."

Peripherally he saw her turn toward him, waiting without speaking.

"I knew you came from money, but until I saw that picture, I didn't have a clue how much." Truth was, the realization had intimidated him. He knew better than to judge a man's worth by his bank balance, knew he could be proud of who he was and the life he'd lived even if he never earned much more than minimum wage. He knew money didn't make a man—James Rich-man proved that—and there were many things in life more important than how much money a person had.

He knew all that, but Crystal had been raised differently. She'd grown up in a society where money and standing were all-important. She'd left that life, granted, and come to his part of the world, but not voluntarily. She hadn't given up the parties, the clothes, the plantations, the jewels, by choice.

She might not be able, or willing, to give it up permanently.

He took a breath, then turned his head so he could see her. "I'd never be able to give you a house like that, or a ring like that, or a life like that. If you settle for me, financially, you're settling for less. A lot less. I make decent money for this job in this part of the country, and I've saved a fair amount of it, but what I earn in a year probably wouldn't even pay for the champagne at that one party. I just think you should be aware of that."

For a long, still moment, she simply looked at him, her expression impossible to read. Then she brushed her hair back, anchoring it behind her ear, and tilted her head to study him. "I don't want a house like that," she said evenly, "but if I did, I could provide it, or something similar, myself." At his incredulous look, she shrugged embarrassedly. "I have a trust fund. From my great-grandmother. It's been invested in the high tech and Pacific Rim stock markets for years. I hear it's done all right.

"As for the ring, what should have been a symbol of joy was a burden instead. I couldn't wear it anywhere unless there was security, and it snagged on everything. And I don't like champagne. And if you think my going out with you means I'm settling, then you're not quite as smart as I thought you were. I've settled all my life, but not anymore. I'm never going to settle again." She paused, then quietly added, "I think you should be aware of that."

Grinning ruefully, he shook his head. "It threw me for a loop, that's all. You seem so normal—"

"Thank you. No matter how my parents disagreed, I like to think that, except for this one little quirk, I *am* normal."

"I've never heard anyone describe being beautiful as a little quirk."

"I was referring to being psychic."

"Oh. You are beautiful, you know."

Her gaze slipped away, then came back, bringing with it a shy smile. "Thank you."

Sliding to the ground, he stood in front of her, planting his hands on either side of her hips. "I can't give you anything in the way of luxuries, but I can give you this promise. If we ever stand together after announcing that we're going to get married, you won't look like you did in that picture. I'd do my best to make sure you never had a reason to look like that."

She lifted her hand, touched his jaw so lightly that he

barely felt it, then let it slide down until her fingers caught in the lapel of his coat. "You're wrong, Sloan," she whispered. "Not feeling the way I felt in that picture, being happy, being accepted—those are the greatest luxuries in my world. And you're the only man who's ever given them to me."

Of course he kissed her. How could he not? He wrapped his arms around her, pulling her against him, and claimed her mouth. She opened to his tongue, and he thrust inside, wishing like hell he could take possession of her body as easily. It didn't ease his sexual frustration any knowing that he *could* seduce her as easily, if only he hadn't put that one condition on their lovemaking.

But he'd never before been with a woman who didn't trust him, who expected him to betray her, and he was too old to start now. He needed her trust more than he needed her body.

Though certain parts of his own body were willing to argue the point at that moment.

Still clinging to him, Crystal lay back on the boulder, her hands urging him to follow. It was a hard bed, and a cold one, but it would be adequate if she would just say the words and make him believe them. But all she said as he settled between her thighs was, "Please...oh, please..." And then he took her mouth again, and for a long time neither of them said anything.

In desperate need of air, and restraint, and something to think about other than how aroused he was and how perfectly she used her hands and body and soft, husky whimpers to torment him, he broke away and rolled onto his back, staring up into the night sky. He dragged in sweet, cold breaths and willed his erection to go away—not likely, as she snuggled closer to him—or at least subside to only painfully intense.

"Kinda like being back in high school, isn't it?" he asked when he thought his voice would be steady. It was, but so thick and hoarse that he hardly recognized it. "Or were Chatham Prep kids too superior to neck wherever they got the chance?"

"I wouldn't know," she murmured. Her hand was tucked inside his coat, right square in the middle of his chest. He wondered if she could feel the thudding of his heart, wondered if he slid his hand underneath her sweater if he'd feel the same heavy beat.

Just the thought made his own heart skip a beat.

"By high school," she went on, her fingers lightly massaging, the tips working their way between buttons to reach his bare skin, "I was already so afraid of the other kids that I never had a date."

"Why were you afraid?"

She loosened one button, then slid her hand inside his shirt. Sloan felt his skin ripple, felt his nipple pucker as she grazed across it. "My earliest memory is of my mother shrieking to my father that there was something wrong with me, that all she'd wanted was a normal child to love and take care of, and instead she'd gotten a little freak or witch or whatever the hell I was."

She smiled faintly. "She had known my father all their lives, and she'd never known that Aunt Winona was psychic. It was a big family secret. When he realized that I shared her psychic abilities, he had to tell my mother. She took to her bed for a week. She forbade me to ever tell her anything, but I was a kid. I'd blurt out that Grandmother was calling and fifteen seconds later the phone would ring. It freaked her out every time.

"My father had been conditioned by his parents to never discuss Aunt Winona's odd behavior with anyone. They convinced him it was something to be ashamed of, something that normal people, good people, weren't afflicted with. He and my mother decided that was the best course of action for me, too. She drilled me every time we left the house to not blurt out anything, to not say anything that couldn't be explained, to never, ever tell anyone I was different. That was the term she eventually settled on. *Different.*"

She'd been an innocent child, too young to know that her abilities weren't so unusual, that they were certainly nothing to be ashamed of. Parents never ceased to amaze Sloan, some with their boundless love for their children, others with their endless mistakes in raising them.

"I got regular lectures on how to behave around other people, instructions for how to cover up if I slipped and warnings about the consequences if I ever confided in anyone. 'The kids will make fun of you and call you names like Crazy Crystal, weirdo and freak,'" she recited, "'and their parents won't let them play with you, and you won't have any friends, and you'll be lonely and sad, and it'll all be your fault for letting them know you're *different*.'"

Sloan muttered a heartfelt obscenity in the heavy silence that followed.

"Needless to say, I wasn't the most outgoing kid at Chatham. I didn't have my first date until college, where I made up for my stunted high school social life in one night, from first kiss to losing my virginity."

"Your parents should be shot."

"Oh, they've been punished. They've lost James. He was the magic that was going to fix everything. He was so perfect that merely being married to him was going to turn me into the perfect daughter they'd always dreamed of." Then she lifted her head and smiled down at him. "More importantly, they've lost *me*. I'm worth knowing, in spite of the premonitions and the visions, but they never figured that out."

And in that moment when she smiled, in that very second, Sloan completed a process that had started the first time he'd ever seen her. He fell in love. He'd never been there before, but he had no doubt that was exactly where he was.

Desperately, passionately, impossibly in love with Crystal.

He sat cross-legged on the boulder and tugged her into his lap. Able to feel her chill from lying on the rock even through her clothes, he cradled her close and simply held her for a time, and she was content to be held. He couldn't find a degree of tension anywhere in her body, and he was touching her just about everywhere.

"You're a remarkable woman, Crystal," he said, his

mouth against her ear making her shiver. "It's a wonder your parents didn't drive you into intensive therapy."

"I'm not remarkable," she disagreed. "I'm a terrible coward. I've been afraid all my life—of disappointing my parents, of letting my secret slip, of being found out for the fraud I've become and the freak I was taught that I am. When things became impossible at home, I ran away rather than stay and deal with them. If they become impossible here, I'll probably run away again."

His arms tightened around her as if he could somehow hold her there and keep her safe. "They won't become impossible here."

"You mean because you haven't found anything to support my vision. But that could change."

"I mean because things are different here. You're not alone. You have Winona, Raeanne and Rafe. You have me. Nothing's going to hurt you with us around. And if you want eight more loyal protectors…"

She tilted her head back to gaze up at him, and he lost his train of thought. She looked exotic in the moonlight—gleaming black hair, delicate china skin, incredibly kissable mouth. He wanted to stop talking and do just that, but too much kissing and he was going to forget that she didn't trust him, that sex without trust was just sex, that he wanted so much more. His bone-deep need was going to persuade him that trust could be worked on after sex, that it might even be easier to cultivate once their physical needs were met.

Clearing his throat, he fixed his gaze on the river a few feet away and went on. "We've been invited to my folks' house for dinner tomorrow. We can go early and do some riding, or we can just make it for dinner, or we can do something else entirely. What do you say?"

"Riding would be nice," she murmured.

He murmured his agreement, too, before giving in to the need and kissing her again, one sweet time after another on the bank of the Little Blue River under a sky filled with stars and a half-moon, with the world a million miles away.

And everything was most definitely peaceful.

In the ten years since she'd last ridden, Crystal had forgotten how different the world could look from the back of a horse. She would probably pay for the reminder tomorrow with aching muscles, but at the moment she was enjoying it tremendously.

Sloan's father was the only one of his relatives who'd met them when they arrived to saddle the horses. The rest of the family, he'd informed them, had gone on their weekly shopping trip into town.

Arlen Ravencrest was a handsome man, taller than his son, broad-shouldered, lean-hipped and black-haired. The resemblance between them was so strong she had no doubt that in another twenty years, Sloan would look exactly like his father did now, except, of course, for their color. Being a full-blood Cheyenne, Arlen's skin was several shades darker than his son's.

After questioning Crystal on her riding experience, he'd singled a chestnut out of the horses who'd come trotting when they'd appeared at the pasture fence. While he'd saddled the gelding, then helped her mount, Sloan had saddled his own horse, a beautiful paint.

Now they were miles from the house, riding alongside the road that cut through the reservation, and hadn't yet passed another house or another person. Such space was daunting and impressive. It made her feel small.

"Tell me about Georgia."

Crystal glanced at Sloan. He was, at the same time, far more relaxed and far more controlled in the saddle than she was. With his black Stetson tipped forward to shadow his face, he looked daunting and impressive, too, and handsome as sin. It was no wonder cowboys were prime hero material in the books she read. Sloan on a horse could certainly win her over.

Gazing back to the countryside, she focused her thoughts on his request. "It's a beautiful state. There are beaches, swamps, rolling hills, mountains. Small towns, big cities. Live oaks, sugar pines, Spanish moss, azaleas, wisteria, kudzu. It's nothing like this.''

''Is that a compliment or an insult?''

Smiling brightly, she parroted his own words back to him. ''Different isn't necessarily better or worse. Sometimes it's just different.''

''Smart ass.''

Her smile turned smug before she returned to the subject. ''We don't have much of this kind of wide open space in Georgia. Most of what isn't developed for housing, industry or agriculture is fairly heavily wooded. This—'' she stretched out one arm to encompass the countryside ''—can take your breath away. It's so open and vast, but kind of lonely, too. So, is this all a reservation is? Land and houses?''

''What were you expecting?'' he asked with a grin.

''I don't know. Towns. Lots of people. Kids and dogs and horses.''

''Tepees? Open fires, drying racks?'' His grin broadened. ''The sort of encampment you see in old Hollywood movies?''

''I know better than that,'' she scolded. ''I just thought there would be something different about a reservation.''

Suddenly he grew serious. ''There is. Whatever problems the surrounding areas have are usually magnified on a reservation. Unemployment on the rez—any rez, not just Laughing Horse—runs from thirty percent to seventy or even higher. The poverty is pervasive. We have severe drug problems, alcohol problems and high suicide rates, especially among our young people. A large percentage of our children are being raised by grandparents or other relatives because their parents aren't able or willing. Even more are living at boarding schools for the same reason.

''On top of that, we're losing our languages, which are the basis of our cultural identity. In the first half of the century, the government forced the reservation children into boarding schools, where they were punished if they spoke their native language. As a result, fewer of their children learned, and even fewer of their grandchildren. Today most young adults on any given reservation can't speak their tribal language. Traditionally, we learn from our elders, but when you don't speak their language, it's hard to benefit from their wisdom."

He broke off to take a breath, then color reddened his cheeks. "Sorry. I didn't mean to lecture."

"Don't apologize. Everyone should feel passionately about something."

Without words he gestured for her to turn onto a dirt road, then urged his horse closer to hers. "And what do you feel passionately about, Crystal?"

You. She was feeling things for him that she had only imagined feeling for James. For three years she had kidded herself and everyone else about how she loved James and how willing she was to live a regimented, following-other-people's-orders-and-other-people's-dreams existence as long as she was living it with him.

But she'd never loved him. She'd loved the idea of being in love. She'd loved being on the receiving end, for once, of her parents' support and approval. But she'd been slowly suffocating, finding the smiles harder to force, finding the restrictions harder to endure. She was lucky things had ended before she and James had actually married, before there were children involved.

But knowing that didn't lessen the hurt. It didn't ease her sense of betrayal. It didn't change the fact that everyone she'd trusted had let her down, and had done so in the most painful way she could imagine.

"I'm not sure I have any passions," she remarked. She'd enjoyed teaching and would still be doing it today if she could, but she'd never been passionate about it. She'd never had any hobbies or interests that consumed her, had never found anything that she simply couldn't live without. She'd been too busy living her life for someone else.

"We'll have to change that then, won't we?"

And he'd already made a good start, she thought but didn't

say so. Instead she turned back to his passion. "Do you speak Cheyenne?"

"Yes, ma'am. My grandmother insisted on it. Dad and Amy's kids are learning, too."

"And your children will also learn, when they're old enough."

"Yes. And maybe their mother, if she has any talent for languages." His steady, intent gaze settled on her face. "Do you?"

Lost in the idea of Sloan's children—beautiful, dark-eyed, raven-haired babies welcomed by both mother and father, by at least one set of grandparents and all the countless Ravencrest relatives—it took her a moment to realize he'd asked a question. She blinked to dispel the image of a chubby-cheeked infant cradled in her own arms—an image that made her heart suddenly ache with longing—and managed to summon up a somewhat haughty look. "Students at Chatham Prep study foreign languages from first grade on. I'm native-fluent in French, and I can squeak by in Spanish and Italian."

"So you could probably learn Cheyenne. They have adult classes at the community center a few miles from here. Interested?"

Was she? She had plenty of free time, and if the other students didn't mind having her join them, she would enjoy the classes. And if things worked out between her and Sloan, if all those adorable dark-eyed, raven-haired babies were hers as well as his, she could help teach them, and she wouldn't feel left out of their conversations.

"Sure," she replied. "I'd like to give it a try."

He stopped both his horse and hers, and leaned over to brush his mouth over hers. "Oh, darlin', my family's gonna love you." After a much too brief kiss, he nodded ahead. "Come on. They're back from town now. I want you to meet them."

Eight

Crystal hadn't realized they'd gone full circle, but there was the Ravencrest ranch a few hundred yards ahead. They were halfway down the driveway when a kid gave a yell. By the time they reached the barn, his family was waiting—three solemn adults, four solemn kids, and Arlen.

Crystal felt far more nervous as she dismounted than she had the first time she'd met James's extended family. The occasion had been dinner at Atlanta's most exclusive club, and she'd spent most of the day getting her hair, makeup and nails done, and a week shopping for just the right dress. The goal hadn't been to make them like her, but to gain their approval—two totally separate things. They hadn't liked her, but they had deemed her acceptable, and so her engagement to James had proceeded.

And now here she was, meeting Sloan's family for the first time in jeans and boots, windblown and smelling of a horse. What if they didn't like her? It would be the kiss of death for their relationship, she imagined. They were far too important for him to disregard their opinions.

As his father, accompanied by the younger two boys, led the horses away to unsaddle them, Sloan slid his arm around her waist and moved her forward with him. When they reached the small group, he released her and hugged first his grandmother, then his grandfather and his stepmother. Crystal was touched by the natural gesture. Hugs had been few and far between in her own family, and the closest James and his father had ever come to an expression of affection was a handshake.

When he returned to her, he took her left hand in his. "Grandma, Granddad, Amy, I want you to meet Crystal Cobbs. Crystal, these are my grandparents, Dorrie and Hank Ravencrest, who promised to be on their best behavior this evening, and my stepmother Amy."

"Who's always on her best behavior," the woman volunteered with an easy smile.

Amy was a surprise. Crystal had pictured…well, a motherly stepmother. Amy might well be motherly, but she was also only a few years older than Sloan. Tall, slender, with jet-black hair that fell past her waist, she was lovely—and, at first glance, appeared better suited to Sloan than his father.

His grandparents were exactly what she'd expected, his grandmother tiny and feisty, his grandfather tall and handsome. Neither of them were smiling. She hoped fervently that wasn't necessarily a bad sign.

Next Sloan introduced his half brothers—Stephen, who was nine, and Hank, eight. Daniel, seven, and Darrell, four, were helping their father.

Amy invited them inside and showed Crystal to a bathroom where she could wash up. With the small makeup kit from her purse, she freshened up the best she could, then went in search of the others. She found Sloan in the living room, talking with his father and grandfather. Catching her eye, he silently beckoned, but she shook her head and instead went through the dining room to the kitchen, where Amy and Mrs. Ravencrest were preparing dinner.

"Can I help with anything?"

It was the old lady who responded. "Can you make biscuits?"

Swallowing hard, she shook her head.

"Here. Peel the potatoes." The woman pushed a tray in her direction, which held a knife, a bowl of peelings, and both peeled and unpeeled potatoes. "How'd you get to be a grown woman without learning how to make biscuits?"

Crystal picked up the knife and a half-peeled potato and went to work. She was trying to think of a legitimate reason, then decided on the truth. If she hoped to ever fit into this family, lying to them wasn't the way to start. "There was no need. The cook always made them."

Both women stopped to look at her. '"The cook?"' Amy echoed.

"What are you?" Mrs. Ravencrest asked sharply. "Rich or something?"

"My—my family was—is."

"And you aren't?"

"I—I work for a living. I have since college. But—" Honesty forced her on after she cleared her throat. "I have some…investments."

"So you're rich, too." Mrs. Ravencrest gave a sorrowful shake of her head. "A rich white woman. Just what my grandson needs."

"Dorrie," Amy chided, but the old lady wasn't listening.

"There's not a single woman on the reservation who would turn Sloan away if he came calling. But no, he goes out and finds himself a rich white woman who doesn't even know how to make biscuits."

Sloan's stepmother, looking flustered and apologetic, caught Crystal's eye and mouthed the word "sorry" behind her mother-in-law's back. Out loud, in an overly friendly tone, she asked, "What brought you to Montana, Crystal?"

"My great-aunt Winona owns the Stop-n-Swap. When she had a heart attack last summer and needed someone to stay with her, I volunteered. I liked Whitehorn, and there was nothing for me back in Atlanta, so I stayed. I still live with her, and I work with her in the shop."

"You hear that, Dorrie?" Amy asked, a subtle challenge in her voice. "A lot of young women wouldn't dream of giving up city life to come live in Whitehorn and take care of an elderly relative. Obviously, family is important to her."

Crystal hoped it didn't come out this evening that she was estranged from her own parents. The fact that it was no fault of her own probably wouldn't count for much with the old woman.

She made it through the rest of the meal preparation without offending Mrs. Ravencrest too much, and the meal itself was enjoyable. With company filling their spots at the table, the four boys were allowed to eat on trays in the living room with the television on. Crystal found herself seated between Sloan and his grandfather, who was every bit as charming as the grandson, and she managed to avoid his grandmother's too sharp look through most of the meal.

But her luck ran out when it came time to do the dishes. She offered to help, but before Amy got halfway through her refusal, Mrs. Ravencrest interrupted. "You and I will do them together, Crystal. We'll talk."

"We'll all three do them," Amy said quickly. "Cleanup will be done in no time."

Mrs. Ravencrest turned a disapproving look on her daughter-in-law and quietly repeated, "Crystal and I will do them together. We'll talk. Just her and me."

Crystal flashed a panicked look at Sloan, who squeezed her hand as they stood up from the table. "Sorry, darlin'," he murmured in her ear while suppressing a grin. "There's not a soul in this house brave enough to go against her wishes, including me. Don't worry. She won't do you any lasting damage."

Crystal gave him a sarcastic smile. "Thanks for all your help, Deputy," she whispered before following his grandmother into the kitchen.

She and the old woman worked in silence the first few minutes, putting away leftovers, scraping scraps into the trash, running a sinkful of hot soapy water. Crystal was about to plunge her hands into the water when Mrs. Ravencrest none too gently moved her aside. "I wash."

Swallowing a frustrated sigh, Crystal stepped back and picked up a dish towel instead. She'd barely dried the first glass when Mrs. Ravencrest spoke again. "You know about Sloan's mother."

"Yes."

"She was a rich white woman, too."

"And a fool. I'm not. I would never give up my own child, and I would kill anyone who tried to take him from me."

The woman's look was speculative. "Easy to say now, but will you feel that way when you have a Cheyenne baby?"

Instead of answering, Crystal concentrated for a moment on drying the glass she held, then set it aside before she got tense enough to break it. Before picking up another, she faced the old woman squarely. "Mrs. Ravencrest, Sloan loves you dearly—all of you. Partly for that reason, and partly because I was raised to respect my elders, I don't want to be disrespectful to you."

"But you're going to, anyway."

Crystal couldn't read the woman's expression and didn't waste much time trying. "Sloan's mother couldn't commit to his father because she couldn't accept that he was Indian. She couldn't raise her own child because he was half Indian. She was racist and intolerant, and you and I both agree, I'm sure, that her attitude and her actions were unforgivable. But it seems you have exactly the same problem with me. You don't like my relationship with Sloan because I'm white. You're not willing to give me a chance. You're not willing to get to know me. You've taken one look at the color of my skin and decided I'm not worthy of your grandson, and that makes you as racist and intolerant as his mother."

For a time everything went silent in the room. The refrigerator stopped running. The water stopped dripping. The clock, or so it seemed, stopped ticking. Dorrie Ravencrest stood motionless, her strong, thin arms in sudsy water to the elbows, her dark gaze locked on Crystal.

Crystal felt sick inside. She wished she'd kept her mouth shut, wished she'd never come here, wished she'd chosen the third option—doing something else entirely—Sloan had offered last night. Now his grandmother was going to tell him what a rude and disrespectful woman she was. She would tell him to stop seeing her and find someone else, and he would listen because, Crystal knew instinctively, if there was one thing he wouldn't forgive, it was showing disrespect to his family.

And she'd really wanted to fit in here.

After a time, Mrs. Ravencrest offered a response—"Humph"—then went back to washing dishes. Crystal was trying anxiously to determine exactly what that translated to when the old lady started talking again. "The secret to good biscuits is in the pan. I use my cast-iron skillet and melt some butter in it—butter, not margarine. If you're worried about calories or cholesterol or any of that garbage, you shouldn't be eatin' biscuits in the first place. Roll out the dough and cut 'em out. You can use a drinking glass, but a rich girl like you might prefer a la-di-da biscuit cutter. Then dredge 'em in butter on both sides and bake—"

"Aren't you angry with me?" Crystal interrupted in a weak voice.

"Why would I be angry? You got backbone. You're not afraid to stand up for yourself. That's important around here, especially for a white girl who intends to marry a Cheyenne. Not everyone's as open-minded and accepting of such marriages as I am."

"Open-minded? Accepting?" Crystal stared at Mrs. Ravencrest, who maintained her unblinking expression for a moment before giving in to a great body-shaking laugh.

She directed her next words behind Crystal. "When I gave you the quilt, I told you to choose well. You listened to my advice."

Sloan wrapped his arms around Crystal from behind. "I always listen to your advice, Grandma."

Mrs. Ravencrest pulled the dish towel from Crystal's nerveless fingers. "Go on now. You two get along and let me get some work done here."

As Sloan pulled her from the room, Crystal bewilderedly asked, "What just happened in there?"

"You just got my grandmother's stamp of approval," he teased, then stopped in the empty hall, pulled her close and bent his head for a kiss. "Welcome to the Ravencrest family, sweetheart."

Sloan was whistling cheerfully when he walked into work on Monday. A command to report to the sheriff's office didn't put much of a damper on his mood, but the look on Rafe's face did.

"The chief just faxed this over," he said, tossing a single sheet of paper to him.

Sloan caught it before it slipped off the desk and read the few paragraphs as he sank into a chair. When he finished, he met his boss's gaze. "They've got to be kidding. Who in their right mind would ever think Homer Gilmore might be involved with Christina's disappearance?"

"Homer's crazy as hell, but he's not a criminal. Unfortunately, the Montgomerys and the D.A. are pressuring both the police and us for an arrest, and because Homer *is* crazy as hell, he's not a bad choice for a frame. He sure can't put forth much in his own defense."

"So what are we going to do?"

"Hopefully, keep him out of jail. Go talk to him. Find out anything you can—every time he saw Christina, where he was when she disappeared, everything he's done and seen since then."

"I'll head out to his place now." He gave the fax back, then left the building once again.

Homer lived northwest of town, about halfway between the Walker and Kincaid ranches and only a few miles from the clearing in Crystal's vision. His cabin was tiny, one room, with a porch and a rocker. Like his good friend Winona, Homer collected other people's junk, but while Winona's junk had value to her customers, Homer's was just junk. Rusted car parts and appliances, a broken-down chair and tires stacked in groups of three, among other discards, filled the clearing around his house. He seemed to have a particular fondness for shiny items. Dented hub caps were nailed to trees as decoration, pieces of broken mirrors hung from the branches, and aluminum cans with their food labels torn off were stacked everywhere.

When Sloan climbed out of his truck, he smelled smoke, coming from a fifty-gallon trash barrel off to one side, and heard the unceasing tinkle of wind chimes. Two dozen sets or more were hung from the porch rafters, catching the morning breeze.

He climbed the steps and knocked, but there was no answer. Old Homer didn't have a car—couldn't get a driver's license even if he had one—so he traveled on foot or got a ride from a friend. Half the county, including Sloan, had taxied him around one time or another. He could be anywhere in the county, could come home in five minutes or five days.

Walking back down the steps, Sloan called, "Mr. Gilmore? It's Sloan Ravencrest. Hello?"

Getting no answer, Sloan turned to go back to his Jeep, then stopped abruptly. Homer was standing less than two feet away. If his reaction time had been a second or two slower, he would have walked right into him. "Jeez, Homer, you scared me," he admonished the man. "I didn't hear you walk up."

"That's 'cause you were yelling. No need to yell when right here I'm standin'."

Sloan couldn't argue his logic with him. "How are you?"

"Couldn't be better. How are you?"

"I couldn't be better, either." He'd spent both Saturday and Sunday with Crystal. His family had liked her. His grandmother had approved her. And he'd gotten plenty more of her kisses...though if they didn't make love soon, his sexual frustration level was going to shoot off the charts and he was going to go as nuts as good ol' Homer here. "Can we sit on your porch and talk a bit, Mr. Gilmore?"

"Nope."

"Why not?"

"Ain't got but one chair. There's two of us. Two of us cain't sit in one chair."

"That's okay. You can sit on the chair, and I'll sit on the steps."

Looking pleased with the idea, Homer led the way to the porch. Before sitting, he pulled a handkerchief from his pocket, dusted the seat and each spindle of the rocker, then shook out the handkerchief, redepositing the dust on the seat, before tucking it back into his pocket. Then he sat.

Sloan restrained a smile as he took a seat on the top step, turning so that he faced Homer. No one was sure how old the man was, Homer least of all. Somewhere in his seventies, Sloan guessed. If he stood straight, he'd be six-three, maybe six-five, but his shoulders were so stooped that he walked in a perpetual crouch. His hair was gray and thinning, and fell past his shoulders, and his beard, also gray and thinning, reached halfway down his chest. He lived in a uniform of overalls, flannel shirts and work boots. On a man about whom everything was unusual, those boots were the most unusual—a size fifteen at least. Homer's feet made Sloan's size elevens look damn near dainty in comparison.

"Homer, do you know Christina Montgomery?"

"Nope. Who is she?"

"A young woman who lived in Whitehorn."

"You live in Whitehorn."

"Yes, I do."

"Do you know her?"

"I knew who she was." From his jacket pocket, Sloan withdrew the photograph of Christina that every police officer, deputy, state trooper and BIA law officer had been given. It was a casual shot, snapped at a party six months before her disappearance.

Homer took it and studied it for a long time, then asked, "Who is this?"

"Christina Montgomery."

"I don't know her."

"You don't remember seeing her around town? Mayor Montgomery's daughter?"

"I didn't vote for the mayor. Don't like politics. Say, did

I tell you I had a run-in with an alien from outer space? Right out there.'' He flung out one bony hand to point off into the woods. ''Lessee now, it was back in September...or was that when the durned UFO zapped Kincaid's cow? Yep, I b'lieve it was. Musta been August, right after them heavy rains. Walkin' through the woods, I was, when all of a sudden, there it was. Had a big ol' alien ray-gun and no hair and eyes... Lord, those eyes! They like to drove me mad just lookin' at 'em. I saw it, and it saw me, and it tried to git me with its ray-gun—'' he lunged forward, both hands lifted above and to the side as if clasping a bat or something similar, and then he sat back with a grin ''—but Homer Gilmore ain't nobody's fool. I never been caught by no aliens yet, and I ain't ever gonna be. Right fast I hightailed it outta there.''

''About the woman, Homer...'' Sloan began, feeling more than a little out of his depth.

''It weren't no woman. It were an alien. They don't got male and female, y'know. Don't need to. They can reproduce anyways. Pro'bly from Jupiter, it was. They's pretty hostile up there. Not like the Martians or the Venusians.'' Homer began rocking and shaking his head in perfect tempo. ''Scared some gray into old Homer's beard, it did. Yes, sir, it was one fierce sight.''

With a sigh, Sloan got to his feet, took the photo from Homer and returned it to his pocket, then headed for his truck. When he looked back just before climbing in, the old man was still rocking, still talking. He didn't have a clue Sloan was leaving and probably wouldn't remember in five minutes that he'd ever been there.

Which made his insistence that he didn't know Christina pretty much worthless.

Hell, how hard could it be to build a case against a crazy man? Even though it was doubtful that Homer would ever be ruled competent to stand trial, the D.A. very well might get him locked up in the state mental hospital for the rest of his life. That would kill an old man accustomed to his freedom like Homer.

So he and Rafe would have to make sure it didn't happen.

He took the northern route back to the highway, then drove to the Stop-n-Swap. For the first time, he hoped Crystal was in the back working. This time it was Winona he wanted to talk to.

He was in luck. There were no customers in the store, and Winona was alone behind the counter. She greeted him with a bright smile as she rose from her chair. "Why, Deputy Ravencrest, how nice to see you. Crystal's in the back. You can go on back or I'll call her up here."

"Actually, Miz Cobbs, I'm here to see you." He gestured for her to sit again, and he leaned both elbows on the counter. "Tell me about Homer Gilmore."

"Is Homer in trouble? Oh, dear, that old fool hasn't gone off and injured himself, has he?"

"No, ma'am, he's fine. I'm just looking for some information. Does he have any family?"

"Not that I know of. He was married once, but his wife's been dead...oh, forty years or more. No children, no siblings."

"Do you know where he came from?"

She shook her head. "He was here when I moved here. He used to work back then, but his mind was starting to go. He's lived the way he does now for about twenty-five years."

"Where does he get his money?"

"Government checks. Handouts from generous neighbors. He pretty much takes care of himself, but people help him out. Why all the curiosity?"

Sloan ignored her question. "Has he ever been in trouble? Ever bothered anybody, gotten into a fight, maybe threatened anyone?"

"Good heavens, no! Homer is the dearest, sweetest man you'll ever meet. He would never hurt a fly. Why, he takes strays home with him, feeds them and cleans them up and finds homes for them. He's absolutely harmless. What is this about, Sloan Ravencrest?''

He debated what to tell her, then settled on the truth. After all, she was Homer's best friend. He might need her help. ''Apparently there's some speculation in town that Homer might be involved in Christina Montgomery's disappearance.''

Winona was speechless. Eyes and mouth open wide, she stared at him, took a deep breath to refute his statement, then simply stared instead.

Then the moment passed, and she burst into speech. ''Why, that's the most ridiculous thing I ever heard! You can't possibly believe that! No one in their right mind could believe it! Homer is incapable of causing injury to another human being! I'd stake my life on it! Why, I—''

''Whoa, Miz Cobbs. *I* don't believe it. But the only way I know to keep the D.A. from looking to charge Homer is to prove that he's innocent. That means finding out who's guilty, and I don't have a clue who that might be.''

Winona's gaze slowly shifted from him to the back room, then returned to him. He could read what she was thinking without the least bit of psychic power. He raised both hands to stop her. ''No. I promised Crystal that I wouldn't ask for her help. I gave her my word.''

''But if I ask, you won't have to.''

''No. Besides, she's told me everything she knows, and it didn't help.''

''Didn't help? You found the clearing where Christina almost surely had her baby.''

''And with absolutely no evidence to prove that she ever set foot there.''

''Well, that's not Crystal's fault, and it's hardly a reason to allow poor Homer to be railroaded.'' Swiftly her expression changed from indignation to pure distress. ''Oh, Sloan, if they lock him up, he'll waste away. He'll absolutely die in jail!''

''He won't go to jail, Miz Cobbs.''

"How can you be so sure?"

He shifted uncomfortably, then finally said, "Because he'll wind up at Warm Springs long before he'll see the inside of a jail."

"The mental hospital?" She sounded shocked and scandalized. "That can't happen! I won't allow it to happen, and you mustn't, either! There's got to be something you can do."

Sure. He could prove Christina was alive and well, or he could prove she was dead and find her killer. Those were his only choices. And his only help in proving either one was a crazy man who ran into aliens with ray-guns in the woods at night.

"Miz Cobbs, do you have a county map?"

"I've got a state map back there in the corner." Rising agilely from her chair, she rounded the counter and headed for the distant corner. "Picked it up in an estate sale over in Missoula. Used to belong to a college professor." Bending, she hefted a heavy frame onto an old soda pop icebox and blew away a layer of dust.

The map was over fifty years old, but not much in Blue River County had changed. Sloan leaned over it, following the thin line of a county road. "Homer lives about here, right?"

Winona nodded.

"And the clearing Crystal saw in her vision is...about here." It was a greater distance than most people wanted to travel on foot at night, and across some rough terrain, but Homer Gilmore wasn't most people. He knew the county better than anyone, and had been crisscrossing it day and night, good weather and bad, for years.

"You're not suggesting..." Winona trailed off when he glanced at her.

"Homer said that one night back in August, right after those heavy rains, he had a run-in with an alien in these woods." He tapped the map between the other two points he'd marked. "Christina disappeared right after those heavy rains, and the last place we can put her is this clearing."

"Do you think Christina was the alien?"

"Maybe. More likely, the person who killed her was. He said the alien threatened him, but he got away. Christina would have no reason to threaten him."

"But her murderer would."

He studied the map a moment longer, then pressed a kiss to Winona's forehead. "Thank you, ma'am."

"We're practically family, Sloan," she said with a girlish laugh. "You can call me by my name."

"I'd like that, Winona. I believe I'll go say hello to your niece before I head back out to work."

"I'll stay here and see that you aren't disturbed." She gave him a wink as he walked away.

When Sloan walked into the store room, music was playing on the radio behind Crystal's desk, and she was keeping time with the sandpaper on a heavy oak bookcase. For a while he simply stood back and watched the flex of muscles as she sanded in long, sure strokes, the sway of her hips as she shifted from side to side, the movements of her fingers as she wiped away dust and tested her work.

Someday she was going to touch him that way—and someday soon, or he'd go nuts. He'd never wanted a woman the way he wanted her, which was only fair, since he'd never loved a woman. He thought about her all the time and dreamed about her—and in most of those dreams, he was inside her, filling her, making her whimper and plead. Sweet hell, someday he *would* have her—sooner rather than later.

Moving quietly, he sneaked up behind her, slid his arms around her and pulled her close. She didn't even give a soft cry of surprise, but closed her eyes, leaned back against him and sighed quietly. "You knew I was there, huh?" he asked, nuzzling her neck.

"Hmm. I felt you."

"How did I feel?"

"Fabulous." She looked up at him then and smiled. It just about buckled his knees. "What brings you out this way?"

"I was just passing by. Thought I'd stop in and see if I could steal a kiss from my sweetheart."

"I'd rather give you one."

"By all means, please do." He released her, and she turned to face him, resting her hands on his upper arms. For a time that was all she did, besides turn a little pink and smile nervously before brushing her mouth across his in the most chaste of kisses. When she started to step back, he caught her and held her fast.

"Uh-uh. No way. I have not fallen in love with a woman who could mistake that innocent little peck for a real kiss."

As she held his gaze evenly, he realized what he'd said. It wasn't the most romantic of declarations, certainly not the scene he would have set or the words he would have chosen, but he wouldn't call them back.

"Have you fallen in love with me?" she asked, trying to be so cool but unable to control the tiny quiver in her voice.

"Absolutely," he murmured. "Does that worry you?"

She tilted her head to one side as if considering his question, then smiled and said, "Not at all. I think it's sweet."

"'Sweet?'" he echoed with a groan. "Ah, Crystal, you sure know how to deflate a man's ego."

That made her laugh. "Your ego is perfectly healthy. I've never known a man with a stronger sense of who he is and of his own self-worth than you. Considering your history with your mother and the prejudice you've dealt with all your life, it says something impressive about you and about your family."

"On behalf of my father, my grandparents and all the other countless relatives who had a hand in raising me, I thank you. Now, how about that kiss?"

For a moment she simply looked at him. The expression in her eyes was lighthearted, and the corners of her mouth were curving into a smile in spite of her best efforts to contain it. After a moment she cupped her hands to his face and murmured, "Pucker up, darlin'." And then she gave him her sultry, Southern best.

Sloan swore the heat generated between them was enough to bring the mercury in the thermometer out front to a boil. If he looked out the window, no doubt he'd see wildflowers poking up through the ground, thinking it was summer again, and the snowcaps on the Crazy Mountains would be turning to slush. Not that he could look at anything, or do anything, besides kiss her back and want her and need her.

When she ended the kiss, he was slow to open his eyes. When his breathing was seminormal again, when his heart had slowed to a gallop, he did open them to find her watching him with a sweet, gentle smile. "We're still here," he said, rubbing his hands up and down her arms. "And not even singed."

"Want to have dinner with us tonight?"

"I'd like that."

"We'll eat around six-thirty. Come over whenever you want." She brushed her fingers lightly over his jaw as she pulled away, then stepped back. She picked up the sandpaper, but didn't start sanding again until he reached the door.

Which seemed fair. After all, he didn't start breathing again until he was through the door.

As Sloan pulled out of the Stop-n-Swap parking lot, his cell phone rang. It was Rafe, wanting to know what he'd found out about Homer. Sloan gave him the gist of his conversation with the old man, then brought up the alien sighting. "Maybe it's nothing, but I'd like to go out to the woods and have a look around."

"You think Christina might have been out in those woods at night? Christina, the shopper princess, whose idea of roughing it was wearing shoes not made in Italy?"

Sloan hesitated, then carefully phrased his reply. "I know. It doesn't seem likely. But remember the vision I told you about?"

"Winona's vision?"

Guiltily he didn't correct his boss. The fact that his next words were less than honest made him feel even guiltier. "She's convinced that Christina gave birth in the woods at night. From the description, I think I know the area, and it's the same general area as Homer's alien sighting. I'd like to go out there and look around. Maybe old Homer was just seeing things. Maybe he ran into Christina. Or maybe he ran into someone who had already run into Christina."

There was a heavy silence. He knew Rafe was weighing the merits of a search based on nothing but the say-so of a woman acknowledged by half the county to be a kook. He was also, no doubt, considering the backlash if it got out that he'd committed county resources to such a search. The sheriff's department would look desperate, or like a bunch of New Age wackos, and Rafe's critics would make the most of it.

"I'm not asking for any help," Sloan said. "Just let me go out and look around. I'll be on the radio. If you need me, I'll be available." Once he'd hiked back through the woods to his unit, then hightailed it to wherever.

Rafe exhaled loudly. "All right. Go ahead. I'll instruct the dispatchers to assign you calls only if there's no one else available. Where is this place?"

"Out by the old Baxter place."

"Near the old trail head?"

"Yeah. That's where I'll be parked. Thanks, Sheriff." After hanging up, Sloan muttered a curse. He hated misleading Rafe, hated being less than honest with a man who was taking a risk by trusting him a hundred percent. But damn it all, what else could he do? He had to protect Crystal, and so far, he hadn't been forced to tell an out-and-out lie.

He'd just withheld part of the truth. Trust Rafe, if he ever found out, to point out that that wasn't much better than an outright lie.

At the makeshift parking lot, he slid his cell phone into his pocket, locked the truck and started up the trail. By the time he reached the clearing, the sun had disappeared and the sky had turned leaden, making the air seem colder than it really was. As he stood in the clearing beside the spot where Crystal had reacted so strongly, a chill shivered down his spine. It was a hell of a place to give birth. Why would she choose it? Why come here in the first place?

To meet someone. It was the only half-logical answer he could think of. But whom? Maybe the father of her baby. But no one had a clue who he was. After her mother's death, Christina had run a little wild, developing a serious fondness for partying, outrageous behavior and men—all a cry for her father's attention. Well, now she had it, but it was too little, too late. Ellis Montgomery would have to live with that knowledge.

Say Christina had come here to meet the baby's father— to make some demand, perhaps—and unexpectedly she'd gone into labor. She gave birth there on the ground and... And what?

She hadn't gone to the hospital in Whitehorn. She hadn't driven to a nearby house to call for help. She hadn't checked into any hospitals within a five-hundred-mile radius, at least not under her own name. She hadn't gone to one of the local midwives for care.

Just how much energy would she have had to go any-where? He would imagine that giving birth was exhausting, to say the least, and if Crystal's vision was accurate, she'd lost a lot of blood. How much energy would she have had to go wandering off?

Sloan turned in a slow circle, then faced the woods. If he headed due east, he would eventually come to the Kincaid ranch. Southwest would lead him to Homer's place. In any other direction was just woods, hills, some canyons. Rumor had it there were some mines in there, too—sapphire, as he recalled—but he'd been all over this area when he was a kid, and he'd never found anything remotely resembling a mine or a sapphire.

If Christina had headed off that way, where in hell had she been going?

And what had happened to her baby?

Another chill passed through him. It wasn't far from here that Rafe's mother had abandoned him. Fortunately, he'd been found little the worse for wear. But no one in the county had shown up in recent months with a new baby whose parents couldn't be accounted for.

God help him, the last thing he wanted to find in these woods was a tiny grave or a pile of rocks protecting a shrouded infant's corpse from predators.

It looked as if the last thing he was going to find was answers, while he had no shortage of questions. With a sigh, he set off through the trees, his gaze scanning from side to side. It would be nice to find a conveniently dropped letter from Christina, saying she couldn't take another Montana winter. "I've gone to sunny L.A. with my healthy baby boy. You can reach me at this number."

Oh, yeah. And as long as he was fantasizing, this evening Crystal would greet him wearing something thin, sexy and easily removed and with the news that she trusted him completely and Winona was gone for the night.

But he found no note. Seven hours of hiking through the woods—or, at least, a small part of them—and he'd found nothing at all. He returned to his truck tired, hungry and empty-handed.

He drove into town, traded the Jeep for his truck and went home. After a shower, he stretched out on the bed just for a minute. He wouldn't fall asleep, he promised himself. He was just going to rest briefly before dinner. Fifteen minutes, thirty tops.

And then he fell asleep.

Nine

Crystal slept in late Tuesday morning after a restless night. By the time she opened her eyes and was willing to keep them open, the sun was high in the sky and Winona had long since gone to the shop.

She shoved her feet into a pair of house shoes and belted her robe over her shorts and tank before shuffling down the hall. The kitchen still smelled faintly of last night's dinner—fried chicken with a buttermilk crust, potato salad, deviled eggs and frosted walnut brownies. Picnic food, Southern style. She'd cooked it all herself—so there, Mrs. Ravencrest—and she'd packed away all the leftovers by herself.

There had been a lot of leftovers, since Winona had had dinner with friends.

And Sloan hadn't showed up.

This morning she just might eat them all by herself.

He hadn't come, hadn't called. She'd tried to call him and discovered that his phone number was unlisted. Worried that something had happened, she'd finally called the sheriff's department, where a disinterested young woman informed her that he'd gone off duty at five o'clock and, no, she couldn't give out his home number and, no, she couldn't call him at home with a message.

Crystal had been stood up, by the last man in the world she ever would have expected it from.

Did he regret that he'd told her he loved her? Was this his way of punishing her because she hadn't said the words back to him? Or had a better offer come along?

Mentally, she kicked herself. Sloan wasn't the sort to punish people for not living up to his expectations, and he certainly wasn't the sort who'd accept a better offer, no matter how much he wanted to. Something unavoidable had come up. It was as simple as that. In James's line of work, he had often had unavoidable conflicts. She was familiar with them.

Bypassing the half-filled coffeepot Winona had left for her, she opened the refrigerator and took a cold drumstick from the platter on the second shelf. She munched it while standing at the sink, then got a brownie. Once it was gone, she returned to the chicken for another drumstick. She was halfway through it when the phone beside her broke the silence and made her jump.

She grabbed it before the second ring. "Hello?"

"Can you come over to the shop, dear?"

"Aunt Winona? What—"

Her aunt had hung up on her. First, Sloan stood her up, and then Winona hung up on her. Sheesh, what was it? Make Crystal Feel Insignificant Week?

On her way past the door, she raised the curtain to look out. Besides Winona's truck and a couple of cars, there were two four-wheel-drives in the lot. Both bore light bars on the roof, and the one closest to her was identified on the side as belonging to the Whitehorn Police Department.

She tossed the chicken away and got dressed and over to the shop in record time. The first person she saw when she walked in was an agitated Homer Gilmore. The second was Sloan, who cast an apologetic look her way. Also gathered around were Winona, every customer in the place, and two men in suits, both strangers to her.

One of the men scowled at her. "Who are you?"

Winona answered before Crystal had a chance. "She's my employee. She's going to watch the shop while we take this into the back room, where we'll have some privacy."

Employee, Crystal thought with surprise. Yep, it was definitely Insignificant Crystal Week.

The two men—Whitehorn detectives, she assumed—headed for the store room. Winona, leading Homer by the arm, followed, and Sloan brought up the rear. He didn't delay even a moment to speak to her.

A shiver of uneasiness ricocheted through her as she watched the door close, but she shrugged it off as she walked around the counter.

All but one of the customers returned to their shopping. That one remained at the counter. "What's going on here?"

"I don't know, Mr. Jefferson. Obviously, you saw more than I did."

"That Indian boy—"

"Deputy Ravencrest," she interrupted.

"Yeah, him. He brought ol' Homer in here, and him and Winona was talkin' to him, and then them detectives come in and told the boy to mind his own business, that they was here to talk to Homer and it was none of his concern 'bout what. They got Homer all upset and confused, and the Indian boy—"

Crystal gritted her teeth and repeated, "Deputy Ravencrest."

The old man fixed a narrow gaze on her. "I *know* his name. But he's an Indian, and he's a boy." He shrugged to show the logic.

"And you're an old—" Biting off the insult, she silently counted to ten, then did it again in French and Italian. Then she took a deep breath and gave the man a chilly smile. "I'm busy, Mr. Jefferson. If you'll excuse me…"

He walked off down one aisle, muttering to himself about ill-mannered youngsters and their sass.

She watched the clock and checked out a customer's selection of Roseville pottery. After another ten minutes crawled by, she rang up half a dozen pieces of Depression glass for a dealer in Wyoming who made regular stops at the Stop-n-Swap.

Finally the two detectives left. So did the few other customers. Crystal was debating whether it was appropriate for her to go back to the store room since she clearly hadn't been invited when the door opened then closed behind Sloan.

He came to the counter and rested his hands on the glass. When he didn't speak right away, she asked, "What's going on?"

"I think I just pissed off two of Whitehorn's finest."

"Finest what?"

He smiled faintly, then said, "I'm sorry about last night."

She shrugged. "It's no big deal. James used to—"

His eyes turned dark and cold so swiftly that she forgot the rest of her sentence. "I'm *not* James." His tone was sharp, warning. "It *is* a big deal. You were expecting me for dinner and I didn't show. I spent most of the day out in the woods, looking for *something*. When I got home, I just meant to close my eyes for a minute, but the next thing I knew, it was morning and I was late for work. I'm sorry, sweetheart. I've never done that before in my life."

She debated whether to nurse her hurt feelings or let it slide. She chose to let it slide. "You've never fallen asleep? Gee, no wonder you were tired."

"Why didn't you call me?"

"I tried. You're unlisted."

"Your aunt's got my number."

"She wasn't home. It was going to be just you and me."

Grimacing, he reached into his pocket for a business card, then grabbed a pen from the counter. She watched him write two numbers in bold, black figures—one his home number, the other, his cell phone. When he finished, he slid the card across the counter. "Now you've got my number, in more ways than one."

His grin didn't have half the charm he was aiming for, and after one wobbly moment, it disappeared entirely. "Crystal, I made you a promise a few weeks back. Remember?"

Her uneasiness increased tenfold. *I won't ask you to go back to that clearing,* he'd said, *or to have anything further to do with the Montgomery case.* He'd promised. He'd *sworn.*

He took one look at her face and quietly said, "You remember. I would rather do damn near anything else in the world than this, but—"

"No." Her breath caught in her chest. "You gave me your word."

"Those two men were the detectives in charge of the police department's investigation into Christina's disappearance. They're being pressured to make an arrest—we all are—but none of us has a likely suspect. So they've decided to create one. Homer."

She shook her head frantically from side to side. "You said you were an honorable man. You said you don't betray people."

"Crystal, you *know* Homer didn't do anything to Christina. But they don't even have to make a case against him. All they have to do is investigate him and bring it to the D.A.'s attention that Homer's out where the buses don't run. Even without bringing charges against him, the D.A. would be justified in asking that Homer be sent to the state mental hospital for evaluation. Trust me on this, darlin'—if they get hold of him, they're not likely to let him go."

Crystal hugged her arms to her middle. She was suddenly so cold. But getting warm wasn't a simple matter of putting on a sweater or wrapping up in a blanket, because this cold came from the inside out. This cold came from the sick, hard lump of betrayal centered low in her stomach, from the knowledge that once again someone who'd claimed to love her had let her down.

And the hell of it was, she couldn't even blame him. He was just doing his job. Protecting an innocent man. And breaking his promise to her.

"When did you find out that they were trying to arrest Homer?" Her voice sounded strangled, strange to her own ears.

"Yesterday morning. Rafe told me as soon as I got to work. Why?"

Before he'd come to see her.

Before he'd told her he loved her.

Numbness spread through her, bringing welcome relief from the all-too-familiar hurt. She breathed and discovered she still could, moved and discovered she could do that, too. She wasn't going to fall apart right there before his eyes, wasn't going to burst into tears or get hysterical. She wasn't going to keep repeating "You promised, you gave me your word, and you lied." At least, not to him. But the anguished little voice inside her couldn't seem to say anything else.

"Crystal…I wouldn't ask this of you if there were any other way. Please, for Homer's sake, you've got to help me."

"Sure," she said softly, distantly. "For Homer."

"I'll be right there beside you, I swear. I'll—"

"Don't," she whispered. "Don't swear." Because she might be tempted to believe him again, and then when he broke his word again, she would be hurt again, and she would have no one to blame but herself.

She had no one else to blame now. James and her parents had taught her a hard lesson, and in a matter of days, she'd let Sloan sweet-talk her into forgetting it. It was all her fault. Just as her mother had warned her. *It'll all be your fault, Crystal.*

"Crystal—"

She turned away from the counter, away from him. Lacing her fingers together, she stared hard into the display case there, willing her mother's echoes out of her head, willing the hurtful, disappointed thoughts—broken promises, letdowns, lies—out of her head.

He came around the counter to stand beside her. "Here. Put this up somewhere."

Her gaze dropped to his hand and the business card he held between two fingers. She returned to staring at a tiny blown-glass figure that was as delicate as she felt. "I don't need it."

"The hell you don't." Catching hold of her wrist, he lifted her limp hand, pressed the card into it and folded her fingers over it. The instant he let go, she very methodically curled her fingers into a fist, crumpling the card, then opened her hand, palm down, and let it fall to the floor.

"Damn it, Crystal!" Grabbing both her arms, he gave her

a shake. "Stop it! I'm sorry about this. I hate it more than you can imagine. But I can't stand by and do nothing while Homer gets railroaded off to the mental hospital when he's done nothing wrong. If you can, then you're not the woman I thought you were."

It'll all be your fault, Crystal. Her mother wasn't the only one adept at casting blame.

When she didn't respond, he hauled her close and kissed her. She prepared herself for a hard, angry kiss—another betrayal—but his mouth was gentle. It fueled her ever-present desire, turned her blood hot and her knees weak, offered her hope that everything could be made right.

When he ended the kiss, she was breathless. He was tender. Resting his forehead against hers, he whispered, "I love you, Crystal."

She wished desperately she could take him at his word. She wished he hadn't just presented her with proof that he wasn't to be trusted. Taking a deep breath that smelled enticingly of him, she lifted her head, met his dark gaze and numbly asked, "Do you? Or do you think I'll be more likely to cooperate with you if you tell me that? Because you have to admit, your timing is curious. If you were me, wouldn't it strike you as odd that, of all the times you could have said 'I love you, Crystal,' you chose to say it after finding out that you needed my help again—the very same help you swore to me you would never ask for?"

He took a step back, then another. He looked offended, insulted, hurt, and she felt a twinge of guilt. Ruthlessly she quashed it. She was the one who'd been lied to. She had nothing to feel guilty for.

"You can't believe…" Letting the words trail away, he gave a disgusted shake of his head. "What am I saying? Of course you can believe it. Because you haven't learned a damned thing about me. Because you haven't even begun to get over what James and your parents did to you. They hurt you, Crystal, and they betrayed you. And you know why? Because they didn't love you. But I'm not them, and I do love you, more than I can say. If you've ever believed anything, believe that.''

He was waiting for some response from her, for some sign that she did believe him. She wanted to, wanted it intensely, but how could she? How could she know he wasn't playing her for a fool? It had happened before.

When she said nothing, a look of grim acceptance crept into his eyes. His mouth formed a thin line and his jaw was taut as he spoke. ''I'm sorry, Crystal. I made you a promise I can't keep. But when I made that promise, I had no clue anyone would try to frame an innocent man. Would you respect me more if I stood back and let it happen? Would it make you think more of me as a deputy, as a man, if I kept my promise to you, and said to hell with Homer?''

''Of course not,'' she murmured.

He stared at her for a moment, then his mouth quirked into a bitter smile. ''With you I can't win for losing, can I? I'm damned if I do, and damned if I don't.'' He uttered an obscenity that made her cringe, then impatiently gestured. ''Get your coat and gloves. We're heading out to the woods—you, me and Homer. Wear sturdy boots, and grab a hat, too. It's damned cold out there.''

It couldn't be any colder outside than she was inside, Crystal thought numbly as she obeyed. She felt as if she might never get warm again.

When she returned from the trailer five minutes later, Sloan and Homer were standing beside the Jeep, and Winona was locking the shop door. ''Miz Winona,'' Sloan was saying, ''it's rugged terrain, and it's awfully cold. It would be better if you'd wait here.''

Winona pulled herself to her full height. ''My niece and my friend need me. I won't slow you down too much, young man.''

Sloan shot an angry, exasperated look at Crystal, and she stepped forward. ''Aunt Winona, I appreciate your concern, but he's right. Those woods are no place for you to be traipsing around for hours. It would do us all more good if you'd stay here and fix a big pot of your famous beef stew so we can warm up when we get back.''

''With fresh cornbread and something sweet and warm for dessert, like blackberry cobbler.'' Winona bobbed her head. ''All right. I'll stay. But, child, what if something happens?''

The look in her eyes made it clear what kind of ''something'' she was referring to. Crystal was worried about that, too. The first time she'd gone into those woods, to that clearing, she'd been overwhelmed. She'd run away, desperate to escape, and when he'd caught her, Sloan had held her, comforted her, made her feel normal again.

He wouldn't be so willing to hold her this time, and even if he was, under the circumstances, she didn't think she would find much comfort in his arms.

But that didn't stop her from smiling reassuringly at her aunt. ''Don't worry, Aunt Winona. Sloan will be there. If anything happens, he'll take care of it.'' She heard the mocking in her voice with each reference to him, and saw with a sidelong glance that he did, too. But Winona didn't. She was too worried.

Crystal climbed into the back seat, leaving the front seat—and the proximity to Sloan—to Homer. She stared out the side window, where Sloan wasn't even a shadow in her peripheral vision, and clasped her gloved hands between her knees.

''Can we turn on the red lights?'' Homer asked. ''Can we turn on the si-rene?''

''Sorry, Homer, not this time.'' Sloan sounded subdued.

''Is this here your shotgun? You gonna take it with us in case we run into that alien agin?''

''I thought you only saw aliens at night.''

''Heck fire, you can see 'em any time they wanna be seen. They ain't like vampires or bats. Them're the creatures 'at only come out at night.''

Crystal blocked out the conversation that followed and concentrated on breathing. If she wasn't careful, she would hyperventilate before they even got to the woods. But maybe that wouldn't be such a bad thing. Maybe it would give Sloan a good scare and force him to return her home.

But no such luck. Before she was ready, Homer pointed with one bony finger. "Right back in there's where the alien tried to git me," he said, and Sloan brought the Jeep to a stop.

"Let's walk up in there so you can show us exactly where. Do you remember?"

The old man puffed up. "'Course I 'member. Not likely to forget a terrifyin' sight like that, I'm not."

Sloan backed up thirty feet, pulled onto the side of the road and shut off the engine. He and Homer climbed out, but Crystal remained where she was until Sloan came around and opened the door. "Care to join us?" he asked stiffly.

"I thought I'd wait here. I don't do mind-melds with aliens. You'll have to find some other freak for that."

He looked neither amused nor patient. Without waiting for another invitation, she got out and followed Homer into the woods. If the old man was following a trail, she couldn't see it, and she couldn't match his pace. Half-buried boulders that he scrambled right up required more energy and effort from her, and the worn soles of her tennis shoes slipped on pine needles and moss.

After a thirty-minute hike that left her breathless, Homer came to a stop in a large clearing, looked around, then grinned. "Right here it was. I was comin' from my cabin over that way, and I come outta the woods over there, and the alien was standing right about there." With big, ungainly hands, he gestured wildly in various directions. "The moon was shining right bright, an' the first thing I seen were its eyes... Oh, Lord, them eyes!" His voice dropped into a low moan, and he clamped his hands over his own eyes as if to block out the sight.

"What was the alien doing when you first saw it?" Sloan asked. There was no hint in his voice that he found the story utterly bizarre. He sounded serious, a true believer.

Just as he'd sounded when he'd questioned *her*.

Homer removed one hand from one eye to gesture again. "It were over there behind them rocks. Doin' what, I couldn't tell."

Sloan started toward the rocks, and Crystal and Homer followed as if they had no choice.

"When it saw me," Homer went on, "it raised up big and fierce and come at me with its ray-gun, and them evil, soulless eyes, they was tryin' to bore a hole right through me. Some of 'em can do that, y'know. Laser vision. That's what they call it."

Crystal stepped around the largest boulder, rested her hand on it and suddenly shivered. "It was a shovel," she whispered.

Sloan, bent over to examine the ground, whirled around to stare at her. Old Homer threw back his head and laughed. "'Tweren't no shovel, girl. Looked like it, is all." He leaned close to her and said in exaggerated tones, "It's called camouflage. They travel across the universe in spaceships. D'y'think they cain't disguise their ray-guns as shovels?" Shaking his head, he went on. "Silly girl don't know nothin' 'bout aliens. Alien try to capture her, wouldn't even be no contest. 'Course, Martians wouldn't have her. They got no patience for foolishness. The Venusians, on the other hand, they like pretty things so's maybe they wouldn't mind so much, but…"

Ignoring him, Sloan stood and took a few steps toward Crystal. Her face was pale, and she looked as if she were in pain. He wanted to wrap his arms around her and hold her until that look was gone, wanted to take her back to the Jeep and back to her aunt's and spend the rest of his life making things right with her. Of course, he did neither. He stopped some distance away and asked, "Are you all right?"

She ignored the question. "It was a shovel, and it wasn't Christina."

"Do you know who it was?"

"No."

"Can you see anything?"

"No."

"Can you tell—"

"No." Jerking her hand away from the boulder, she rubbed her temples, then walked away. Twenty feet later she sat on a rock, brought her knees up and huddled into a tight ball.

Sloan watched her for a moment before reluctantly shifting his attention to Homer. The old man was rambling on in a singsong voice and moving his thin, gangly body in an aimless, arrhythmic dance. Harmless or not, the old guy *was* crazy. Would it really be so bad for him to be locked up in a mental institution? To have someone to look after him and keep him safe? To get treatment that might help him become again the sane, rational man he'd once been?

Quit dancing around like that old man and get to the real question that's bugging you, Sloan silently admonished himself. The question he was ashamed to put into words.

Was saving Homer worth losing Crystal?

He wanted to say no and believe it, but he couldn't lie to himself. Homer was crazy, not guilty, not dangerous. He loved these woods, loved his freedom to come and go as he pleased. As long as he could take care of himself, as long as he wasn't causing anyone else any harm, he should be allowed to live the way he wanted. He shouldn't be confined, restrained, medicated.

And if Sloan really had lost Crystal over this... He would be better off without her, because she couldn't possibly be the woman he'd thought she was. If he lost her because of this, he'd be a lucky man to have found out the truth before he'd done something foolish such as persuade her to marry him.

But he didn't feel lucky. He felt as if his whole life had gone straight to hell, and he didn't know how to get it back.

So he would concentrate on work instead. Turning his back on both of them, he wandered around the rocks, looking for footprints, signs of digging, anything to suggest that Homer's alien was flesh and bone.

He found it a few yards away—extensive digging. Under the circumstances, his first thought was that the overturned dirt was a grave, but the disturbed earth didn't appear large enough to conceal a body, not even one as petite as Christina's. No, it looked as if the alien had been searching for something. But what? Hidden treasure? The proceeds of an earlier robbery? A mysterious fortune?

Anything was possible. A criminal hiding his loot to protect it in case he was caught wasn't unusual. Hadn't he sat out in the woods a week or two ago awaiting the return of just such a crook? And who hadn't heard stories of eccentric people dying in poverty on a mattress stuffed with a fortune in cash? Hell, for all he knew, old Homer could be richer than sin and keeping it all in Mason jars buried around these hills.

He returned to the clearing, where Crystal was trying with little success to persuade Homer to stay there. "Let him go," he said as he approached them.

She released the old man's arm, and he wandered off, jabbering nonsense.

"His cabin's not far from here. He knows his way home." Sloan stopped near her, but not near enough. "You were right. Someone was digging back there. I don't have any idea why. Do you?"

She shook her head without looking at him.

"Crystal—"

"Now what?" she interrupted. "Look around here? Or head for the clearing?"

He kept the great, frustrated sigh to himself and answered her in a flat voice. "Let's look around here."

Searching a heavily wooded area was a job that called for a lot more manpower than the two of them could provide. A person could pass within a few yards of someone else and not see him. The kind of clues they were most likely to find—threads from clothing snagged on a branch, something small enough to drop unnoticed, signs of a struggle, even,

God forbid, a newborn's grave—could be easily overlooked amid the rocks, brush, canyons and hills.

By midafternoon, they'd found nothing but a couple more sites where Homer's alien had been digging. Crystal had walked through and around them, but she'd picked up nothing new. Sloan supposed that was the way it worked. Sometimes the visions or the knowledge came, and sometimes they didn't.

Kind of like life, where sometimes an intelligent person believed what was before her eyes, and sometimes she didn't.

"Want to break for lunch?" he asked.

She shook her head.

It was just as well. He didn't think he could stomach food just now.

They searched for another two hours and covered maybe four more acres before he called it quits. Instead of trying to retrace their steps, they headed east until they hit the dead-end road that led to the clearing, then walked back to his Jeep in silence.

They made the drive back to the Stop-n-Swap in silence, too. The instant the Jeep came to a stop, Crystal jumped out and headed for the trailer. Sloan got out, too, debating whether to follow her, to try to talk some sense into her, or to just go home and forget this day from hell. Before he could decide, Winona came out of the shop.

"Find anything?"

He shook his head.

"Did she have a bad time out there?"

He gave the old woman a bitter smile. "Only because she was with me. We didn't go to the clearing. We'll do that tomorrow."

"She's angry with you."

"I made her a promise, and I broke it. She thinks that means I'm like James."

"That's ridiculous. Homer's life is at stake! You have no choice!"

"Convince her of that, would you?"

Winona sighed, and for the first time that he'd known her, he thought she looked her age. "Then I guess you won't be staying for my beef stew and cobbler."

"No, ma'am. I'm going to head home and have a hot shower and a cold beer." Maybe two or six or eight of 'em. However many it took to get the hurt in Crystal's eyes out of his mind.

"Don't go do anything rash, Sloan. Give her some time. She's hurting, but she'll get over it. She'll see reason. Just don't go do anything to make it worse."

"What do you think I might do?" he asked sarcastically. "Find another woman to ease the pain?"

She shrugged. "That's the solution to every problem for a lot of men."

"Miz Cobbs—Winona, I'm in love with your niece, and if we get through this, I fully intend to marry her and spend the rest of my life with her—though I'd prefer you not say anything to her about that before I get the chance to. I'm not interested in other women. I would never do that to her." He gave a rueful shake of his head. "You Cobbs women don't think too highly of me, do you?"

She had the courtesy to blush. "I fear we've judged you by other men's behavior. I do apologize, Sloan. I won't make that mistake again."

He acknowledged that with a nod, then climbed into the Jeep. "Tell Crystal I'll pick her up around nine tomorrow morning."

"I will. And, Sloan? Thank you."

He didn't ask for what. He just nodded, closed the door and drove away.

Ten

Crystal locked herself in the bathroom for a long soak in a hot tub and refused to get out until the water had gone cold and there was none left in the hot water tank to replace it. After dressing for bed, she wrapped her robe around her, then curled up under the covers with nothing exposed but her nose and eyes.

She didn't have any tears to cry, which came as a surprise. If asked to predict her own behavior once she was away from Sloan, she would have guessed tears until her nose was stuffy, then a pig-out on Winona's cobbler and the half gallon of vanilla ice cream in the freezer, followed by more tears and self-pity.

But she was dry-eyed as she lay there. And empty. And soul-tired. She wanted to sleep for four or five days, wanted to wake up to a whole new world, one where she had no powers for people to take advantage of. A world where she would never forget that people betrayed the people foolish enough to trust them. Simple rule. Easy to remember. But it had brought her heartache too many times.

There was a knock at the door, but she ignored it. It wasn't so easy, though, to ignore the overhead light when Winona switched it on, or her aunt's round, concerned face peering at her from the side of the bed.

"No tears. That's a good sign." Winona plopped down onto the floor. "If I'd behaved the way you did today, I'd hide my head under the covers, too. You should be ashamed of yourself, Crystal."

If Crystal's own reaction to her heartache surprised her,

Winona's left her speechless. She emerged from the covers to stare at her aunt.

"Yes, dear, I said ashamed. You heard right, so close your mouth. Do you realize what you were asking of that young man? That he choose between his principles and you. That he turn his back on the job he's taken an oath to perform, and on an innocent man whom he's sworn to protect. Poor Homer could be locked away for the rest of his life when he's done nothing wrong, and you'd rather see that happen than get involved with this investigation. You'd prefer that Sloan let an innocent man's life be destroyed rather than break a silly promise to you that he never should have been forced to make."

Feeling vulnerable because she couldn't argue those points adequately, Crystal sat up. It didn't help much, though, because Winona immediately moved to sit on the bed so they were on the same level. "It doesn't matter whether the promise was silly," Crystal said primly. "The fact is he lied to me. He swore on his honor that he wouldn't ask for my help, and he lied to me."

"He didn't lie. The circumstances changed."

"It was a simple promise—"

"A foolish promise, born of his desire to be with you."

"—and he broke it. If he can't keep the simple promises, how in hell can I expect him to keep the ones that matter?"

Winona looked at her for a long time, her expression somber and the slightest bit disapproving. "Perhaps you could start by acting like a mature adult instead of a hurt little child. In your heart, you know that breaking his promise was the right thing—the only thing he could do. You would have lost all respect for him if he didn't do everything in his power to help Homer. He had no choice, and you know it, and yet you're blaming him anyway."

I can't win for losing, Sloan had said, and the look in his eyes had been bitterly disappointed. *I'm damned if I do, and damned if I don't.*

"The mature thing for you to have done was to release

him from that promise. You should have offered your help instead of making him ask for it. In your heart, you know that, too.''

The last of Crystal's bravado slipped away, leaving her shoulders rounded, her head bowed. She did know Winona was right, and Sloan was right. Circumstances had left him no choice but to break his promise, but *she'd* had a choice. As her aunt had pointed out, she could have released him from the vow, could have volunteered her help. Instead, she'd put him in a situation where he was damned if he asked and damned if he didn't.

She *was* ashamed of herself. And frightened by the thought of the harm she might have done. Angry with herself for being so selfish. And yet still hurt that, when forced to make a choice, he hadn't chosen her. Just once in her life she wanted someone to choose *her*.

Reaching out to clasp her hand, Winona softened her voice. ''As you said yourself, it was a simple promise,'' she said gently. ''Are you willing to lose a good and honorable man over something so foolish?''

She didn't want to answer, but she couldn't help it. ''No,'' she whispered.

''Then go see him. Tell him you're sorry. Tell him you respect his honor and his willingness to do the right thing, no matter how painful it was for him.'' Winona chucked her under the chin, forcing her to look up, then smiled. ''Tell him you love him.''

There was one thing he wanted to hear more than that, Crystal thought—that she trusted him. And she did, or the whole incident this morning wouldn't have been so difficult for her. She'd come to believe that he was, indeed, a man of his word, that he was honorable, that he would never let her down. She'd believed that, unlike James, she could trust Sloan with her heart, her body, her life, and he would never give her reason to regret it.

Slowly she pushed the covers back and swung her feet to

the floor. Before heading to the closet, though, she bent to hug her aunt. "Thank you."

"My motives are quite selfish, actually. I never had any children of my own, and so I can never have grandchildren. But I think great-great-nieces and -nephews are surely the next best thing, and I couldn't pick a better father for them than Sloan Ravencrest. Besides, the boy's in love with you. You're in love with him. Go be happy together instead of moping apart." Winona walked as far as the door, then turned back with a lascivious grin. "Don't worry about getting the truck back before morning. I'm not planning on going anywhere."

Crystal changed into jeans and a sweater, ran a brush through her hair and did a quick makeup job. For a moment she hesitated, then removed the ring from her index finger and tossed it on the dresser. Within five minutes she was walking out the front door...to as far as the porch. There she turned back. "What if he doesn't want—"

Winona interrupted her, making shooing motions with both hands. "He wants. Trust me." Then she added, "Trust yourself, Crystal. Trust your heart."

Trust yourself. She hadn't done that in a long time. The idea was scary, and enticing and full of promise.

Her aunt's truck was ancient, but reliable. She made the trip into town in good time, but when she reached Sloan's apartment complex, there was no sign of his truck in the parking lot. A drive by the sheriff's department turned up nothing more than his Jeep, parked in the back lot in its usual space, so at least he wasn't working late. She drove past the Rawlings's house, the Hip Hop Café and Neela's restaurant, all with no luck.

With a disappointed sigh, she pulled to a stop at a stop sign on the edge of town. She wouldn't put it past him to be back out in the woods, searching for evidence or maybe even hoping for a run-in with Homer's alien. He could be at his dad's house, or his grandparents' place, or even at his own property, sitting alone in a starlit meadow. It would take her only a few hours to check them all out.

Or he could be at the Branding Iron catercorner from where she sat.

She stared at the red pickup in the bar's parking lot, certain it was Sloan's. She would have preferred to find him alone, but if she had to face him with his friends, well, then, she had to.

After looking both ways for traffic, she pulled into the parking lot, found a space at the rear of the lot and walked through the cold night to the front entrance. The Branding Iron was, she imagined, a typical bar, not that she'd ever been inside one to know. Dimly lit, smoky, with loud country music, neon signs and a crowd of people having a good time. It was probably not so typical with the hundreds of brands burned into every wooden surface, from walls to booths to the floor.

She stopped just inside the door, gathering her courage for a search of crowded booths and dark corners, but then her gaze went straight to Sloan. He was part of a small group at the bar, three other men and four women, and one of the women, seated on the stool next to where he stood, was artfully draped over him. Her arm was across his shoulders, her fingers idly playing with his hair. Her long, tanned, stockinged legs were crossed, with her knee pressed to his thigh. She was blond, beautiful, sexy, and obviously quite taken with him, but he was so deep in conversation with the young man beside him that he hardly seemed to notice her.

Until he noticed *her*.

The other man saw her first and pointed her out, and Sloan shifted his gaze her way. He didn't look surprised, or guilty at getting caught with another woman, or even particularly happy to see her. In fact, she couldn't read any emotion at all in the dispassionate set of his features.

Part of her wanted to turn around and walk out, but the fear that he would let her go held her in place—that, and emotional fatigue. She'd come to make up for that morning,

and he was entitled to make it as difficult as he wanted. That
didn't mean she could run away again. She was so damn
tired of running.

She crossed to the bar, weaving her way between tables,
aware of the weight of his gaze increasing with every step.
By the time she stood in front of him, her palms were damp,
her lungs hurting, and she thought maybe she could run away
one more time. But, as his friends turned their attention to
her, too, she held her ground. She even managed to sound
halfway steady when she spoke. "Can I talk to you?"

For a moment, she knew he was considering ignoring her,
or making her speak her piece right there in front of them
all. She wouldn't blame him if he did, but it would hurt.
She'd been publicly humiliated before, and it was no fun, but
she could go through it again.

Slowly he straightened, pulling away from the blonde, and
gestured for her to lead the way. With no privacy to be had
inside, she went back out, breathing in the frigid night air,
clearing her lungs of alcohol and smoke. Too bad the nerves
weren't so easy to get rid of.

Across the street was a small park, with benches underneath trees that had lost their leaves. She crossed the street,
and he silently followed, but when she reached the nearest
bench, she didn't sit. Instead she leaned against the tree trunk,
shoved her hands into her coat pockets and fixed her gaze
on a distant street lamp. He stood behind the bench, hands
in his own pockets, and waited.

She took a deep breath, then started, though not with an
apology. "Eighteen months ago a young woman about Christina's age disappeared from the town nearest Boonesville.
She'd had a very public breakup with her boyfriend, and he'd
threatened to kill her. He was the last person seen with her.
His neighbors had reported a disturbance the night she disappeared, and the police found fresh blood that matched her
type in his house and in the trunk of his car.

"They arrested him, the D.A.'s office brought charges
against him, and James was given the case. Because of his

family name and his political ambitions, he got all the high-profile cases—and this was the highest profile of them all. The girl was beautiful. Her family was wealthy and influential. The boyfriend was a drunken, tattooed ex-con. James had a perfect circumstantial case. There was only one thing missing—the girl's body. Only the boyfriend and one other person knew where he'd dumped her body, and he wasn't talking.'' She fell silent for a long time before quietly adding, ''Unfortunately for him, *I* was.''

Risking a glance at Sloan, she saw that he was staring at the yellow grass fifteen feet in front of him. Little light reached his face, making his expression once again impossible to read. Was he remembering the day they'd found the clearing, when he'd asked if she'd ever had a vision like this one before, and she'd said no, not like this? The day she'd lied to him?

''I—I'd had a vision of her, obviously dead. I'd recognized her immediately. Her face had been on the news, in the papers, in photographs that covered James's desk. I tried to ignore it at first. My parents had always insisted that that was the *only* thing I could do. But the vision kept returning, with more details, until I was able to recognize where she was. Finally I made an anonymous call to the police, but they wrote it off as a crank call. They didn't even send an officer out to check. The trial was scheduled to start soon, and James was fairly worried. The girl's father had promised his considerable support if James got a conviction. He made even bigger promises if James could get a confession and a guilty plea from the boyfriend and spare the girl's mother the nightmare of a trial.

''Finally, I told him what I'd seen. Told him that I'd had visions all my life, that I knew things…I told him where to find the girl's body, and he passed the information on to his two detective friends who had made the arrest. When they found the body, the boyfriend confessed and pled guilty, and there was no trial for the grieving mother to endure. But everyone, from the girl's parents to the D.A. to the media, wanted to know *how* they found the body.

"James knew the truth would be the kiss of death to his political career. A prominent assistant district attorney from one of Georgia's oldest and most illustrious families relying on psychics, weirdos and freaks?" She made a scandalized sound. "The detectives were none too eager to be tarred with the same brush, and so they decided to go with the anonymous informant story. The only one who disputed it was the boyfriend, who *knew* no one had seen him dump the girl's body. But, hey, he'd just confessed to murder. Who would believe him?"

Now Sloan was looking at her, but she still couldn't tell what he was thinking. She knew one thing, though—there was more distance between them than the ten physical feet that separated them.

"So James and the cops told their story, and everyone believed them, and I thought it was over. I was safe. I'd told the man I was going to marry the truth about me, and I hadn't lost him. He still loved me, still wanted me. He was even willing to lie to protect me. Then…one day he made an appointment to meet me for lunch. He told me over the salad that he was breaking our engagement. The case had given him the type of positive publicity that money couldn't buy. It had boosted his political standing tremendously. There was just one small problem. He'd told his advisors about me, and they'd told him to get rid of me. I was too big a liability. He was certain I would understand that he had no choice, and he thought I would go quietly."

She impatiently wiped away the tear that had seeped down her cheek. "For the first time in my life, I didn't go quietly. My parents would be so disappointed. They would stop loving me again, and they would blame me. 'I can't believe this,' I told him. 'If I weren't psychic, you never would have found her body, you never would have gotten that confession or that guilty plea, and now you're dumping me for it?'"

She smiled bitterly at the memory. "Who knew there was a reporter seated in the booth behind me?"

"Crystal—"

"I'm almost done. Let me finish, please." Taking her hands from her pockets, she hugged herself tightly. For much too much of her life, she'd been the only one around willing to do that. Hopefully that wouldn't be the case—please, God—for the rest of her life. "It was on the front page of the evening paper. 'Assistant District Attorney Makes Psychic Connection.' All the media picked it up and ran with it. Within a day, James and the two detectives called a press conference. They insisted I was *not* involved in the case in any way. They even played a tape of their anonymous informant. My words. A man's voice.

"James stood there in front of all those reporters and TV cameras and told them that I was unstable. Delusional. That I'd had emotional problems since I was a child. He said that was what he'd meant when he said he'd told his advisors about me. That was why he'd broken our engagement, because he feared I wasn't strong enough to handle the stress of being a politician's wife. And my mother and my father stood there beside him, and said, 'Yes, she's sick. She always has been.'

"I lost my friends, my family, my job, my future, all in one swoop. I moved to Atlanta, but I couldn't get a teaching job there, not with my former employer saying I'd been fired because I was crazy. So that's how I wound up here."

Heedless of the cold or the numbness in his fingers, Sloan didn't seem able to let go of the back of the bench. It anchored him, kept him from going to her and dragging her into his arms, whether she wanted to be there or not. He just gripped it harder and wondered what the hell he could say. "I'm sorry" was too damned inadequate. "I love you"— hell, who could blame her for not believing that? "I'll never hurt you" was another promise he couldn't keep. He *had* hurt her, and would probably do so again in the future. After all, he was only human.

But he wasn't a bastard like James. He wasn't cold-hearted and selfish like her parents, or dishonest and unethical like the two Georgia detectives.

No wonder she wanted to keep her psychic abilities secret. No wonder she'd wanted to stay hell and gone from the Montgomery case. The only wonder was that she'd survived the ugly mess—a little the worse for wear, no doubt, damaged but whole.

Finally, when the silence had gone on too long, he found his voice, forced some steadiness into it and quietly asked, "Why are you telling me all this?"

In the dim light he saw the corners of her mouth curve up, but it was too sad to be a smile. "You're a smart cop. You figure it out."

Why did a woman confide her worst nightmare in a man? For sympathy. Understanding. So he'd know why she did the things she did. So he could know her better. So he'd know what he was up against.

He suspected that, to some degree, all those answers were right, but there was one more that was even more right. Because she trusted him to know all her secrets and not leave her because of them. Because she trusted him to guard that information and never use it to hurt her. Because she *trusted* him, period.

Desire stronger than anything he'd ever felt swept through him, burning, making his muscles taut, making his body ache. His fingers uncurled from the cold, unpainted wood, and he started toward her. "Say it," he demanded.

Sticking close to the tree, she backed away one slow step at a time. "You already know."

"I want to hear it from you. Say it."

"Sloan—"

"Just say it once and put me out of my misery." He caught her one hand, then the other, and used them and his body to pin her against the tree trunk. Pressing his erection against her, he nuzzled her hair back from her ear, then murmured, "Jeez, you're killing me here. Say, 'I trust you, Sloan.'"

With little effort, she freed her hands and cupped his face. "I trust you, Sloan, and I am so sorry—"

He realized in that instant that her fingers were bare. James's ring—the ring that reminded her every day to trust no man, to give her heart to no one, the ring he'd never seen her without—was gone, and he fiercely kissed her in mid-apology, thrusting his tongue into her mouth, lifting her tight and hard against his body. He felt starved, as if he'd never had such a kiss, as if he might never have one again. Greedily he stroked her tongue while his hands found their way inside her coat and beneath her sweater. When his cold fingers came in contact with her warm skin, she shuddered, but when he tried to withdraw them, she made a sound of protest deep in her throat.

He'd just reached her breasts when a wolf whistle from across the street made him stiffen. "Hey, Sloan, get a room!" Eugene Elkshoulder called to the accompaniment of feminine laughter.

Though he ended the kiss, Sloan didn't move, aware that his body shielded from view what he was doing to hers. Crystal stretched onto her toes, though, to see over his shoulder.

"Blondie's leaving with your friend," she commented, her voice husky and thick in his ear. "Do you mind?"

"'Blondie?'" he repeated in a daze. "Oh…Marita. No. I don't mind."

"If I ever catch her with her arm around you again, I'll break it," she said so matter-of-factly that he couldn't help but grin. Then, bringing her mouth into contact with his ear, she murmured, "Slide your hands up a bit…a little more…oh, oh, there."

He stroked her nipples, making her breath catch, raising tiny goose bumps across her breasts, then pulled his hands free of her clothing. When she started to protest, he silenced her with a kiss and a rough-edged warning. "If we don't go someplace private soon, I'm going to make love to you right here against this tree and we're both gonna wind up in the city jail. Will you come home with me?''

She smiled at him then, the sweetest, most delicate, innocent smile. ''I don't know. Since that first Saturday when you showed up at Aunt Winona's to give me a tour of all the clearings in the county, I've had this fantasy about making love with you under the stars. We have stars here. You don't have them in your apartment.''

Crystal, lit only by starlight, wearing nothing but the quilt his grandmother had made for them. It was an image powerful enough to make his knees weak and erotic enough to push him dangerously close to the edge. ''Do you know how cold it is?'' he asked hoarsely.

''Do you know how hot you make me?''

''I know a place...'' His place. *Their* place. It was fitting that he should make love to her for the first time in the place where they were going to share the rest of their lives.

Grabbing her hand, he started for his truck, his strides so long she had to ask him to slow down. They made one stop at his apartment, where she waited in the truck while he went inside to gather his sleeping bag and an armload of blankets, and then they headed out of town.

They made the journey in record time. Once he shut off the engine, the night was utterly silent, then gradually the sound of the river reached him. The sound of her breathing. The thunder of his heart beating.

''Wait here.'' He left the truck, carrying the blankets with him. In warm weather he sometimes camped out here for the simple pleasure of sleeping in a place that belonged to him. His usual spot was near the river, with a rise to the northwest that offered shelter from the wind and a stone ring for campfires. He kept a stack of wood just for that purpose nearby. Now, after spreading first the unzipped sleeping bag, then the various blankets and quilts, he knelt beside the ring and used a lighter and a pile of dried leaves to start the twigs he'd laid out. He was adding small chunks of wood to the blaze when he suddenly became aware that he was no longer alone.

She hadn't made a sound, but he knew Crystal was behind him. Slowly he turned and saw her as he'd imagined her, wrapped in his grandmother's quilt and nothing else. The log he held in his left hand fell into the fire, sending up showers of sparks, but he didn't feel them. He was too dazed.

She left her shoes at the edge of their makeshift bed, then gracefully sat down, tucking the quilt around her until no part of her was exposed except her beautiful face, and then she smiled at him. "The fire is nice."

"Y-yeah." Blankly he turned back to it, trying to remember what in hell he was doing. Oh, yeah, adding logs. Building a blaze. Providing heat, when he already felt feverish, when his skin was already starting to get slick with sweat. He tossed on a few more logs from the pile he'd gathered, then slowly stood, dusted his hands and gazed down at her.

"You are so damn beautiful," he murmured.

She freed one slender pale arm from the quilt and extended her hand to him. "Come here."

He let her pull him down onto the makeshift bed, let her slide his coat off his arms, then unbutton his shirt, one torturous button at a time. When she tugged it free of his jeans, then pushed the sides apart, the cold air made his breath catch. The gentle caress of her hands made it catch again, and made him forget the cold.

"Take off your clothes and come under the covers and make love to me," she invited, her voice husky as she managed to gracefully, modestly, slide out of the quilt and under the pile of blankets. "I want you inside me, please."

"'I want you inside me, please,'" Sloan mimicked, the words sending a powerful surge of lust through him. "You Southern girls, so polite and proper in every circumstance." He tugged off his boots and socks, shrugged out of his shirt, undid his belt and jeans and shucked them and his briefs in one long, controlled movement.

She laughed as he slid beneath the covers, then pulled her into his arms. "I bet every woman you're with says please and gives thanks because you're so perfect and handsome and sweet and they can't help but love you.''

Gently he tilted her head back so he could see her face. ''Is that a roundabout way of saying *you* love me?'' When she shyly lowered her gaze, he placed a kiss on her forehead. ''I know the last three people you said it to all hurt you deeply. You don't have to say it to me.''

Seconds passed as they simply looked at each other. She did love him. Sloan could see it in her eyes, could feel it in her touch. She loved him more than she'd ever pretended to love her bastard fiancé, and he intended to see to it that she loved him for the rest of their lives.

''I haven't yet apologized for the way I acted today,'' she said, but he shook his head.

''I don't want an apology. I just want you.'' He wasn't sure what was so right about his words, but they brought her a sweetly delighted smile that he couldn't resist kissing. Gathering her close, he deepened the kiss immediately, sliding his tongue into her mouth as he slid his hands over her body. Even without seeing, he knew she was a marvel of perfection. Her skin was soft and pale, her curves nicely rounded, her muscles long and lean. Her breasts were soft, her nipples incredibly hard, her waist narrow, her hips womanly.

As he memorized the way her skin quivered when he stroked over her belly, the way her heart pounded beneath his hand, the way he could make her muscles tighten, then relax, then tighten again, she was doing the same to him, touching him as he'd fantasized since seeing her that long-ago day in the grocery store. There was no hesitance as she glided her hands over his stomach, no tentativeness as she slid one hand to his groin. She touched him with the certainty of a woman who knew what she wanted. She aroused him, made him hard, hot, hungry as hell. The way she was stroking him, cupping him, making him swell, he knew this first time wasn't going to be slow and leisurely…but the next would be.

By mutual unspoken agreement, they were moving into place, her long, slender body underneath his, her hips cradling his, her legs twining with his, when the last bit of common sense he possessed crept to the front of his mind. Twisting free of her mouth, he breathed deeply, then squeezed his eyes shut to regain some bit of control so he could gasp, "I don't…have any…any condoms…"

She touched his face, a series of light, gentle touches that both soothed and tormented. "James never forgot condoms," she murmured, "and since him, I've been alone. If it's protection you're worried about, I'm clean. If it's birth control…" Her smile was loving and wistful and wishful. "Let's not worry."

The thought of Crystal pregnant was a powerful one. He gave her a hard, possessive kiss at the same time he entered her. Once he'd filled her, once her body gloved his in a perfect, snug, made-for-each-other fit, he murmured, "I never forgot, either, and I've been alone a long time, too. I've been waiting for you."

She'd been right that the cold didn't matter. They generated their own heat. His skin was damp and slick, and slid against hers with a friction he felt all the way to his toes. She matched his rhythm and increased it, urging him with her hands, her mouth, her body, to thrust deeper, harder, faster. Already on edge and unbearably aroused, he was happy to comply, sliding his hands underneath her, pressing her flesh to his, taking her for a greedy, demanding, frantic ride. With her soft cries and his ragged breaths echoing in his head, he stiffened, gave a great groan, then filled her. With her own great groan, she came, too, her hands clutching his arms, her body clinging to his, with intense shudders ricocheting through her, intense emotion claiming her.

For a long time he remained where he was, braced above her, still inside her, until his arms began to tremble from the effort. Gentle waves of pure pleasure replaced the thundering rush of need. Languid satisfaction, both physical and mental, claimed his body, made it heavy, as he slowly sank to lie half on their makeshift bed, half on Crystal.

Nuzzling her shoulder, he opened one eye to see that her own eyes were closed. A single tear slipped from the corner and left a trail across pale china skin before it disappeared into her hair, and her mouth was curved into the sweetest, most satisfied-woman smile he'd ever seen. Understanding both the tear and the smile, he grinned. "What does a polite and proper Southern girl say after making love?"

She turned her head to look at him. "I think a heartfelt 'Wow!' sums it up. I can't move." He automatically started to shift his weight off her, but, belying her pronouncement, she caught hold of him and pulled him back. "Every nerve in my body is tingling. Even the soles of my feet feel different."

"And we've hardly even started," he teased.

She slid her fingers into his hair, combing, playing, and oh, so seriously spoke his name. "Sloan? I know you said I don't have to say it, but...I do love you. Just so you know."

He turned onto his side and pulled her onto hers. Her thigh was between his, her belly pressing against his rapidly reviving arousal, her breasts rubbing his chest. With a bit of maneuvering, he was inside her again, and his hand was covering her breast, making her nipple harden and her breathing go shallow. "I know," he murmured as he watched her eyes flutter shut and he began a slow, lazy thrust that filled her through her soul. "I'm glad you know, too."

Crystal lay on her back, her head pillowed on Sloan's arm, and gazed at the millions of bright stars sparkling above. She'd always found the Montana sky an impressive sight, but never more so than tonight. Every cold dark night the rest of her life, she would think of Sloan and this night, and she would smile...or drag him off for an encore performance.

"Aren't they beautiful?" she asked, her voice so small and insignificant in the big meadow under the big sky.

"Hmm."

She glanced at Sloan and found him looking at her with such tenderness. Swallowing over the lump in her throat, she said, "I mean the stars."

"Yeah, them, too."

She directed her gaze up again. "To think that they're so far away, that this light we're seeing started its journey to earth ages ago, that some of these stars we're seeing don't even exist any longer. It's incredible."

"Hmm." He grinned when she gave him a chastening look. "I know. You meant the stars. But you're pretty damn incredible, too."

She turned onto her side and snuggled as close to him as she could get. She opened her mouth to say something about how utterly amazing he was, but the words that came were a total surprise. "What is Marita to you?"

He needed a moment to shift gears, then gave an awkward shrug. "At the risk of sounding callous, nothing. I've known her all my life, but we've never been friends."

"She was clinging to you."

He made a dismissive gesture. "She's playing a game. She's looking to see how many Indians she can have sex with before she settles down and marries the respectable white guy her father's picked out for her."

"Does your friend know that?"

"Everyone knows. Tonight Elkshoulder just didn't care." He stroked her back, rubbing with even pressure over every vertebra, making her stretch like a cat against him. "Do you want to ask if *I've* slept with her?"

She gave him a reproving look. "I have more respect for you than that."

"Respect?" he teased. "For a lowly Cheyenne cop who lacks ambition, a pedigree, a fancy college degree and everything else women like you are supposed to want?"

"Oh, darlin', you have *everything* I want," she replied with a throaty laugh. Finding soft, warm skin beneath her hand, she began rubbing his stomach in slow circles. "I thought you were going to make me apologize in front of your friends.''

"I have to admit, the thought crossed my mind. But it would have been cruel, and I was afraid you'd leave and, of course, I'd have to go after you.''

"I was afraid I'd leave and you *wouldn't* come after me.''

"That'll never happen.'' He said it quietly, with no great emotion, no emphasis. Just a simple statement of fact. A promise she could believe in. And she did believe him—believed in him.

Savoring the comfort and pleasure of that fact, she raised her head to tell him so. The grimness of his expression stopped her, though. Feeling a tiny shiver inside, she waited for him to say whatever had turned him so bleak.

"If I had known your history with James, I never would have threatened to tell the Montgomerys anything about your vision. I never would have bluffed about exposing you to gossip and ridicule.''

She considered his solemn words for a moment, then cheerfully disagreed. "Sure, you would have.'' When he opened his mouth to argue, she silenced him with her fingertips on his lips. "You wouldn't have carried through, but you would have made the threat, because it was the only way to get me to cooperate, and you needed my cooperation. I don't blame you, Sloan. I would have played it out the same way if I'd been you. You've got nothing to be sorry for.''

"I never would have hurt you.''

"I know that now. Don't worry about it. If you hadn't threatened to expose me, I never would have helped you, and we wouldn't be here like this tonight.''

"Yes, we would,'' he replied. "Maybe not tonight, but sooner or later.''

"How can you be so sure?''

"It was inevitable. From the first time I ever saw you, I knew you were meant to be mine.''

She looked to see if he was teasing, but there was nothing

but bold confidence and smug certainty in his expression. *Meant to be mine.* She couldn't think of anything nicer.

Silence settled between them then—comfortable, warm, peaceful. She and James had had a lot of silences between them, but never like this. She'd been too busy worrying that he would find out she was pretending to be someone she wasn't, or that she wouldn't measure up to his standards, or that she would disappoint her parents again, and he...

The truth was he had gone long periods of time without thinking of her, even when she was right beside him. The plainest, simplest truth was he had never loved her, had never really wanted her, had never given a damn about her. Just as he had been the means of winning her parents' approval, to him she had been one more step along the journey of his political ambition. He'd had the right family name, the right upbringing, the right education, the right job and the right support. All he'd needed was the right wife...but she'd turned out to be very wrong.

For the first time she could smile about it.

"What are you grinning about?" Sloan asked.

Before she could answer, a light streaking across the sky caught her attention. "Look, a shooting star."

"Make a wish."

Closing her eyes, she did. When she felt him move, when his gentle, talented fingers closed over her breast, rousing her nipple, when he slid down to take it in his mouth, she gasped, then gave a deeply satisfied sigh. "Hey," she said delightedly, threading her fingers through his hair in a silent plea for more. "How did you know what I wished for?"

Eleven

Wednesday was the day before Thanksgiving and offered little to be thankful for. It was cold, without even a hint of sun, and a drizzle was coming down, not heavy enough to call off their search, but enough to make a person miserable.

Sloan and Crystal sat in the Jeep at the end of the narrow road. She'd asked for a minute before they headed for the clearing, so for several moments they'd sat there, motor and heater running. His arm was stretched between the seats, his hand on her neck under her hair. He'd made love to her again last night and slept all night with her in his arms, but he couldn't get enough of touching her. It seemed to fill some need in him and, at the same time, double or triple it. The more he touched her, the more he wanted to touch her.

Right now, as pale and uneasy as she looked, he really *needed* to touch her.

Sometime after midnight the cold had overcome the romance, and they'd packed up and gone to his apartment. After an early breakfast there, he'd driven her to the Branding Iron to pick up Winona's truck. He'd pointed out Marita's car a few spaces away, and she'd shaken her head. "Shameless woman," she'd said with a sexy smile. "Gone off to spend the night with some handsome Cheyenne, and she doesn't care who knows it."

He'd pulled her close and murmured, "I like shameless women," and she'd blushed. So innocent, and so bold. So proper and polite, and so incredibly passionate. So delicate, and so strong. He loved the contradictions that were her. Hell, he just plain loved her.

With a deep breath and a shaky sigh, she turned to him. "Shall we go?"

He shut off the ignition, zipped his yellow slicker and climbed out. She was out, too, by the time he circled the truck. Her slicker was hot pink and belonged to Winona. It was big enough to allow for warm clothes underneath—jeans and a heavy sweater—and the sleeves fell practically to her fingertips. She pulled the hood over her hair, but didn't tighten the drawstring.

He brushed a strand of hair off her forehead. "I'd give anything if I didn't have to take you up there again."

With a feeble smile, she wrapped her fingers around his wrist. "I'll be all right." But she didn't sound very convincing.

They followed the trail to the clearing without conversation. What could he say to make her feel better? What could she say to make him stop worrying?

There Crystal walked straight to the place where Christina's presence was strongest. She stood there, eyes closed, arms folded over her chest. Sloan went to stand behind her and wrapped his arms around her, holding her tightly. Without opening her eyes, she turned her face toward him and smiled a thin, sickly smile. "Thanks. I need that."

After a time—he couldn't say whether it was one minute or ten—she asked, "Is there another road out here besides the one we used?"

"I don't know. There may be a logging road or a utility right-of-way. Maybe an old ranch road. Why?"

"There's a car, parked on a road where no one will see it."

That would explain how Christina had gotten to the clearing, Sloan thought, and how she'd planned to leave. They'd done an aerial search of the whole county shortly after her disappearance, but it was easy to miss a car from the air. Park it under some trees, still leafed out in August, and the sharpest eyes in the sky wouldn't see it.

Shrugging out of his arms, Crystal took his hand and left

the clearing, following a faint trail. He'd walked it for a couple of miles on Monday, finding nothing, but he didn't tell her that.

All through the hills, trails crossed and circled around on each other. Periodically, she stopped and gazed around, seeking clues that he couldn't begin to guess at. After a time, the path they were following diverged into two. They ran parallel, like different tracks of the same path, for a few hundred feet, then gradually separated.

She stood motionless, gazing from one to the other, seemingly unaware of the drizzle, the cold or him. Finally she took a hesitant step to the right, followed by another. As she walked on, her manner became more confident, her step surer.

Where the path was wider, Sloan moved to walk beside her. "What are you seeing?" he asked quietly.

"I'm not. It's more of a feeling, actually—a sensation. I can *feel* that Christina was here. She walked along this trail. She knew where she was going. It was familiar to her at night, but this time she was..." Her forehead wrinkled into a frown. "Not afraid. Tense. Afraid of being disappointed. And hopeful."

Where the path from the road to the clearing had been a steady climb, this one was a gentle slope. It was easier going, no more strenuous than a walk in the park. Trees were scarcer, so the sky was visible overhead. On a moonlit night, Sloan figured, a person could move with reasonable care at a decent pace without the aid of a flashlight.

The trail came to an end between two tall boulders that looked as if they'd been deliberately placed to hold a gate, and just on the other side was a narrow, primitive road.

Sloan gave Crystal an admiring look. "You're good, darlin'. This road is perfect for someone who wants to get in and out of here without being seen."

She looked neither pleased nor satisfied. "Where do you suppose it comes out?"

"God only knows. It's not on any county maps that I've

seen." He stood in the center of the grassy lane, looking first one way, then the other. "So Christina arranged a meeting out here, possibly with the father of her baby, to…"

"Ask him for money. To ask him to take the baby. Maybe to marry her and give his child his name. But why all the way out here? And why at night?"

"To avoid being seen. She never even confirmed for anyone that she was pregnant. She sure as hell never gave anyone the name of the father. It was obviously their secret. But why the big deal?"

"Maybe he was married. Maybe he was too old for her."

"Or too young. Or maybe he was Indian." His smile was no more than a quirk. "Mayor Montgomery will tell you himself that he's the least prejudiced man in all of Blue River County. Why, he likes Indians just fine. But he sure doesn't want his daughter bringing one home to join the family, and he probably wouldn't feel any more kindly toward an Indian grandchild than my mother's parents would have." He returned to lean against one boulder while she took up position against the other. "So Christina comes out here to meet someone. Does he show?"

"Yes," Crystal replied. It didn't sound like a guess.

"She goes into labor and delivers the baby. Surely he doesn't go off and leave her and a newborn in the woods."

"Maybe he's already gone before her labor starts. Or maybe he stays with her, then takes the baby away to care for it. Maybe—" She rubbed one hand across her forehead.

"Are you all right?"

"Yeah. I just feel…unsettled."

He put his arms around her. Even through the layers of clothing separating them, he could feel that she was chilled. "Let's go back to the truck and have some of whatever Winona put in those thermoses, then see if we can find out where this road goes."

Though she nodded, she didn't look as if she found much relief in the suggestion. "We're not through in these woods," she whispered.

They wouldn't be, Sloan agreed, until they found Christina.

With the trail made slippery by rain, it took them nearly an hour to hike back to the Jeep. There he once again started the engine and turned the heat to high while Crystal opened the basket Winona had packed for them.

The thermoses held hot coffee and cocoa, and there were foil packets of oatmeal raisin cookies, fresh-baked banana nut bread and brownies. Winona packed the good stuff, he thought with a grin. Caffeine and sugar.

By the time they finished their snack, they were warm and the windows were fogged over. He was thinking idly of the fun they could have making sure the windows stayed that way when Crystal spoke.

"How are we going to find out about the road if it's not on any maps?"

"Homer. He knows the county better than anyone, and unless it makes a hairpin turn somewhere, it's got to run within a mile or two of his house. Let's see if we can catch him at home."

They did. In spite of the wet day, the old man was out in his yard, arranging his collection of cans as if their order was of the utmost importance. He stopped to watch Sloan park, then greeted them with a wide grin as they got out. "Ain't it a beautiful day?" he asked as rain dripped from the brim of his old straw hat.

"It's beautiful," Sloan agreed. "Think we might get some snow?"

"Nah. Too warm for it."

"Too warm, huh?" Sloan watched the fog that formed with each puff of breath. Warm compared to what?

Homer turned his faded blue gaze on Crystal. "UFO ain't gotcha yet, I see. Be careful, or they will. You see a bright light in the skies, best be hidin'."

"I saw a bright light streaking across the sky last night," Crystal said. "It was a shooting star."

"Didja wish on it?"

"Yes, and it came true."

Sloan smiled at her before he moved closer to the old man. "Mr. Gilmore, Crystal and I were over in the woods at the trail head where the road dead-ends. You know the place?"

His old gray head bobbed as if it were on a spring.

"We came across an old road up in there. Thought it might be a logging road. Do you know where it goes?"

Homer's head continued to bob.

Sloan noticed that Crystal had wandered off toward the house and the shelter of the trees there and didn't blame her. Getting sensible answers from Homer could be a long, tedious process, and even when he gave them, there was no way to know whether they were truth or fantasy. "Can you tell me where it goes?"

"Off through the woods it goes. It surely does. Uphill and downhill, over streams and under trees. Through the woods, yessir."

"Where does it start?"

"At the beginnin'."

"And where would that be?"

"Why, where it starts, of course."

Sloan took a breath for patience. "If I wanted to drive on that old road, how would I get to it?"

Homer took his hat off, sluicing water over his head, and scratched his ear for a minute before asking, "Why would you wanna do that? They's better roads in the county. Paved ones, and all."

"I know, but I want to drive on that road."

"Well now, I don't rightly know. If I was gonna do it, I'd likely go down past the Walker ranch, where the road starts, or maybe out to the reservation, where it ends. But I don't drive, so I cain't really tell you how to do it."

They were closer to the ranch than the rez, Sloan estimated. Surely someone there could point out the road to them. "Thank you for your time, Homer. I appreciate—"

"Sloan."

The odd quality to Crystal's voice made him turn to face

her. She stood next to the raised porch, where the contents
of a canvas duffel bag had been dumped out for sorting. More
of Homer's junk, he supposed.

Except for the item she held between both palms. He recognized the thin metal as a license plate right away. Then
she turned it upright so he could see it was a Montana tag.
A personalized Montana tag.

Chris 37.

"Christina Montgomery," he murmured. "Her birthday
was March seventh." How many times had he seen her driving too fast down the highway with that tag attached in the
rear? State troopers who worked the local roads had commented that it was her way of warning, Don't dare give me
a ticket or Mayor Daddy will make you sorry.

The tag may have protected her from tickets and soaring
insurance rates, but it'd done nothing to save her life. It could
go a long way toward destroying Homer's.

"Ain't that purty?" Homer asked, following Sloan to the
porch. "You know, lots of aliens have numbers for names.
I ain't never knowed a Chris 37 before, but ya' never know.
I might meet one, and then I'd have me a purty gift to give
'im or her."

"It's short for Christina, Homer. Do you remember when
I came here two days ago? I asked you about a girl from
town who was missing—a girl named Christina."

His expression blank, Homer shook his head. "I weren't
home Monday last. Was over at my friend Winona's place,
I was. Do you know Winona?"

"You were there yesterday," Sloan disagreed. "Remember? With me and the two detectives from town?"

The old man stiffened, and his hand gestures grew agitated.
"Don't wanna talk about them. Bad men tellin' bad lies
about Homer. I'm puttin' it outta my mind." He pressed all
ten fingertips against his forehead, then jerked both hands
away with a flourish. "Gone. Outta my mind. Didn't happen."

"Can you show me where you got this?"

"I found it. It's mine. Finders keepers, losers weepers. You cain't have it."

"If you show me where you found it, I'll get you a tag that has your name on it," Sloan offered.

The idea obviously intrigued the old man. He considered it a moment, then said, "All righty. Can we turn on the lights and si-rene this time?"

The turnoff to the old road was several miles past the entrance to the Walker ranch and was nothing more than a narrow gap in the bushes that lined the road. If Crystal had been creeping by at a mile an hour looking for it, she would have missed it.

For a seldom-used road, it wasn't in bad shape. There were a few jarring bumps, but for the most part the travel was smooth enough for any car. She sat in the middle of the back seat and gazed ahead, trying to tell if anyone had used it in the last few months. Was the yellowed grass beaten down a little more in places, or was that merely her imagination?

No, not imagination. The farther they went, the more certain she became of it. Someone had used this road—someone besides Christina.

In the front seat, Homer was droning on about cattle, Martians and Incans and actually making some sense. She was grateful for his chatter, for the distraction that helped her ignore the clamminess of her hands and the knot in her stomach. This trip was significant. They were going to find something, but what was difficult to guess. Something that might make the detectives' case against Homer? Something that might take away the Montgomery family's last hope?

No bodies, she silently prayed. She didn't want to be present when Christina's body, or that of her baby, was discovered. She didn't want to add that to the memories that already haunted her.

They'd been on the road for more than half an hour when Homer commanded, "Stop here."

When Sloan obeyed, they all climbed out of the Jeep. "Do you know exactly where we are, Homer?" he asked.

The old man tilted his face up to the sky. "The boy don't have a clue where he's taken hisself, and people say *I'm* crazy. We're on the old Blue River Timber logging road."

"Where is your house from here?"

Homer took a good look at the woods, then decisively pointed to the southeast. "Not too far thataway."

"And where did you find the tag?"

"Up there." He turned and pointed ahead. "'Bout fifty yards or so."

"How did you find it?"

"I was walkin' along, lookin' for treasure, and there it was. Chris 37. I thought maybe Chris 37 was the alien what tried to shoot me with its ray-gun that night. Maybe next time I meet up with one of 'em, it'll be Chris 38."

Sloan laid his hand on the old man's arm to get his attention. "Homer. Was the tag just lying in the road? Could it have fallen off the car it belongs to?"

"Don't b'long to no car. B'longs to me. Finders keepers, losers weepers."

"Okay. You were walking down the road—"

Homer gave a great exaggerated sigh. "Nope. I was walkin' through the woods, lookin' for treasure. That's when I saw the tag, right there on the ground, like it'd fallen from the sky."

"So someone had thrown it into the woods," Sloan remarked to Crystal. "It's not unusual for car thieves to ditch the tags one way or another."

"Wouldn't it make better sense to just switch tags with another car in town?"

"Crooks don't always show good sense." His grin faded as he turned to Homer once again. "Homer, if you found the tag in the woods up the road, why did you tell me to stop here?"

"'Cause the car's across the road."

They turned as one to look at the opposite side of the road, where the ground sloped away into a thicket of trees, both evergreens and hardwoods. The yellowed grass and hard ground showed no sign that any person or vehicle had passed that way recently, but if Homer was telling the truth, both had.

They started walking in that direction. Sloan was quiet, Crystal apprehensive. Even Homer fell silent. With the advantage of knowing what to look for, he spotted it first, some thirty yards away from the road, and alerted them with a whoop, followed by a cackle of laughter. "See? I told you so. There it is."

Sloan seemed to realize immediately what they were looking at, but Crystal needed a moment to look beyond the piled-up brush, to see that the dusty silver underneath wasn't gray sky showing through. There was a car under there, well-hidden, difficult to see from the ground and impossible from the sky.

Sloan stopped them some distance away and walked on by himself. He removed enough branches to check the license plate on the front bumper and to see the vehicle identification number, then pulled his cell phone from his pocket.

Crystal moved close enough to hear his end of the conversation. "Quick question, Rafe. Have you got the VIN on Christina's car handy?... Read it to me, would you?"

He checked the number visible at the bottom of the windshield, his expression growing grimmer with each second. Looking at Crystal, he nodded once, and she turned away.

She'd believed from the first vision that Christina was dead, but some small part of her had wanted to be proven wrong. She'd wanted Christina to be alive and well, wanted her own psychic abilities written off as just so much bunk.

Not much chance of that happening now, because those same abilities were telling her that the last person to drive the car hadn't been Christina. He—or she—had been excited, both panicked over what he'd done and, at the same time, oddly remorseless, untouched by it. It was just one of the costs of doing business.

Still on the phone, Sloan came to stand beside her. "We're out on the old Blue River Timber logging road that starts near the Walker place. Are you familiar with it?" He listened for a moment before grimly going on. "We need the evidence guys out here. We've located Christina's car."

Within an hour, the remote country road looked like a parking lot for a convention of cops. The sheriff and his senior investigators showed up, as well as the two deputies who routinely handled evidence collection. The police chief was there, along with his two detectives, Wilkins and Blakely, and other officers, and the district attorney came, too, with Ellis Montgomery and his son in tow.

Crystal sat in the back seat of Sloan's Jeep, her fingers tightly knotted together. Homer was in the front seat. The sight of the detectives had frightened him into silence. Their frequent dark scowls weren't doing much for her peace of mind, either.

The brush had been pulled back and the car had been photographed, dusted for prints, examined and searched. Now it was being loaded onto a wrecker for the trip into town.

"Don't like it here," Homer said abruptly. "Too many people. I'm goin' home."

He was out of the Jeep before Crystal could react. She jumped out, too, and hurried after him. "Mr. Gilmore, wait. Sloan and I will take you home."

He shrugged off her hand. "Don't wanna wait. Bad people here. Gonna go home and tend to my supper."

"Why isn't that man in handcuffs?" Ellis Montgomery's voice was loud, sharp, angry. It cut through all the chatter, through the very air itself, and it brought both Crystal and Homer to a sudden stop.

They turned to find everyone watching them, their expressions ranging from sympathy to outright hostility. Sloan was the first to respond, casually moving between them and the others. "Mr. Gilmore isn't a suspect, Mr. Montgomery."

"That's not what the chief tells me."

"Well, the chief is—"

Rafe Rawlings stepped up and smoothly broke in. "Mr. Gilmore found the car, Ellis. He came out here to show Deputy Ravencrest where it was. He's just a citizen cooperating with the authorities." His smile was equally smooth. "We generally try not to lock up cooperating citizens without probable cause."

"I want him behind bars until he tells us what happened to my little girl," Montgomery insisted.

Sloan's scowl matched the detectives'. "He can't tell you what he doesn't know. This is the first real clue we've found since your daughter disappeared, and we wouldn't have it without Homer. If we lock him up for helping us, anyone else who might know something will think twice before sharing."

Montgomery looked ready to argue, but his son murmured something to him that made him back down. He wasn't done yet, though. He merely redirected his attention. "What is that woman doing here? Is she also just a citizen cooperating with the authorities?" he asked snidely.

Everyone turned to stare at Crystal except for Sloan. She felt her spine stiffen and her face color.

"Crystal is a friend of Homer's," Sloan replied. "She came with him as a favor."

"If you're through asking questions," Rafe said, "we need to get this road cleared so Tiny can get his wrecker out. Mr. Gilmore, Crystal, would you wait in Sloan's Jeep?"

Homer let her lead him back to the vehicle and help him into the front seat. Not more than a minute after she settled in the back seat, both driver's side doors opened. Sloan slid into the front while Rafe climbed in beside Crystal. He fixed his dark gaze on her and mildly asked, "What *are* you doing here, Crystal?"

She looked at Sloan, whose face was impassive, but his eyes were active. He was trying to come up with some explanation that his boss wouldn't recognize as an outright fabrication. She saved him the trouble. "You know about the vision."

"Ms. Cobbs's vision about Christina?" He nodded.

"For reasons I'd prefer to not go into now, my aunt and I decided to pass it off as hers, but the vision was mine. Sloan figured that out and asked for my help. I'm not like Aunt Winona. I consider my psychic abilities a curse rather than a gift. I didn't want people here to know, so Sloan agreed to keep my name out of it as much as possible."

"So, while he's been out in the woods looking for clues...?"

"I've been helping him."

Sloan spoke up then. "That's how we found this road. We went over to Homer's to ask him about it, and Crystal saw the license plate there. He brought us here."

"Anything else you haven't been putting in your reports, Deputy?" Rafe asked mildly.

"No, sir."

"I hope not. When I get back to the office, I'll be organizing search parties to check out the woods here. Do you want to help, or would you prefer to continue with what you've been doing?"

"I'd rather continue what we've been doing, if that's not a problem."

"As long as you keep me informed—or *start* keeping me informed—it shouldn't be." Glancing out the window as the last of the other vehicles drove away, Rafe opened the door. "Mr. Gilmore, Crystal, thanks for your help. Sloan, can I speak to you out here?"

Crystal watched through the glass as they took a few steps toward the sheriff's car. They talked earnestly for a minute or two before Rafe went to his car and Sloan returned to them. He fastened his seat belt and started the engine, then waited for Rafe to drive away. When he pulled out, though, he didn't back into the clearing to return the way they'd come. He headed on down the road as yet unexplored.

After long minutes passed in which he didn't speak, she

did. "I'm sorry if protecting me has caused problems with Rafe."

"We'll get over it." His dark eyes were guarded when he looked at her in the rearview mirror. "You didn't have to volunteer the truth."

"Yes, I did. It was something Aunt Winona said the other day—that when you told me Homer was in trouble, I should have volunteered my help rather than making you break your promise and ask for it. She was right. I was so hurt that you'd gone back on your word, but you did it only because I left you no choice." She smiled faintly. "I may be slow, but I do learn."

They drove another few minutes in silence, then Homer abruptly demanded, "Stop here."

Sloan automatically obeyed before asking why.

"I'm goin' home. Gonna tend to my supper."

"We'll take you right up to the house, Homer."

The old man gave him a patronizing smile. "You cain't drive right up to the house, not through these here woods. If'n you was to do that, you'd have to go all the way to the reservation, then come all the way back. Why should I wait that long when my house is right through them trees? I can be home and sittin' down to my supper before you even git off this road."

"Thanks for your help, Mr. Gilmore."

The old man started to climb out, then abruptly looked back. "Don't forgit. A tag with my own name on it. You promised." Then with a grin, he added, "I'm kinda partial to red and gold. You know, with sparkles."

"I won't forget."

Crystal moved to the front seat and gave a soft sigh. It had been a long day in a series of them, and she was tired, hungry, cold and damp through and through. At least tomorrow was a holiday. Sloan surely wouldn't expect her to go back into the woods on a holiday...would he?

When she asked, he grinned. "My grandmother would have my head if I worked on Thanksgiving when I didn't

have to. Any chance I can persuade you and Winona to come
out and have dinner with the family? You can meet more
Ravencrests than you'll ever keep straight.''

"Aunt Winona has invited Homer over for dinner. Maybe
you can sneak away and have dessert with us."

"I'm sure I can."

After another brief silence, she returned to a subject she
was dearly learning to hate. "Christina's car... She wasn't
the one who hid it there. Her killer was."

He looked at her, but didn't speak, instead patiently waiting for her to go on.

"I couldn't tell if it was a man or a woman, but whoever
it was got a thrill from it. He was excited, afraid of getting
caught but enjoying the adrenaline rush. The one thing he
wasn't was sorry. She brought it on herself. If she hadn't
interrupted whatever he was doing, he wouldn't have had to
kill her."

"Do you think it was Homer's alien?"

She shrugged. "He's the only other person we can place
in those woods at that time."

"So someone was out there digging for...treasure, for lack
of a better word, and Christina... How did she come in contact with him? The alien was digging quite a ways from the
clearing. Could she have taken a wrong turn on her way out
of there?"

"She'd just given birth. She wasn't in any condition to go
wandering around. Could he have been digging closer to the
clearing at a site you haven't found yet?"

"Sure. Anything's possible."

Up ahead the two stone columns that marked the entrance
to the trail came into view. Crystal closed her eyes and focused everything inward, seeking answers, a flash, a sensation, anything. "Maybe, like Christina, he drove this road so
no one would know he was here. And he saw her car and
thought she was after his treasure, and he waited for her."
Her breath caught in her chest, and she gave a sad sigh. "Oh,
no, no. The feelings I had of Crystal on that trail... That

wasn't when she was leaving that night. It was when she'd arrived. She was afraid of being disappointed and, at the same time, hopeful. When she was leaving, whatever had happened between her and the baby's father had happened. If he'd disappointed her, she would have been disappointed, not expecting to be. She would have lost hope. And if he *hadn't* disappointed her, she would have been relieved. Maybe even happy.''

"So Christina didn't come back this way."

She shook her head. "Where the trail split, I wasn't sure at first I'd chosen the right one. It seemed I was picking up leads from both sides, but the farther I went, the stronger I could feel her. I thought the confusion at first was because the two paths ran so close together. But she could have taken the other trail that night."

"You said she knew the trail. It was familiar to her at night. Why would she take the wrong trail?"

"She was in pain. She'd lost a lot of blood. She could have been confused. Maybe her meeting hadn't gone well and she was disappointed, heartbroken, crying. She veered off on the wrong trail, and by the time she realized it…it was too late."

She opened her eyes to see that Sloan had stopped beside the stone pillars. A few hundred yards up the trail, they could connect with the other branch and maybe discover what had happened to Christina. But, God forgive her, she didn't want to do it. She didn't want to set one foot in those woods again today. She was weary physically, emotionally, psychically. She just wanted to snuggle up somewhere with Sloan and forget everything and everyone else.

But she took a deep breath and hoped she'd hidden the reluctance well before she turned to face him. "Shall we go look?"

Shaking his head, he put the truck in motion again. "Not this evening. With the cloud cover, it'll be dark before long. The last thing I want is you wandering around with Homer's alien possibly in the same woods."

"I don't mind—"

"I do. We'll come back Friday."

Her sigh was filled with heartfelt relief.

As the road neared its end, it became rougher, almost impassable in places. A car couldn't travel the last two miles, but the four-wheel-drive Jeep did okay. Once they reached a dirt road, Sloan knew exactly where they were and shook his head in surprise. "I've ridden my horse on that trail a ways, but never far. I always thought it probably went to an old abandoned homestead and wasn't worth exploring to the end." He grinned. "Want to stop by and see my folks?"

"No, thank you."

"Want to stop by and see Winona?"

"No, thank you."

The grin broadened. "Want to go home with me and make love until we're both too weak to move?"

She couldn't resist smiling back at him. In her best Southern belle voice, she said, "Five minutes ago I thought I was too tired to do anything more strenuous than curl up, but I find I have an unexpected resurgence of energy. I'll take you up on that last offer. If you don't mind, though, I'd like to stop at home and change into some dry clothes."

"I don't mind at all, darlin'. Put on whatever you want. I'll enjoy taking it off again as soon as we get home. I'll also enjoy helping you put it back on in the morning."

She did more than just change. While Sloan caught Winona up on the day's activities, Crystal showered, dried her hair and smoothed her favorite scented lotion everywhere. She didn't bother with makeup—with the activities they were planning, she didn't think it would last long—but tucked her makeup bag into a straw tote, along with a change of clothes and a toothbrush.

In her bedroom, she chose her clothes carefully—her favorite lingerie, a camisole and tap pants in creamy silk and lace, with her most comfortable jeans and a V-neck sweater that revealed a touch of camisole lace. She secured her hair from her face with a headband, added earrings and a necklace, and, on impulse, picked up the gold nugget ring from the dresser.

Both Sloan and Winona looked up to watch her come in the door. His look was appreciative and more than a touch possessive. Winona looked every bit the proud matchmaker.

"You ready to go, babe?" Sloan asked.

Babe. She was quite certain that never once in James's life had the word "babe" crossed his lips. She was also quite certain that if it ever did, it would be condescending and demeaning.

From Sloan it was simply sweet.

"Just a minute. Aunt Winona, I have something for you to add to your jewelry counter." Unfolding her fingers, she revealed the nugget ring. Winona's beaming smile seemed to make it shine even brighter.

"I'd be happy to sell that for you, my dear. In fact—" She gazed around the room, then called, "Vern Jefferson, you have a fondness for gold. Come and look at this fine ring my niece is placing with me for sale."

The old man rambled over from the back, his gaze less than friendly for both Sloan and Crystal. He lit up when he saw the ring, though he quickly tried to hide it. "Nice-lookin' piece."

"Probably just about fits you, too," Winona said. She handed it over so he could try it on. It was a bit of a squeeze over his arthritic knuckle but otherwise fit fine.

"How much you want for it?"

Winona started to name a price, but Crystal stopped her. "How much are you offering?"

He examined it on his hand, then took it off and held it to the light. "It's not the best quality I ever seen," he said, and ignored Winona's scoff. "My granddaddy was a gold miner, and he had some nuggets that were a sight to see. I'd only be interested in the ring 'cause I feel sentimental toward my granddaddy, of course." He studied it for a moment, then said, "I'll give you fifty dollars, take it or leave it."

Winona puffed up like an angry hen. "Fifty dollars? Why,

I can sell a ring of that size and quality for easily five times that without even making an effort. If I tried, I could get a whole heck of a lot more. Fifty dollars! Why, that's insulting!''

"I'll take it," Crystal said firmly.

Winona turned to stare at her while the old man's face lit with delight. He immediately dug into his pocket and removed two wadded twenties and a ten, slapping them on the counter before he put the ring on again. "You shoulda listened to your aunt, little girl, 'cause you just got took. This ring's worth a whole lot more than fifty bucks."

She dropped the bills into her purse before giving the old man her friendliest smile. "Not to me, it isn't. I would've given it to you for five." Linking her arm through Sloan's, she started toward the door. "Come on, Sloan. Let's go work up an appetite, and then I'll take you to Neela's. Mr. Jefferson's treat."

Once they were outside and out of sight, he pulled her close for a hard kiss. "I noticed you weren't wearing it last night. That's when I knew for sure that you loved me."

"You did, huh? And here I thought it was when I jumped your bones."

His smile lasted briefly, then faded. "I never would have asked you to get rid of it."

"You didn't. It was my choice. It no longer had a place in my life because you do." She touched his face gently, then caught his hand. "Come on. Take me home and undress me. I think you'll like what you find."

He gave her a damn near sizzling look as he helped her into the Jeep. "Darlin'," he drawled before closing the door. "I already love what I'll find."

Twelve

Once they reached his apartment, Sloan took a shower, then wrapped a towel around his waist before leaving the bathroom. He didn't make it farther than the bedroom door, though, where he leaned against the jamb and watched Crystal as she studied the scene outside the window. He would have sworn he hadn't made a sound, but she knew he was there.

"Will you take me camping in the Crazy Mountains sometime?" she asked without turning toward him.

"Next summer, when it's warm."

"Will we take our kids camping there when they're old enough?"

He swallowed hard over the lump that formed instantly in his throat. "You bet."

She turned and offered him a nervous smile. "That's awfully presumptuous of me, isn't it? No one's said anything about kids...or marriage."

"Only because I made them promise they'd let me ask you before they started making plans."

"Made who promise?"

He answered as he pushed away from the door and started slowly toward her. "Dad, Amy, Grandma and Grandpa, Winona. By now, I imagine a hundred people or so know."

She choked on a laugh. "You've told all those people that you're going to marry me without even mentioning it to me first? What if I turn you down?"

"Then you'd break my heart. But I wouldn't give up. I'd woo you until you'd had no choice but to say yes."

"You wouldn't want me to say yes because I had no choice. You want me to say yes because you're the best of all possible choices."

"Babe, I'll take you any way I can get you." He stopped in front of her and shifted his gaze to the vee of her sweater. The bit of lace showing there was pale, delicate and feminine. Like the woman wearing it. Hooking his finger in the vee, he pulled her to him. "What have you got on under there?" he asked, tugging the sweater out far enough to see more lace covering the swells of her breasts.

"Take it off and see."

He reached past her for the cord that closed the drapes, enveloping the room in darkness, then turned on the bedside lamp and did just what she'd suggested. He curled his fingers around the ribbed hem of the sweater and slowly inched it up, then forgot the sweater and began exploring. He found soft silk clinging to her middle, cupping impossibly soft breasts. As he slid his palms higher to the lace, he felt her nipples pebble and harden, enticing him to replace his hands with his mouth.

"You don't need this." Returning to the sweater, he peeled it over her head, carefully straightened it, folded it, then carelessly tossed it aside on the corner chair.

Smiling sensuously, she unknotted the towel at his waist and gave it the same attention before dropping it to the floor. "You don't need that, either. It's not as if it was hiding anything."

There wasn't a towel made that could hide how he was feeling at that moment. He'd never been so hard, so needy, so impatient, so greedy. He'd never felt so tender, both toward her and inside himself, as if he were being remade from the inside out into a better man, someone who just might someday, if he worked hard enough, deserve her.

Pressing her hand to his chest above his heart, she said, "Lie down. I have it on good authority that the rest is better watched."

James's authority? he wondered, but the thought couldn't

stir even an instant's jealousy. She'd never loved James, had never looked at him the way she looked at Sloan, had never touched him or kissed him or made love with him the way she did with Sloan. She never would have lived happily ever after with James the way she would with Sloan.

He retreated to the bed, pulling the pillows free of the quilt to tuck under his head. She balanced delicately on the edge of the chair to remove her shoes and thick white socks, then stood and undid the button-fly front of her jeans one metal button at a time. Sliding her thumbs inside the waistband at her hips, she pushed the denim slowly down, revealing more silk and lace and pale, delicate skin. After turning her back to him, she worked the snug fabric down each leg, bending to tug it free of one foot, pulling the insubstantial silk tight over the curve of her bottom. Straightening, she repeated the process with the other foot, then removed her headband and gave her head a shake before facing him, bringing a tousled, combed-by-a-lover's-hands look to her silky black hair.

She looked incredible. Was incredible. Was his.

Sometime in the last few seconds, his arousal had become painful. It made his muscles taut, his nerves quivery, and his throat was tight when he finally asked, "Whose authority?"

With another of those sensuous smiles, she let the weight of her gaze glide slowly over his chest and abdomen to the erection that strained with a life of its own. "Yours. I love a shamelessly aroused man."

He knew that was no generalization, along the lines of "I love cowboys" or "I love a man who knows what he wants."

She came to him then, placing one knee on the bed beside his hip, swinging the other leg over him, then settling astride his groin. The silk was soft and quickly became warm with the heat from her body, the fire from his. He couldn't help moving just slightly—one tormenting inch—against her, couldn't stop the gasp of pure pain—or was it pure pleasure?—the movement brought him.

Still moving with a lithe, catlike grace, she placed one

hand above his left shoulder, brought the other above his right shoulder, then bent over him. He felt the silk of the tap pants come into contact with his belly, then the slight scratch of the lace hem of the top. Cool silk fell against his chest, then her breasts pressed heavily against him, immediately turning his skin sultry hot, scorching him, promising destruction and rebirth as that better man for her.

Tiny delicate straps curved over her shoulders, just right for such a delicate garment and such a delicate woman. With a soft, sweet, hungry sigh, she touched her mouth to his in the most innocent, and most wicked, of kisses. Just a taste, a promise, a torment.

When she pulled back, he followed her, raising his hands to stop her, trying to capture her mouth for more. She was quicker, though. She caught his hands and evaded his mouth and sat up with the same nerve-racking slowness that made his entire body throb. She sat upright, bringing the most intimate part of her into snug, damn near perfect contact with the most intimate part of him, and lifted his hands to her breasts, molding them gently, firmly, one finger at a time, until she was satisfied. Then she thrust her hips once, long, slow, lazy, against his erection, dragging hot, damp silk along the length of him, making him jerk convulsively against her.

"Come inside me," she murmured, her head thrown back, her eyes closed, her face exquisitely beautiful, "and play with my breasts. Show me how much you want me. Show me how much you—" Her request ended in a gasp as he shoved the delicate fabric aside and plunged deep, hard, frantically, inside her. That one thrust, and his hands on her breasts, was enough. He felt her body clenching his in tight spasms, felt the shudders of pleasure that washed through her, felt her hot moisture seep over him.

So easy, he marveled. So perfect. So exquisite.

When the tension holding her body so stiff began to ease, her eyes fluttered open. He cradled her face in his palm. "I love a shamelessly satisfied woman," he murmured.

She gave him another of those cut-him-off-at-the-knees

smiles. "Not as much as you're going to love being a satisfied man," she promised.

And then she made good on it.

Thanksgiving Day had provided Crystal with a badly needed break. For one day life had been relatively normal again. After a lazy breakfast with Sloan, she'd gone home to help Winona fix the turkey trimmings, and then they'd driven together to pick up Homer at his place. Later in the afternoon, Sloan had joined them, and when Winona had left to take Homer home again, they'd made love on her cramped twin bed. They'd barely gotten their clothes back on as she'd returned.

It had been different from any Thanksgiving she'd ever known. Excruciatingly formal dinners with her own family that, in recent years, were repeated with James's family. Boring conversation, stressful company, little to be thankful for until the day was over.

This Thanksgiving had been sweet. Special. Spent with people she loved who loved her back.

But this Friday morning, she and Sloan were back at work. Back in the woods.

To cut down on hiking time, they'd taken the logging road to the trail's end, coming in once again from the reservation end to avoid the joint sheriff's office/police department search at the site where Christina's car had been ditched. The temperature was a frosty thirty-three degrees, and his grandfather, Sloan had mentioned, was predicting snow.

She wouldn't mind a nice, heavy snow, especially if she was stranded with the right person.

They reached the point where the trail split and silently turned onto the other branch. By the time they'd gone twenty yards, she knew their theory was at least partly correct. In pain, dazed and burdened by overwhelming guilt, Christina had missed the trail and come this way the night she'd died. She hadn't known she was walking into danger, hadn't even realized she was going the wrong way.

As Crystal's steps quickened, Sloan caught up with her, taking hold of her elbow. "It's not a race, darlin'," he said quietly, forcing her to slow her pace.

She brushed him away, veered to the side to avoid him when he reached for her again, then stopped suddenly, wrapping her arms around her middle. "She doesn't have her baby," she blurted, feeling the intensity of Christina's pain.

"What do you mean?"

"I don't know."

"She gave birth?"

"Yes."

"Did the baby die?"

"I don't know. She lost it, gave it away, abandoned it, I don't know. But she doesn't have it, and she'll never have it again, and she'll never be able to live with that." She took as deep a breath as the tightness in her chest would allow. She felt so empty and, at the same time, so filled with sorrow, as she whispered, "She never got the chance to even try."

Her voice broke on the last word, and she started walking again, her pace faster than was comfortable.

Sloan caught up with her, stopped her again, and she jerked free again. Trying not to notice the faint hurt in his eyes, she held up one hand warning him away. "I can't handle her and you and me all at once. Please, let me do this my way. Later... I'll need you later."

He backed off. "Maybe you shouldn't be trying to handle her at all. Let me take you back to Winona's. You've narrowed the search area quite a bit. I can go on from here."

"It could take you days, maybe weeks, to search even a narrower area, and you still might miss her." She took another breath, then smiled shakily. "I'm all right."

"I don't want to see you hurting."

"If I could tell you exactly what to expect, I would. But I don't know myself. I'll be all right." She could see he wanted to question her, to doubt her, but, with a grim set to his features, he nodded once and gestured for her to go on.

Unlike the other branch of the trail, open to the sky, this

one wove through trees stretching overhead—hardwoods, some barren for the winter, others cloaked in dried brown leaves, and scraggly cedars and tall pines. The undergrowth was tangled, restricting easy passage to the trail in most places. Crystal couldn't imagine deliberately walking through these woods alone at any time, but especially at night. What was merely oppressive during the day would terrify her in the dark. Just as she'd done the day they'd discovered the clearing, after five minutes out here in the dark, she would find herself running willy-nilly in a full-fledged panic.

When the trail split again, she came to a stop. "She doesn't remember this place. She wonders if she's taken a wrong turn. She's supposed to go right, but this doesn't look right. But maybe it just looks different tonight. Hell, she just lost, left, gave up her baby. The whole damned world should look different tonight. She, who knows better than anyone, how much a child needs her mother, just walked away from her own child."

Christina's indecision practically consumed Crystal, along with her desperate need to be out of this awful place. It was that desperation that had made her take the right-hand trail, Crystal knew, that had let her believe, in spite of what her own eyes had told her, that it was the correct trail.

Crystal turned that way, too, but her steps were slower. Christina had been tired, weak, aware of the blood seeping down her legs. She'd begun to wonder how big a mistake she'd made, whether she would make it to her car, whether she should try to return to the clearing. She needed to sit, to catch her breath, to give the pain and the bleeding a chance to subside, but if she sat down, she was afraid she wouldn't find the energy to get up again. She had to keep moving, keep going, and surely the end of the trail would be just ahead, just around the next curve....

Around the next curve, the narrow trail suddenly opened into a clearing. Boulders were scattered about as if dropped by a careless giant, and pine needles covered the ground.

Except where it had been scraped away and turned over by a ray-gun camouflaged as a shovel.

Sloan brushed past Crystal when she stopped and left the trail to examine the digging. It was more extensive than at the site where Homer had confronted the alien—larger piles, deeper holes. Sloan crouched to examine one that was roughly the right size for a small adult, using a stick to judge the depth of the loosened dirt.

"That's not a grave," she said emotionlessly. She walked straight ahead, feeling bone-weary and heartsick. Pine straw gave way to moss-covered rock, which, after ten feet, took a steep turn down, forming one side of a small, familiar canyon. Lifting her arm took more energy than she thought she possessed, but she managed to point to a shallow depression below, managed to flatly say, "But that is."

Then the last of her energy drained away and she sank to the ground in a heap.

Sloan stood in the canyon and felt an overwhelming sense of regret. He'd long believed Christina Montgomery was dead, but some part of him had hoped... Now the hope was gone. He hadn't touched the grave yet, but he was as convinced as Crystal was that he would find her body there. She hadn't been wrong yet.

He looked back at her, sitting on a rock some dozen feet away. He'd wanted her to wait up above, wanted to take her back to the truck, back to Winona's, back far, far away from here, but she'd insisted on staying. She'd brought him this far. She wanted to see it through. Even though he'd given in and helped her down the narrow trail into the canyon, he wondered if he should have refused. She was so pale, so shaken. When she'd crumpled up above, his heart had damn near stopped beating in his chest. If she'd been hurt, if she'd fallen over the bluff's edge...

But she hadn't. She was all right. She *would* be all right.

The canyon floor was rocky in places, thick and heavy with clay elsewhere, and plain, Montana soil in still other places, and it had yielded the first clue. With all the rain preceding Christina's disappearance, the ground had been muddy, and the stiff consistency of the clay had captured some excellent footprints. Two sets, to be exact, one wearing regular street shoes, the other in ridged-soled hiking boots, and neither anywhere near as big as his size elevens. That ought to help clear Homer, with his three-times-bigger giant clown feet.

The street shoes, he assumed, belonged to Christina. The hiking boots, he'd bet, would have to belong to an adolescent boy…or a woman. He had to believe no adolescent boy around here could kill a woman in cold blood, bury her body and never let on to his family or friends that anything had happened. Hell, he knew all the kids who lived within ten miles of here and was related to plenty of them. Not one of them was that cold, that brutal or sick.

Which left a woman. Christina had run wild after her mother's death and had taken up with plenty of men. Maybe one of those men had had an angry wife or a jealous lover. Or maybe the woman had been connected to the baby's disappearance. Maybe Christina had sold or given away the baby, and while someone else had taken off with the child, the woman had followed Christina to make certain that she never tried to renege on their deal.

But that wouldn't explain the digging up above. More likely, the woman had been searching for something and Christina had surprised her at it. Maybe her death had been an accident—for which the killer felt no remorse, according to Crystal. Maybe it had all been senseless, wasteful, a classic case of being in the wrong place at the wrong time.

Careful not to get close to the footprints, Sloan followed their trail. In only a few feet, the street shoe prints disappeared, giving way to two shallow grooves. Drag marks.

On a dark August night, Christina Montgomery, twenty-two, beautiful, privileged, with the brightest of futures ahead of her, had died in the mud where he stood.

The drag marks and boot prints led to the depression. The

killer had moved Christina some distance, across clay that sucked at her feet and would have been difficult to dig in to the softer soil at the canyon's edge. Looking around, he found a piece of granite that fitted well in his hand, a curved piece with some heft to it and one edge that came to a vee. He knelt about at the middle of the depression, took a deep breath to steady himself, then began gently scraping away layers of soil. He'd gone down three, maybe four, inches when he found what he was looking for.

Do you see Christina? he'd asked Crystal that Friday a lifetime ago, when they'd sat at the table between the shop and the trailer, and she'd answered yes. *What is she wearing?*

A dress. Navy blue, pleated, too big for her. It's covered with blood.

The fabric his rock had revealed was navy blue and stained dark.

He laid the granite aside, stood and turned to find Crystal watching him. Though he could see from her face that she already knew, he nodded once. The simple confirmation seemed to take something from her. She suddenly appeared smaller, weaker, insubstantial. She let her head fall forward into her hands, exquisitely sorrowful, then suddenly stiffened.

"Sloan..." As he started toward her, she rose from the rock and bent to look down. She was reaching toward the crevice formed where the rock met another when he caught her hand and bent to see what was there.

Tucked in the shelter of the stone was a gold locket, its chain broken and curling around it. He wrapped his fingers around hers. "Don't touch it. It might have fingerprints." Maybe Christina's. Maybe her killer's. "Come on." He started pulling her toward the path that had brought them down from the bluff. When she tried to tug free, he simply held her tighter, pulled harder.

"We can't leave her there, Sloan. We can't—"

He turned and brought her into his arms. "She's dead, Crystal," he said gently. "Nothing's going to hurt her. I have to get out of this canyon to pick up a signal on the cell phone." He touched her face and felt how cold she'd become. "I have to get *you* out of this canyon. Christina's beyond pain and fear now. You can't do anything more for her."

For a long moment, she looked as if she wanted to argue, but instead she slowly nodded, then started up the trail.

Within an hour, the site held more deputies and cops than it was ever meant for. After calling Rafe on the cell phone, Sloan had called Winona and asked her to come in from the reservation end to pick up Crystal and take her home, then had taken her back to the truck to wait. The cops had arrived first, forcing him to leave her there to await her aunt while he showed them to the canyon. He'd hated leaving Crystal like that, locked alone in his truck, but she'd assured him she would be all right. A call to the shop fifteen minutes ago had confirmed that she was home safe.

Now he stood on the bluff, watching as the evidence techs, two from the sheriff's department, two from the Whitehorn P.D., made casts of footprints, shot photographs from every angle and meticulously began to uncover the body. Rafe's investigators and the P.D. detectives were down there, too, searching the site, and other officers had spread out into the nearby woods. He was the only one doing nothing. Truth be told, he thought he'd done enough. Now he only wanted to go home.

To Crystal.

Rafe came to stand beside him, the tagged-and-bagged locket in his hand and a curious expression on his face. "Pretty necklace."

Sloan glanced at it but didn't respond.

"The chain must have broken in the struggle. Takes a lot of force to break a chain like that." Turning the bag over, Rafe studied the front of the locket, the back, the chain and its broken link. "Ellis doesn't know if it belonged to Christina. Of course, he's pretty broken up now, and men don't pay that much attention to jewelry."

Some men, Sloan thought. Rafe was looking at that piece

as if it might magically point them to the killer. Who knew? If the killer was a woman, as he suspected, it just might. "Maybe Christina's sister will recognize it, or one of her friends."

"Maybe." Rafe stared at it a moment longer, his eyes narrowed in a frown, then, with an abrupt shrug, he pocketed the bag. "You have any theories?"

Wearily, Sloan told him what he knew, what he suspected, what Crystal knew.

"What kind of treasure would someone hide in these woods?"

"Anything. Nothing. I don't know. It's just a theory."

"So Crystal's the genuine article, huh? A bona fide, certified, true-blue psychic."

Before Sloan could respond to that, an angry voice behind them cut in. "You think you're a real hotshot, don't you, Ravencrest?"

He slowly turned to face the two detectives who'd been assigned the case. He'd never liked Terry Wilkins or Mark Blakely. There was nothing worse than a cop who cared more about his own glory than justice, and that description fit both men to a T. "I was just doing your job for you," he said mildly. "Since you didn't seem capable of doing it yourself."

"Seems real convenient that when we start making a case against crazy old Homer, your girlfriend suddenly, magically, leads you to Christina's body." Wilkins turned an innocent look on Blakely. "How do you suppose she did that? All these trained investigators working full-time on this case, and some civilian just walks into the woods and says, 'There. That's where Christina's buried.'"

"Unless what she really said was, 'There. That's where I buried Christina after I killed her,'" Blakely said before turning an accusing stare on Sloan. "But of course that *can't* be how it happened, because that would put Deputy Ravencrest in quite a dilemma. Which would be more important? Arresting a murderer? Or getting laid every night by the hottest piece of—''

Sloan didn't wait to hear another word. He lunged toward Blakely, but connected instead with Rafe's solid weight.

The sheriff backed him away, warning, "Calm down, Sloan. They're just pissed because you blew their sorry excuse for a case against Homer out of the water and made them look like fools." Over his shoulder, he said sternly, "This is a crime scene. If you two don't have a job to do, you can get the hell out."

"Oh, we've got a job," Wilkins said, "and it looks like it just might be making a case against Ms. Crystal Cobbs. Think about it, Rawlings. How the hell did she know? How in the bloody hell did she know that Christina's body was buried out here in the middle of nowhere?"

"Unless she buried it there," Blakely added. "Nobody had any reason to look out here. There wasn't any evidence to suggest that Montgomery had ever set foot in these woods. And yet little Miss Crystal leads Ravencrest straight here. How?"

"That's a question I've been wondering myself," the police chief said as he and the district attorney joined them. "Would you care to explain, Deputy?"

Sloan looked at each of the men, then noticed for the first time the other officers watching from nearby and, behind them, the handful of reporters who had arrived to cover the story, and he felt sick at heart. He'd promised Crystal that he would try to protect her, try to keep any mention of her name and her psychic powers between him and Rafe.

But he wasn't going to be able to keep that promise any longer. There was no story that could conceivably explain how they'd found Christina's grave, no investigative work so brilliant and thorough that it could have led him from the few clues he'd started with to this place. Any hedging he did to try to keep his promise would only serve to make the detectives more suspicious of Crystal. They would start harassing her, start looking into her background and her reasons for leaving Georgia, and they would find out James's version of the truth, and Marabeth and Andrew Cobbs's version. He had no doubt they would turn an already sordid story into something even uglier and nastier, and they very well might destroy her.

And so might he. No matter how desperately he wanted to protect her.

"Well, Deputy?" the chief prodded.

He looked at Rafe at last, who slowly released him, then nodded. They weren't going to be satisfied until they had an answer, and he had only one answer to give.

He opened his mouth, but the words didn't want to come. He had to force them against his better judgment, had to give them voice despite his tremendous guilt. "Crystal..." He steeled himself against the rush of betrayal and stiffly continued. "Crystal is a psychic. She had a vision of Christina, and that's what led us here."

For a moment there was utter silence, then reaction set in. Murmuring from the reporters, a skeptical laugh or two among the other officers, a disgusted curse from the D.A.

"A 'psychic?'" Blakely echoed, his voice loud enough to carry to everyone. "Hear that, folks? That's how the Blue River County Sheriff's Department solves crimes these days. With fortune-tellers. Kooks. Lunatics. Isn't that a fine way to spend the taxpayers' hard-earned dollars?"

"At least the Blue River County Sheriff's Department solves crimes," Rafe said coldly. "They don't try to frame innocent men."

That wiped the grin off Blakely's face and brought back the hostility. "We don't really know who's innocent in this case, now, do we?"

"We'll find out," Rafe replied. "We'll have all kinds of evidence from this scene. We might even pass the reports on to you when we're done."

"Now wait a minute," the chief said. "This is a joint investigation. You can't withhold evidence from us!"

"This was a joint investigation because we didn't know in

whose jurisdiction the crime took place. Hell, we didn't even know if there was a crime. Now we know. And this is Blue River County, boys. That makes it my department's case.''

Rafe started to walk away and gestured for Sloan to follow, but the D.A. stopped them both. ''Let's not get into any jurisdictional arguments here, Sheriff, Chief. Right now we need to worry about damage control. I want to see both of you in my office. Deputy, you come, too.''

Sloan held the D.A.'s gaze for a moment, then walked off, pushing his way past officers and reporters alike, ignoring their comments and questions. He made it back to his truck in record time, climbed behind the wheel and simply sat there, head bowed. Crystal's scent still lingered faintly in the air, and it hit him with the force of a blow to the gut.

This was twice he'd made her a promise. Twice he'd broken it. He prayed to God she would find it in her heart to forgive him one more time.

But this time he wasn't sure he could forgive himself.

The news of the discovery of Christina Montgomery's body spread through town like wildfire. It was the sole topic of conversation in the Hip Hop all day long. Emma Stover had already heard the bare facts more times than she could count, along with a dozen or so embellishments. The customers were saying Miz Cobbs's niece Crystal was psychic, like Winona, and that she'd been the one to find the body. If it was true, Emma wondered grimly if Crystal might be persuaded to take a look into her future and give her answers to a few questions.

Like whether to visit her mother. Whether Lexine was as guilty of murder as the juries had believed. Whether she cared at all about the daughter she'd given away so many years ago. Whether meeting her at last would be the end of Emma's search...or the beginning of more heartache.

She'd gone round and round on the subject for so long that it hurt her head to think about it, but most of the time it was all she *could* think about. Even the details of discovering the missing girl's body couldn't distract her after hearing about it for the twentieth time. She was sorry the girl was dead, really she was, but she hadn't known Christina, and she had problems of her own.

She was distractedly pouring refills for a tableful of regulars, old men who lived for gossip, when a hush spread over the dining room. Along with everyone else in the place, she looked up to see Ellis Montgomery's children, Max and Rachel, heading for a table at the back of her section. She gave them a moment to get settled, then approached with menus. Rachel waved them away. "We'd just like coffee, please."

Emma nodded and left to get mugs and a pot of fresh coffee. Rachel looked as if she'd been crying, and Max...Max didn't look as if he felt a thing. But Emma knew from experience people could feel things deeply but never let them show.

After serving them, Emma retreated to the end of the counter, totaling tickets and taking a breather before making the rounds of her customers. Though she tried to ignore the Montgomerys' quiet voices, it was impossible to not overhear their conversation.

Rachel began, her tone determined. "We have to try to find the baby."

"We don't even know for sure there is a baby," her brother replied.

"There's a baby. Everyone suspected Christina was pregnant except you and Dad."

"And that's our fault?"

Rachel's patience-seeking breath was clearly audible. "It's not anyone's fault, Max. But Christina's baby is out there somewhere, and we *have* to find it."

"You heard the sheriff. They don't know even know where to look. Whoever killed Christina—" Max's voice quavered just the slightest bit "—might have taken the baby or even killed it, too."

"We have to have faith that the baby is all right. I want to hire a private investigator," Rachel said earnestly. "The sheriff's department can't give a search like this the time and attention it deserves. I want to hire someone who will devote all his time and energy to finding Christina's baby and bringing it back home to her family, where it belongs.''

"We can discuss this further some other time. After we bury—'' Max broke off in a quiver that made Emma wish she was anywhere else at that moment, even at the women's prison in Billings.

Searching. Everyone was searching for something—the Montgomerys for their sister, now for some sense from her death, and for her baby. The authorities for her killer. Emma for her mother. At least she knew where to look, if she could just find the courage. But she didn't have to decide tonight. It wasn't as if Lexine was going anywhere.

But maybe the Montgomerys had thought that about Christina. No need to make time for the spoiled kid sister, the demanding daughter, the needy young woman. Their lives were busy with other responsibilities. Christina was young, and she wasn't going anywhere. They could always find time for her later.

But now *later* would never come.

Emma didn't want to find herself at some point in the future lamenting the *later* that would never arrive. According to the letter from the prison, all she had to do was write to her mother and request that Lexine add her to her visitors' list. It was that easy. And that hard.

But she would do it.

Crystal waited the rest of the morning and all afternoon to hear from Sloan. Finally she called his cell phone, but got his voice mail. Shortly after shift change at four o'clock, she called his apartment and got his machine. She tried to tell herself that he was busy, that working a murder scene was a complicated, time-consuming job. She assured herself that he would call or come by just as soon as he could. She promised herself that nothing was wrong.

But something *was* wrong. She felt it in the pit of her

stomach, in the tightness in her chest that made taking a deep breath impossible. Something was terribly wrong.

Finally she called the sheriff's department and asked for Rafe. After taking her name and putting her on hold, the dispatcher told her that he was in a meeting and couldn't take any calls, but he did give her a message. If she was looking for Sloan, she should try the Hip Hop Café. He'd sent him over there with Deputy Elkshoulder to finally get some food.

The relief she should have felt didn't come. Instead of going back to waiting, or calling the restaurant, she borrowed Winona's truck and drove into town.

The Hip Hop was more crowded than usual. Of course, it *was* Gossip Central, according to Winona, and the discovery of Christina's body was juicy gossip. The fact that it was the day after Thanksgiving, another holiday for a lot of folks, and that most of them had eaten all the turkey they could stand probably didn't hurt business any, either.

She paused inside the door to peel off her gloves and unbutton her coat, then looked around for Sloan. Slowly she became aware that the diner had gone silent—completely, utterly silent—and everyone was staring.

At her.

She'd heard those silences before, had felt those stares before. Some were curious, some repulsed, some just a bit frightened. They knew. Oh, God, they *knew!* It was Boonesville all over again.

She didn't know whether to turn and run, or to walk on into the place and look for Sloan. Her strongest impulse was to run, exactly the way she'd run from Boonesville, to race back to Winona's, pack a suitcase and catch the next plane leaving Montana. But there was no place for her to run to. No other loving relative out there willing to take her in and help her make a new life. No other man like Sloan out there to accept her the way she was and love her anyway. No other place she wanted to be, no other place she wanted to call home.

As she slowly began moving away from the door, the silence gave way to whispers, murmurs. She heard the sibilant S's and the hard K's—psychic, strange, kook, freak, crazy— and they nearly drained her of the strength to keep walking. But a glimpse of Deputy Elkshoulder in a distant booth kept her moving. Even if Sloan wasn't with him, perhaps he could tell her where to find him.

Sloan was still with him. He sat facing the wall, a plate of food untouched in front of him, and he looked... Lost. Distraught. Hopeless. When she stopped beside the table, it took him a long moment to realize she was there, even longer to bring his gaze to her face. The look in his eyes turned bleaker and sent a chill through her. "Sloan, what's wrong?" she whispered.

"Aw, you should know that." The answer came from behind her and made Sloan stiffen. "After all, you've got the power." The last word started in a low, spooky tone, then exploded into the last syllable.

She didn't spare a glance for the detective. "Sloan?"

"You'll have to excuse Deputy Ravencrest's manners," the second detective said. "He got suspended from the department this afternoon, and he's pouting."

Finally she did look at the men. "Suspended for what?"

"Gee, where shall we start? Bringing a civilian into a criminal investigation without proper authority. Tainting the case against Christina Montgomery's murderer. Subjecting the department to public ridicule." The man leered at her. "How does it feel to be the one responsible for 'public ridicule'?"

She held his gaze for a moment, then quietly, clearly said, "Go to hell." She started to turn back to Sloan, but the man's next words left her frozen.

"He was using you, you know. Using you to get ahead. To score points with his boss. Maybe get a promotion, a better job, more respect. He knew about you and that murdered girl in Georgia. He figured the freak did it once. Maybe she could do it again. And, hell, even if she couldn't, he'd get something from her for his efforts—a few hot nights, a little fun.''

The other one took it up then. ''But damned if you didn't come through for him. You must be the queen of freaks, Crystal, you and your crystal ball.''

They were lying. Crystal repeated the words in her head as if they were a mantra that might save her from this public humiliation—or was it public heartbreak? They *must* be lying! Sloan hadn't had a clue about her psychic abilities until Winona had let it slip...or had he? He was a good deputy. If he'd wanted to find out everything about her before he'd come to the Stop-n-Swap that first day, it would have taken only a few phone calls. Plenty of people back in Boonesville would have been eager to share all the sordid details with him. He would have learned enough to know how to approach her, how to treat her, how to talk to her. He certainly would have learned that romance and acceptance were the ways to gain her trust, and once he had her trust...

Hell, there was nothing she wouldn't have done for him. Nothing she *hadn't* done for him.

And he looked so damned guilty right now.

''What's wrong, Crystal-ball?'' one of the men taunted. ''You get visions of other people's lives, but you can't foretell the betrayals in your own life?''

She wanted to cry, to hide, to beg Sloan to tell her it wasn't so. But she'd cried in Boonesville. She'd hidden, and she'd begged James and her parents not to destroy her, and she'd been destroyed anyway. She wouldn't give these two bastards the satisfaction of watching it happen again.

She straightened her spine and gave them her coldest, most invulnerable look. ''You're right. I came through for him, while you tried and failed in your pathetic attempts to frame Homer Gilmore. Even poor, harmless Homer came out of this looking smarter than the two of you.''

A few titters and chuckles agitated both men. ''Oh, yeah?'' one of them blustered. ''Finding the body's not even half the case. Why don't you go crystal-balling again and tell us who murdered Christina?'' He poked the other man in the ribs. ''Get it? Crystal-balling and balling Crys-''

Sloan stood up, looking darker and more dangerous than Crystal had ever imagined he could. His voice sent chills down her spine. ''Go ahead and say it. Give me an excuse.''

Neither man had the courage to speak.

After staring them down a moment longer, Sloan laid his hand at the small of her back. ''Let's get out of here.'' He shoved both men out of their way, then guided her toward the door and onto the street.

They walked one block, then another, his long legs eating up the sidewalk practically faster than she could keep up. In that one small contact with his hand, even through her coat, she could feel the tension in him and guiltily wondered if it was because what the men had said was true. Had he been using her from the start? Had he given her his time, his attention, his gentleness, his kisses, his patience, all for the sake of his investigation? Which was easier to believe—that he'd wanted something from her, or that he'd honestly fallen in love with her?

No one but Winona had ever loved her. Not her parents. Certainly not James. Why should Sloan be any different?

The first tear slipped down her cheek unhindered. When the second fell, she wiped it away, then refused to be pushed along one step further. She came to a sudden stop, holding her ground when he bumped into her, waiting until he'd taken a step back before she looked up and helplessly asked, ''Is it true?''

His laughter was stunned and bitter. ''Well, hell. That makes it pretty clear what you think of me,'' he said scornfully. ''Do you think I used you, Crystal? Do you think I made love to you and took you into my family so you would *help* me?''

She gazed at him, at his handsome face and sexy mouth and wicked dark eyes, and searched inside herself for the best, most honest answer she could give. Once she got past the embarrassment, the reality of her worst nightmare coming true again, the old insecurities and wounded feelings, it was an easy enough answer to find. "No."

He didn't believe her. He'd seen the doubts, and he wasn't buying the change of heart. "The way you looked in there... All that bastard Wilkins had to say was, 'He was using you,' and you believed him. Four little words from a lying son of a bitch you don't even know, and you looked at me like—" Breaking off, he compressed his mouth in a thin line and turned away from her, as if finishing the sentence was too painful.

"You're right," she said quietly. "For a moment I believed him. I've been betrayed before. I couldn't help but wonder if I'd been betrayed again."

He swung back around and hotly declared, "I *love* you! Maybe that doesn't mean much to you, but it means everything to me!"

"It means everything to me, too! That's why I'm so terrified of losing it! Because I've lost before, Sloan. I know what it's like to have nothing. I know that after having you, I couldn't bear to not have you."

Even angry and hurt, he couldn't not reassure her. That fact made her love him even more. "That's never going to happen."

"Then why did you look so damn guilty in there?"

He stared at her a moment, then got that sorrowful look again. "Because everybody knows. The cops. The D.A. The newspapers. The TV stations. Everybody in the whole damn town knows about you being psychic, about your part in finding Christina's body, and they know because—" His voice broke, and he needed a deep breath before he could continue. "They know because I told them. I promised you I'd protect you, I promised I'd keep your name out of it, but when they asked, I told them."

She stared at him for a long time, at the guilt that shadowed his eyes and the regret that etched the corners of his mouth, and she gradually felt about a thousand pounds lighter. "You did no such thing."

He looked at her as if he thought she was so desperate to believe that she was lying to herself. "Sweetheart, I know what I did. I told them—"

"You told me you would keep my name out of it as much as you could, but if anything came from my vision—any clues, any evidence—that you would have to include it, and me, in your report. Well, something came of it. I'd already told Rafe that the vision was mine. I knew there weren't any secrets left to keep. I thought you did, too."

He was slow to understand. "Then...you're not angry?"

"How could I be angry? Sloan, you kept your word. You did exactly what you told me you would do. Even though you wanted to protect me, you did what was right—for your case, for you and for me."

"I saw the way those people looked at you. The way they whispered. The way Wilkins and Blakely talked to you."

"They weren't talking to *me*. They were talking to the woman Deputy Ravencrest loves," she said with a gentle smile. "The same Deputy Ravencrest who blew their case out of the water and made them look like the idiots they are. They don't give a damn about me. They were just trying to get to you through me."

"I do, you know," he said earnestly as he took a step toward her. "I love you so damn much."

"I know. I love you even more." She met him halfway, wrapping her arms around his waist. "So tell me... What does a suspended deputy do with himself?"

"If he's a smart man—"

"The smartest."

"—he takes his best girl home and makes love to her for, oh, sixty hours or so, until he has to go back to work on Monday."

She pulled back to look into his face. "Rafe suspended you for two and a half days? Two of them a weekend when you were already off?"

He grinned. "I brought an unauthorized civilian into an investigation. That was a big strike against me. And she led me to the mayor's missing daughter. That canceled out the strike." He shrugged, his body pressing against hers in all the right places. "It's all politics. So what do you say? Will you come home with me? Make love to me? Make me feel like the luckiest man alive?"

Rising onto her toes, she gave him a kiss so needy, so greedy, that no words were necessary. She offered them, anyway, with a flutter of lashes and a dose of Georgia peach in her voice. "Why, Mr. Ravencrest, I would be honored to come with you..." She kissed his jaw. "Or before you..." Her next kiss landed on his cheek. "Or after you..."

He caught her face in his hands and claimed her mouth with a fierceness that swept through her. "With me," he commanded hoarsely. "Always. Until we die and beyond."

Until we die and beyond. The two of them together forever, in body, in spirit, in soul. The idea brought her a peace and security she'd thought she would never know. With warm satisfaction flowing through her, she linked her arm through his and they started walking once again. "Now *that*, Deputy Ravencrest, is a promise I'll hold you to."

Epilogue

Sloan was leaving work three weeks later when the dispatcher flagged him down. "This came in the afternoon mail for you," she said, leaning over to hand him a heavy cream-colored envelope. It was addressed in an unfamiliar hand, with no return address and a postmark too smeared to make out. If he could read it, though, he knew it would say Boonesville, Georgia.

He waited until he was inside his truck before he opened the envelope. Inside was another envelope, one addressed in his own writing, and inside it was a single sheet of paper, folded in half, then in thirds. He recognized the precise folds because he'd made them himself.

Though he hadn't really expected any response at all, he was disappointed that Marabeth and Andrew Cobbs had lived down to his expectations. What kind of parents cared so damn little about their own child that they would ignore such an important event in her life?

Crystal's parents. His own mother. Rafe's mother. Maybe Christina Montgomery. God knew, there was no shortage of bad parents in the world. The only wonder was that they sometimes managed to turn out the best kids. Crystal was a better daughter than the Cobbses had any right to wish for. He was a better son than his mother could ever deserve, and he intended to be the best damn husband ever.

After starting the engine so the truck could warm up, he unfolded the letter.

Dear Mr. and Mrs. Cobbs:

It had felt odd starting a letter to his future in-laws with such formality, but they were strangers, and probably destined to remain so. What else could he have said?

My name is Sloan Ravencrest. I'm a deputy with the Blue River County Sheriff's Department in Montana. I'm twenty-nine, half Cheyenne, and on the Saturday before Christmas, I'm marrying your daughter.
I love her more than words can express.

Apparently, ol' Marabeth and Andrew had *not* been impressed, he thought dryly. After skimming the rest of the letter, he returned it to its envelope, then slid that into the larger envelope. As he stuck it inside the glove box, he realized something was missing. Along with his note, he'd sent one of their wedding invitations. The Cobbses hadn't returned it.

Maybe they'd thrown it away in disgust that their only child was marrying so far beneath them. Maybe they'd torn it to bits or burned it to ash to demonstrate how little they cared.

Or maybe they'd kept it because, in spite of all the disappointments, in spite of their bad parenting and Crystal's bad fortune to be *different*, she was still their daughter and somewhere in their narrow, selfish souls, they loved her at least a little for it.

He would like to think that was the case.

He went home, showered and changed clothes. By the time the doorbell rang, he was ready and anxious to go.

His father stood there, dressed in his cowboy best. He looked somber, and damn near teary-eyed. "Everyone's waiting over at the church. You ready?"

Sloan took a deep breath. "Yeah. I am."

On the drive to the church, Arlen said, "You know, I always thought when one of my boys got married, I'd have

some words of advice to offer. You know, work hard but
don't let your job keep you away from her too long. Don't
go out drinking with your buddies. Help her with the house-
work when you can. Remember any kids you bring into this
world are your responsibility, too. That sort of thing. But you
already know all that. So I'm just gonna tell you two things.
Thank God every day for sending her into your life, and
thank her for staying there. 'Cause you know, these women
don't need us the way we need them. They're strong and
capable and can do anything, but without them, we're just
poor fools.''

"Amen," Sloan agreed.

There were far more people at the church than one small
wedding rehearsal required, virtually all of them his family
and friends. His cousins were there to make sure he didn't
make a run for it, they good-naturedly teased him. His aunts
and uncles had shown up early for the dinner that would
follow at Neela's and didn't want to miss out on one minute
of family company. His grandparents had come because...well, because nothing happened in the family unless
Dorrie Ravencrest was front and center.

"Sloan, Arlen, Rafe, come and take your place at the
front," the pastor—Sloan's uncle Martin Walksalong—
called. "Everyone have a seat, and we'll get you to your
supper as quick as possible."

His palms damp, Sloan followed his father down the aisle.
Rafe was already waiting, Skye in his arms. "Hey, Sloan,"
she said, leaning across to swing into his arms. "Mama says
you gotta 'nother best girl an' you're gonna marry her and
kiss her every night." She screwed up her face and made
smacking noises, bringing laughter from those seated nearby.

"Your mama didn't say that part," Rafe mildly scolded.

"Well, that's what you and her do every night." Turning
back to Sloan, she cupped his face in both hands. "You
gonna marry Crystal?"

"Yes, ma'am."

"And have babies?"

"Yes, ma'am."

"Have girl babies, so's I can have some to play with, okay?"

Rafe took her back then, settling her on his hip. "Babies aren't like puppies, Skye. You can't go taking the pick of someone else's litter."

"All right," Martin spoke up. "When it's time, the organist will start playing, and the doors back there will open—" he gave the cue, and Amy swung them open "—and the attendants will come down the aisle."

Raeanne entered the sanctuary first, followed at a sedate pace by Winona. It was only the rehearsal, and already the old lady was crying.

"And now the bride," Martin called.

The room hushed as everyone turned to look. For an instant the doorway remained empty, and then Crystal stepped into view. Like the rest of them, she wasn't wearing anything fancy—black jeans, a sweater that matched the green of her eyes, boots with soles to handle the snow outside.

She was beautiful. Unbelievably, incredibly, heartachingly beautiful.

"It's not too late, buddy," one of his cousins called. "You can still escape the noose."

"Sure, it is," someone else responded. "Just look at him. He's already a goner."

Crystal was smiling gently when she reached Sloan's side. "He's right," she murmured. "It's not too late to change your mind."

"Oh, darlin', it's been too late for that since the first time I saw you. Besides, I don't want to wind up a poor fool."

She looked puzzled, as if she wanted to ask for an explanation, but Martin didn't give her a chance. "Turn to face me and put your hand in his, Crystal. I'll start with 'Dearly Beloved, we are gathered here' and go on with 'Do you take this woman?' and 'Do you take this man?' and the I do's and 'let no man put asunder' all the way to 'You may now kiss the bride,' and then—"

Sloan pulled her to him, wrapped his arms around her and

gave her a sweet, tender, perfectly innocent kiss that roused sweet, tender, perfectly wicked feelings in them both. He heard snickers from the younger males in the church, along with a delighted giggle from Skye, and a good-natured ''They always do this'' from the pastor, and even though it was impossible, he would have sworn he heard Crystal's soft Georgia whisper.

I do love you, Sloan. Always.

Or maybe it wasn't impossible. Because judging from the glow in her eyes when he ended the´kiss, he'd swear she'd heard his response.

Until we die and beyond.

MONTANA MAVERICKS:
WED IN WHITEHORN

continues next month with

THE BABY QUEST
by Pat Warren

Turn the page for an exciting preview...

One

Rachel Montgomery sat by the fire in the house of her childhood drying her hair, alone for the fifth night in a row. Her father had had a dinner meeting in town and hadn't wandered home yet, which apparently was a pattern with Ellis. Where, she wondered, did he go every evening, especially on the Sunday night after Thanksgiving?

Actually, she didn't mind. She enjoyed her solitude, even in Chicago in her apartment. Not for days or weeks on end, of course, for she had friends to go out with, to dinner, a movie. She interacted with lots of people at work so evenings alone were often welcome. Yet back here in Montana, they seemed more lonely.

Seeking familiar comfort perhaps, she'd taken a long hot bath and wrapped herself in her old chenille robe that she'd found in the back of her closet. Her feet in scruffy Garfield slippers lovingly saved from her teens, she'd come downstairs and made herself a pot of tea before curling on the couch in front of the fire she'd built earlier. She no longer thought that fires were wasted on one person. In this house, she could shrivel up and blow away waiting for someone to share a fire with.

Since hearing the news a few days ago that her missing sister's body had been found, she'd avoided giving in to the sorrow that was waiting in the wings to overcome her. While Ellis and Max turned from their memories, Rachel now invited them.

Sighing, she felt regret move through her. So many things to regret. That her father had always been more interested in politics and business than his family. That Max, who'd been a warm, loving brother when they'd been children, had grown into an arrogant workaholic much like their father. That their mother had died four years ago when her sister Christina had been eighteen. Maybe if Mom had lived, Christina wouldn't have become quite so flighty and irresponsible. However, the truth that Rachel had finally had to face was that Christina was starved for affection and attention since she got very little from her family, so she'd turned to men and found an unending source.

Why couldn't her family have been more average, more normal? Rachel wondered. The prerequisites had all been in place, the small Montana town where they'd grown up, a place where nearly everyone knew everyone else. What had gone wrong?

Rachel sipped her tea, then returned to her hair brushing. She couldn't help but think of Christina. Her sister had been the pretty one with beautiful, thick chestnut hair. She'd been only thirteen when Rachel had left Whitehorn, yet already beginning to develop very feminine curves.

Christina had been difficult, or so Mother had written to Rachel, but she'd been a good kid at heart. But Mother's death had hit her hard and though Rachel had tried during her short visits home, she hadn't been able to reach Christina.

I should've tried harder, Rachel thought now, tightening her lips to hold back a sob.

The fire slowly dying, she got up to get the poker and spark some embers just as the doorbell rang out twice rather insistently. She glanced at the mantel clock. Who'd be dropping by at nine thirty?

With the damp towel draped around her shoulders, Rachel opened the door just slightly, yet the cold November wind slipped past the tall man standing in the porch light. Her first impression was that he was big with broad shoulders and long legs. He had on a sheepskin-lined jacket hanging open, seemingly oblivious of the cold night, and neatly pressed jeans. He wasn't from around here, she decided, despite the western appearance. No one in her hometown wore tassel loafers.

"I'm Jack Henderson," he said, his hazel-green eyes assessing her just as intently as she'd looked him over. "My sister, Gina, said you were in need of a private investigator." His gaze swept over her again from head to foot. "I guess you weren't expecting me."

Rachel wished she could slam the door closed and pretend she hadn't heard the bell. Gina had called yesterday and said her brother was intrigued by the case and would be arriving soon. But Rachel certainly hadn't expected him to show up on her doorstep the very next day. Gina had told her that for the last eight years Jack Henderson had been running a successful P.I. business out in L.A., the same business, in fact, that she herself had been a partner in, until her pregnancy and marriage to Trent Remmington.

Suddenly conscious of how she must look in her ratty ancient robe, fuzzy slippers, her damp hair hanging every which way, Rachel felt heat move into her face.

"No, I mean, yes, Gina said you'd be arriving, but I thought you'd call first." With an unsteady hand, she clutched at the opening of the robe at her throat. "It's kind of late."

Jack's lips twitched as he checked his watch. "In L.A., nine o'clock's considered the shank of the evening. I heard you're from Chicago. Isn't it the same there?"

Rachel wanted to remind him that they weren't in L.A. or Chicago, but she decided he wasn't going to go away until she talked with him. "All right, come on in. For a few minutes," she amended, opening the door wider.

Unfortunately, as Rachel backed up, her floppy slippers caught on a throw rug and she felt herself falling. Oh, no! Not in front of this smooth Los Angeles P.I.! But down she went in a heap on the polished floor, landing unceremoniously on her bottom and her bruised dignity. Gazing all the way up the more than six feet length of him, Rachel saw amusement on his tanned face and she felt like bopping him a good one.

"I think I'm going to enjoy working with you, Rachel," Jack said, offering her a hand up.

Coming in November 2000
Based on the bestselling continuity series

An original
Silhouette Christmas Collection

36
HOURS:
The Christmas
That Changed
Everything

With stories by

MARY LYNN BAXTER
MARILYN PAPPANO
CHRISTINE FLYNN

'TIS THE SEASON...
WHERE TIME IS OF THE ESSENCE
IN THE SEARCH FOR TRUE LOVE!

Available at your favorite retail outlet.

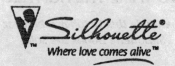

Silhouette®
Where love comes alive™

You're not going to believe this offer!

In October and November 2000, buy any two Harlequin or Silhouette books and save $10.00 off future purchases, or buy any three and save $20.00 off future purchases!

Just fill out this form and attach 2 proofs of purchase (cash register receipts) from October and November 2000 books and Harlequin will send you a coupon booklet worth a total savings of $10.00 off future purchases of Harlequin and Silhouette books in 2001. Send us 3 proofs of purchase and we will send you a coupon booklet worth a total savings of $20.00 off future purchases.

Saving money has never been this easy.

I accept your offer! Please send me a coupon booklet:

Name: _____

Address: _____ City: _____

State/Prov.: _____ Zip/Postal Code: _____

Please send this form, along with your cash register receipts as proofs of purchase, to:
In the U.S.: Harlequin Books, P.O. Box 9057, Buffalo, NY 14269
In Canada: Harlequin Books, P.O. Box 622, Fort Erie, Ontario L2A 5X3

(Allow 4-6 weeks for delivery) Offer expires December 31, 2000.   PHQ4002

#1 *New York Times* **bestselling author**

NORA ROBERTS

introduces the loyal and loving, tempestuous and tantalizing Stanislaski family.

Coming in November 2000:

The Stanislaski Brothers
Mikhail and Alex

Their immigrant roots and warm, supportive home had made Mikhail and Alex Stanislaski both strong and passionate. And their charm makes them irresistible....

In February 2001, watch for
THE STANISLASKI SISTERS: Natasha and Rachel

And a brand-new Stanislaski story from Silhouette Special Edition,
CONSIDERING KATE

Available at your favorite retail outlet.